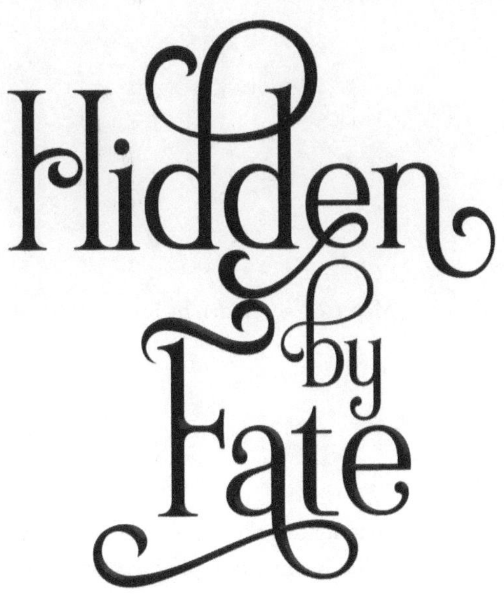

Hidden by Fate

NEW YORK TIMES BESTSELLING AUTHOR

SHANNON MAYER

CHAPTER 1

Diana

The waves slapped at the sides of the boat, a steady sound of *hurry, hurry, hurry,* beside the nearly silent motor running at full capacity. I gripped the fore railing, staring north, hoping to catch a glimpse of the Vanator's ship. Hoping that Myrr, Nicholas, and my new but faithful hell-hound Kevin had not been harmed. When we'd first realized Nicholas and Myrr had been taken, we had no idea Kevin had been snatched too. At least...that was what I was hoping. That he'd been taken and not summarily killed.

Even with my eyes as good as they were, in the dark of the night, there was nothing on the far horizon of the ocean.

The moon above us was just over half full, and light coming through splits in the clouds here and there gave me glimpses of something more in the sea below.

Scales, deep green and gray flashed, and my pulse kicked up a notch.

"Sal?"

I stared, not sure I was really seeing what I was seeing. Saldraenaen, the dragon we'd rescued Maverick from, had dove into the ocean as her mountain lair had exploded with lava. We hadn't been sure she'd survived.

Here she was though, not a mark on her that I could see. For a second, I gripped the railing and considered hollering to the others. But as I watched her, I got the very clear sense that she hadn't come to hurt us. Though why she was following along with us was beyond me.

The water dragon swam to the right of the boat, her body gliding along easily, despite our speed. She rolled as if she were a dolphin using the waves off the boat to help her keep up, her white belly scales catching the light of the moon. The clouds slid over us again, and she seemingly disappeared.

Ever since we'd left her cave, I'd had this nagging sense of grief for her that I couldn't shake. Now, I embraced the small bit of relief that flowed through me. At least she had lived. But my relief was short-lived.

Her emotions rolled into me, as they had when we'd been under the mountain. I pressed my palm to my aching chest, feeling her heartbreak and loneliness anew, the loss of her one true love, George. The infamous dragon-slayer had fallen for Sal in a love that transcended all else. But a jealous woman from George's past refused to let him go so easily. If he followed his heart to Sal, his jilted lover would stop at nothing to see the dragon slain. So George was left with a choice.

Risk Sal's life by returning to her, or protect her by pledging his heart to another.

I could still feel her agony as she waited for him, only to realize he was never coming back. The only solace I had, was the fact that we'd at least given her the truth. She now knew that George never stopped loving her. He'd even written a song about it.

"Fat lot of good that does her. She still spent her life alone," I whispered.

The sadness lingered and I leaned against the railing as the weight of her sorrow mingled with my own. The need to rescue our missing friends was driving me forward, but there were other facets of my suffering that I'd been trying to ignore.

Was I destined to be alone forever, like Sal?

The fleeting blood bond with Raven had faded, but I could still sense him. So close, yet just out of reach.

Seeing him with that buxom redhead on his lap hadn't just enraged me and my wolf...it had broken something inside me, too. As if...well as if he'd meant more to me than the moments we'd spent together. Moments I'd sworn were just to get him out of my system.

I couldn't leave myself vulnerable like that. Time and time again—from the pain of Mav's betrayal to watching

Sal now, and seeing Evangeline's devastation after losing Lycan–the universe told me the same story;

Love equals pain.

And I didn't have the luxury of coddling myself right now. Our world desperately needed saving, and like it or not, I was a big part of the solution. Love would have to wait.

If it was even meant for me at all. Because there was another piece of me that wasn't just scared. It was resigned.

Resigned to the fact that maybe I'd met my one true mate hundreds of years ago...

The young vampire lord who had saved me from Edmund. The one who had risked it all, and was almost certainly executed for his bravery. The weight and pain in my body erupted, tingling through me leaving me uncertain of everything I knew about my past.

"If that story is true, even if we never meet again, just let him be alive," I whispered the plea into the wind, wishing it would send a reply.

A spray of salt water splashed up and over my face, cooling my skin and stealing my breath. I blinked and looked down to see Sal herself there, her big eyes staring up at me, holding my gaze, almost pinning me in place.

A strange calm flowed through me, a calm that was not my own, but as it slid through me it *became* my own, and my erratic thoughts settled.

"Thank you, Sal. We are headed toward danger. You shouldn't follow us. Go, be safe."

She rolled and dove, a flick of her tail sending one last spray up to me. A wave goodbye in her own way?

Strange to feel the loss of Sal, for how little time I'd spent in her company. But I had no doubt it had more to do with the near-violent emotional connection we'd shared as Raven had read the words that George had written for her. Words that had waited over a hundred years to be read.

I shook my head and wiped my face clean of the salty spray.

Raven was steering the boat, up on the second level. I didn't look back over my shoulder to see if he was looking at me. I could feel his eyes on me every time he so much as glanced my way.

Gabriel had said the blood bond was gone, and I believed him. I knew the power of fae blood on a vampire as well as anyone–and Raven had drunk a good deal of it to burn the bond between us.

So what the fuck was this thing between us still?

And maybe Raven wasn't lying when he said that he didn't even remember the red-haired buxom girl. That he'd gone for a drink, she'd approached him, but nothing had come of it...

Nope. I was not going there, not today, not tomorrow. There was no time for the complications any of these men brought to my life. I had a job to do, and I was going to do it.

As if he'd heard my thoughts, Maverick's voice sounded over my shoulder.

"Diana." I turned to find him making his way over to me, favoring his ankle. "You should try to sleep. We might not come on them for hours yet. Or...or days."

I turned my gaze from his eyes, one blue, one green, to stare back out over the ocean between us and our friends. Myrr, Nicholas, and Kevin had been taken only hours before, right from under our noses.

Right from under Maverick's nose, to be precise.

As much as I'd defended Mav from Raven's fury...I couldn't help but feel that Raven wasn't wholly wrong. Yes, Mav had been malnourished and injured, but how had the Vanators boarded our ship and taken them without a sound? Especially with Nicholas there. Surely, there would've been a struggle...Not to mention Kevin's barking?

Unless they'd dispatched Kevin right as they boarded to ensure he didn't let out a warning...

I refused to go down that line of thought. He might have been Gabe's hell-hound before, but he was mine now, and the thought of losing him...having failed him so completely made me want to puke.

"You truly heard nothing? Not a sound..." I did turn to him, because I wanted to see his face when he replied. He'd fooled me once, so completely. But I was different then. I knew better now.

His brows shot up over his dark multi-colored eyes. "Diana, I would have fought for them if I had. I was out cold. Exhausted." He reached out and took one of my hands, almost tentatively as if he expected me to throw his touch off. "I wish I *had* woken up. Maybe that would have made the difference, and we would be off looking for Jade instead of chasing down these bastard Vanators."

Jade...the girl who held the next key to stopping the destruction of not just the Alpha Territories, but the Human Realm as well.

And we had no idea where she was.

"Have you considered where we might start searching for her?"

He did a quick blink. I realized that I'd changed my stance and settled into my persona of queen.

Problem-solving.

Matter of fact.

Curt.

And, instead of responding to his declaration of innocence, I'd launched into another direction of questioning. Better that he know now, I was Wolf Queen first, woman second. I was on a mission.

"Actually, I might have one idea. It has to do with the gem," he cleared his throat. "Your father's gemstone that I..." He leaned in closer, lowering his voice, his mouth brushing my jaw as he whispered, "I'm so sorry, Di. I want to earn your trust back if you'll give me a chance."

I turned my head to reply, our lips almost accidentally brushing when the ship's horn blasted. I clapped my hands over my ears, instinctively stepping back from Maverick as he grabbed at his own head too.

Ears ringing, I could have strangled our captain.

I glared up at the wheelhouse to see Raven smiling down at us, though smiling would imply he was happy. His teeth were bared, and through whatever stubborn, inexplicable bond was left between us, I could practically feel his anger sizzling. Apparently, he didn't appreciate how close Mav and I had gotten. In spite of my fresh resolution to not give a shit about what the men in my life were doing, I couldn't deny the sense of satisfaction that coursed through me.

Good for the goose and all...

Raven held my gaze and then jabbed a finger toward the northeast. I turned and saw what he was pointing at, forgiving him for the blast.

Because on the horizon, I could just make out the silhouette of a familiar-looking vessel skimming the water in the distance.

We'd nearly caught up to the Vanator's ship.

I turned and ran toward the stairs that led up to the main cabin and burst into the wheelhouse. "That's them?"

Raven stared out the window. "You'd have seen them if you weren't so busy letting numb-nuts paw all over you."

"He wasn't pawing all over me," I snapped. "He thinks he might have come up with a way to track Jade using Lycan's gem."

Raven did look at me then, his blue gaze sharp.

"Really? And he wanted to trace the map on your skin with his mouth?"

I glared right back at him. "Fuck you, Raven."

His mouth curled and a fang peaked out and he leaned toward me. "On your word, Frostbite."

My chest tightened and I forced myself to look away from him, to ignore the ache that slid through my body at the thought of...anything with this infuriating man.

"How far are we from them?"

He grunted and a laugh slid from him. "Oh, to change the subject so smoothly. We are within an hour, perhaps a little less."

I took a pair of binoculars and lifted them to my face. The distance between us and the ship shortened and I stared at the back of their ship. I could see figures moving, but no details. "Do you think they've seen us?"

"We're running dark. It will depend on how cocky they are and knowing Vanators as I do...they will think they got away scot free."

His hands adjusted the controls on the dash, angling us more to the northeast, smooth and confident, as though he'd done this a hundred times. His forearms were bare to his elbows and the muscles in them flexed as he worked quickly, holding us steady on the new course he'd set.

Why the fuck was I staring at his hands? How the fuck was him running a damn boat turning me on? How could a pact I'd made with myself less than one minute ago already feel so wobbly?

Heat. Holy fuckery, not again…

Or was it still? I'd thought it had finally passed on Isla Naranja, but here it was, rearing its hot, horny head again.

"Frostbite."

"What?" I snapped the word. Tried to, found myself flustered and staring up at him.

His eyebrows were high. "Unless you want me to mouth fuck you right now—and to be clear, I'd gladly do it—I think you should go. Your desire is fogging the windows."

My jaw dropped and I spun, and all but sprinted from the wheelhouse, self-disgust and lust chasing me all the way to the back of the boat. Raven wouldn't be able to see me from his position in the wheelhouse. And I needed a minute.

Or ten.

Gripping the railing yet again, I struggled to get my body under control. My heat came on randomly, but never this close together. Was it just being in his presence now making me a mass of seething need? Because it was a damn struggle to admit how very much I wanted Raven to do…anything and everything he'd ever said he could do to me.

Mouth fuck me.

Make me scream his name.

Every position, every flavor.

The railing cracked under my grip and I couldn't help the groan that escaped me or the way my body arched and flexed. Fucking heat! If we weren't chasing down the Vanators, I'd have dove right off the side of the boat and let the icy ocean cool my overheated flesh.

Because the problem with a heat like this, even when a queen had made a pact with herself, there was only so much she could do.

How strong was I expected to be when my body and mind were so torn up with the idea of getting railed repeatedly by the vampire in the wheelhouse, it left little room for other thoughts? Important thoughts.

Like rescuing our friends.

Completing our quest.

Saving the world.

You know, little things like that.

"Get it together, Diana," I grumbled under my breath.

I didn't have the inclination for a true dip in the ocean, and retiring to my quarters for a cold bath when we were hot on the Vanator's trail would be a waste of time, but at least I could cool off a little. Stiff-legged, body on fire with Raven's words, I made my way down to the ladder that led to the skiff launch pad.

The pad trailed just above the water, and the skiff for whence it was named took up most of the room on it. But if I went to the edge, I could sit and dangle my legs in the sea.

I climbed down the ladder to the launch and on that wobbling platform, made my way to the edge. There was a railing on my right side that led to the open portion. I clung to it as I lowered my butt to the launch pad.

With my body halfway down, the boat hit a hard wave and bucked, a ripple going through the boat and the launch pad.

I didn't even have time to scream as I was flung forward, straight into the ocean.

CHAPTER 2

Diana

The cold water had an amazing effect on my mind, clearing it of everything that had scrambled it. I tumbled down, over and over in the water, the boat leaving me in its wake as I fought to get to the surface of the ocean, unsure of which way was up. I kicked furiously as I searched for some sign of the moon for guidance.

Watch me die here...I was a fucking idiot.

What in the ever-loving gods of heaven and hell had I been thinking of?

Raven.

And his mouth.

And his hands.

Which meant that, yet again, this was his fault. He'd consumed me, even without that fucking blood bond. It had to be some leftover bits still humming under my skin to be so affected by him—still.

I broke the surface, took in a deep breath, and stared at the boat as it sped away from me. Neither Raven nor Maverick had any idea I'd taken an unscheduled dunk into the ocean and I was already too far from them to bother wasting my breath on screaming. All I could do was start swimming and hope that one of them noticed that I was missing.

"I'm an idiot!" I yelled to the sky, saltwater pooling in my mouth for my troubles. "I should be relieved of my crown for this stupidity!"

Survival though, that's what I had to focus on, not how foolish I'd been.

I stripped off my shirt and shimmied out of my pants and boots while treading water. They would not only weigh me down, but the gods only knew how long I'd be in the water.

The thing was, I wasn't the strongest swimmer, so I knew I had to make this as easy on myself as possible.

Funny enough but my early childhood trauma at the hands of my brother, Edmund, seemed to have burned itself into my subconscious and I didn't like being in deep water. I'd learned to swim as a necessity, not because I liked it. I preferred long hot baths as my deepest immersion in water.

Now, here I was in a situation of my own making in about the deepest, darkest water I could have found. My fear spiked and I fought it back with anger.

"Numbskull. Fool. Stupid girl!" I kept up the litany

of insults at myself. It was all I could do. I couldn't even look at how far the boat was from me.

Something bumped along my right side.

Fuuuuuuck.

If I thought I'd been scared before because of the deep water, it was nothing to the idea of something larger than me being in it right next to my side. Something I couldn't see, something that might be hungry.

The Kraken would have been welcome, but he was all the way back in the Alpha Territories.

My throat tight and my mouth dry I managed one word in desperate hope. "Sal?"

"Nope!"

A head burst out of the water next to me and I screamed and swam backward, flailing and splashing. Green hair and a sharp-toothed smile framed by a familiar, pixie face came into view.

"Xefia?" I murmured, relief rolling through me.

"Yes! You came to swim with me?" Her hair trailed around her shoulders as she floated next to me.

My heart was hammering out of control, and I was afraid I might have peed a little. Not exactly a queenly reaction, but this was a lot for my nervous system to take all at once.

"No, I...fell off the back of our boat."

Her eyes went wide, and she turned to look in the direction of the speeding boat. "That's not good, is it?"

"No...we're chasing the Vanators still."

"Oh yes! Me and my friends are slowing those ones down!"

I stared at her. "You're...what?"

"That's why you're catching up! We tangled their motors with kelp and tried to cause mischief. They're dead in the water." She grinned and took my hand under the water. "Come on! I'll help you get to your boat! This will be fun!"

She started to swim and while I kicked my feet, I'm not sure how much good I was doing. Xefia laughed. "You're terrible at this! Sorry to be mean, but I think we need more help."

I spluttered, another mouthful of water keeping me from replying. She wasn't wrong.

The smooth sleek body of something slid underneath me and I was lifted partially out of the water, my head clear enough that I could breathe better.

"Hang onto his fin!" Xefia pointed at the dorsal fin in front of me. I wrapped my fingers around it and the dolphin took off, like I'd grabbed his accelerator. Xefia laughed and swam beside us, leaping into the air. "This is fun! I'm so glad you fell in."

I wasn't sure I would call it fun, but I was grateful for the help and wasn't about to correct her.

It didn't take us more than ten minutes and the dolphin had me next to the skiff launch.

"Raven! Maverick!" I screamed their names. Raven would be able to hear me, I was sure of it.

The boat slowed and I tried not to gasp with relief.

He'd heard me.

"Frostbite?" he bellowed that ridiculous nickname, and I'd never been so happy to hear it.

"Here!" The boat had slowed enough that I managed to get onto the launch pad on my own before he saw me in the water. "Thank you, Xefia, and thank you to your friend, too."

I patted the dolphin on the back as he dove away from the boat. Xefia smiled. "Is that handsome one...oh... hello!"

She waved and I looked over my shoulder to see Raven there, his eyes wide as he took me in. Of course, I was soaking wet and in nothing but my bra and panties.

"I can explain."

His lips twitched and he held back a laugh. "What the fuck did you do?"

Okay, it was kinda funny, but this was *not* the time.

"Listen. Xefia and her friends have wrapped the Vanator's propellers in kelp. They've stalled them for us. We have to go now and take advantage of this."

Raven chuckled, bowing at the waist to Xefia. "Saved by the beauty again. Thank you, little one."

She giggled and then sighed, before diving back under water. Another heart taken by Raven, with ease.

"I can't wait to hear how this came about." Raven stared hard at me, his eyes tracing water droplets as they raced down my skin. "But it'll have to wait. You're right, our friends need us."

Without another word, he climbed back up to the

main deck and headed to the wheelhouse, leaving my skin pebbling and reacting as if he'd traced the droplets with his fingers.

I all but ran to the captain's quarters, not seeing Maverick the entire time. Had he gone back to bed as he'd suggested I do? It made some sense, even though a small part of me was irritated.

I yanked dry clothes on, noting that my impromptu dip had at least calmed all my emotions and hormones— or at least until Raven had eyed me up and down.

Dressed, with new boots on, I headed to Maverick's quarters and banged on the door. "We'll be upon them soon."

I didn't wait for his response, just went to the weapons stash Hamish had brought with us. Now that we were almost on the Vanators, I wished we'd been able to reach Hamish and the others. A full crew against the Vanators would have been preferred. But there was Nicholas, he was a vampire too—it would have to be enough.

Assuming he hadn't been hurt.

Or worse.

Gritting my teeth against the possibilities, I hurried to pull weapons out that would be most useful in the situation.

Two short swords for me, and three smoke bombs. Raven and I would be able to work in the chaos. It would leave Maverick at a disadvantage, but...I pulled a long-range weapon from the stash. The crossbow would allow him to stay on deck and cover us. With his ankle, that would be best.

I turned and Maverick was behind me. "With my leg..."

I shoved the crossbow at him and the bag of bolts. "Go to the crow's nest. Cover us."

His shoulders slumped. "I wish I could fight beside y—"

"No!" He winced and drew back. Just because I was a mess of emotions on the inside, didn't mean I had to let it show. I needed to keep my cool under pressure, through angst and fury, sadness and, yeah, even heat. "Look...you're injured. You'll be more help as a lookout. But I know you would stand beside me, Mav." I wasn't sure that was a hundred percent true, but being a leader meant diplomacy in the worst of times.

Either way, he bought it because he smiled and kissed me on the cheek. "Good."

With a turn, he limped up toward the stairs. I followed him, feeling the warmth from his kiss on my cheek. A steady, calm warmth, nothing like the raging inferno Raven stoked within me.

Back on deck, I could see how close we were to our quarry.

Raven leaned out of the wheelhouse side window, all business. "Throw the grappling hooks as soon as I turn the engine off."

I gave him a thumbs up then bent and picked up the first of the hooks.

We were maybe a hundred yards from the boat now, and they hadn't noticed us. Their boat was turned sideways to us, and everyone on deck was leaning over the motor.

Fifty yards.

A bellow from the Vanator's boat and a light flared our way.

Raven didn't slow the boat, he *sped up* so we came in hot, our hull slamming flat sideways into theirs. The impact tossed me to the deck and from my knees I threw the first grappling hook, yanking it tight and tying it off.

Raven was at my side in a flash and threw two more hooks so we were flush to their ship.

"Myrr! Nicholas! Kevin!" I yelled for them, hoping to pinpoint them. I didn't care if we killed all the Vanators. I just wanted our people back.

Two Vanators jumped across to our ship. The whizz of a crossbow bolt shot between us, and I leaped back, drawing the enemy deeper onto our deck.

Raven snarled and engaged the other Vanator, but I couldn't watch what he was doing. No, these Vanators weren't quite human and we had to be on our guard.

They were possessed with Lilis' power—the goddess who seemed to have it in for us— having taken some of George's ashes and eaten him like some unholy communion between themselves and the dark goddess.

The Vanator across from me was young, his face speckled with spots and his eyes fevered with obsession.

He held a small glass vial. "I will kill you all," he cooed, as if speaking to a lover. "And I will be rewarded."

I pulled both swords. "I doubt that."

He snarled and leapt at me, no weapon in sight with the exception of the vial. I stepped out of his way, caught his foot with mine, and sent him flat-faced onto the deck.

He screamed and flailed as if I'd run him through. He pushed to his feet and faced me, horror written across the marks on his face. His chest was bubbling, skin and clothing melting off in chunks. I could see through his ribcage, could see the edge of his heart as it beat frantically.

"Griffin acid," Raven yelled. "How the fuck did they get griffin spit?"

Good question. But the young Vanator was not going to make it. There was no antidote for Griffin's acid, and his death would be long and painful. His eyes met mine and he lunged forward, as if to embrace me, soiling me with the same foul poison that covered him. With a roar, I swung my sword with all my might and took his head, sending his body tumbling toward the rail. His screaming ceased as he fell. It was a mercy more than anything.

The deck where he'd lain continued to bubble and froth. It would go straight through given the chance.

I turned to dive across to the Vanator's ship when a boom not unlike thunder tore through the air, the concussion of it flinging me backward. I slammed into the bottom of the wheelhouse, a wave shoving our boat around. The lines between vessels straining, hulls rubbing hard on one another, wood and metal screaming.

The grappling lines snapped, and the two boats swirled around each other like we were caught in a whirlpool.

"What is this?" Raven was crouched, holding his balance.

I mimicked him. The wind whipped up, and the skies opened as the waves shoved us around. It was a storm, but...

Xefia launched herself part way onto our deck. "Flee! This is no natural storm! The waves are...they are not ours. They belong to the dark one! She will kill you!"

Fucking Lilis strikes again.

"Go, Xefia!" I yelled. "Find safety!"

She gave a quick nod and flung herself back into the water.

The two boats were parted now and if we wanted to survive long enough to try again, it was time to retreat.

"Raven, the engine. Get it going!" We were going to need all the power we had to survive this—already the waves were washing over the deck, taking me out at the knees.

He bolted for the wheelhouse, his vampiric speed giving him the edge we needed. The engine started and he fought to get us out of the whirlpool.

Laughter rolled through the skies along with the

thunder. I looked up to see Maverick still in the fucking crow's nest.

Crouched, unmoving.

"Mav!"

Lightning cracked, striking the base of the mast.

He seemed to fall in slow motion, clinging to the edge. The mast only fell part way, hanging at a ninety-degree angle.

Gods' mercy, and I had been the one to send him up there.

I opened my mouth to yell...to tell him to climb, but I couldn't. His face was lit by the lightning as it struck all around us in a freakish show of power, which was the only reason I saw the massive wave.

A hundred feet tall, the rogue giant was silent as it slowly gathered itself and rose over us a behemoth on a quest to crush all in its path.

I threw myself to the deck, scrambling to tie a rope from the grappling hooks to my waist.

There would be no coming back from this if I was swept overboard. I'd sent Xefia away, and I had no doubt that Sal was long gone too.

I looked to the wheelhouse, desperately searching for Raven...I couldn't help it. Because through this all, he'd saved me more than once.

But this time...this time I didn't think there would be any saving us.

CHAPTER 3

Diana

The sound was unlike anything I'd ever heard before. A groan of metal and wood as it did its best not to implode under the sheer power of the sea's fury. I took one last look at the black wave about to swallow us whole and then flung my arms and legs around a pipe that traveled the perimeter of the ship. Then, I closed my eyes and whispered a prayer.

For my shipmates. For my people. For the Territories, and their endurance.

"I've got you. Just hold on!"

The voice barely registered over the howl of the winds and the roar of the wave about to consume us, but I didn't have to hear much to know who it belonged to. I felt his presence an instant before he spoke.

Raven.

Strong arms closed around me in a viselike grip, pinning me even tighter to the pipe. And then all hell broke loose as a wall of water slammed over us. My face smashed against the metal pipe hard enough to rattle my teeth. There was no time to even think about it as brine water blasted up my nose and filled my mouth even as the monster wave tore at my limbs with greedy hands, desperate to pull me free and into its gaping maw.

Raven's grip tightened and his legs followed suit, closing over mine. So safe, so strong, making me feel like just maybe we had a chance. If only I could breathe...Already, my lungs burned, like I'd inhaled hot coals instead of cold salt water.

Fuck you, Lilis.

Almost as if the bitch heard me, the violent wave doubled down, nearly tearing my arms from their sockets.

And then almost as quickly as it had come, it was gone. My head broke above water as the wave ebbed, pulled back, and sluiced off the deck in a wash of foam.

Instantly, I started hacking, lukewarm water shooting out of my nostrils and mouth in a rush.

"You're bleeding." I dimly heard Raven's voice over the sound of my coughing. "Where is the blood coming from?"

I wriggled hard to loosen his death grip on me and finally managed to suck in an excruciating breath. "My lip, I think. It's fine. I'm good."

I could almost feel the tension in his body release as he slowly pulled away.

"Mav, though..." I swiped my forearm over my

bloodied mouth and turned to search the broken crow's nest, only to find it completely gone. "Oh, gods, no!"

I struggled to stand, tearing at the grappling hook around my waist, but Raven's hands were closing over mine.

"Hold tight!" he shouted, not two seconds before we connected hard with something even harder.

The whole ship shuddered as my feet flew out from under me and I crashed into Raven's unmoving body like a sack of stones.

"What the fuck!" I snarled, frantically searching the skies for another wave and finding none.

"We hit something. The Vanator's ship maybe..."

Myrr, Nicholas and Kevin were on the ship.

Raven cupped my chin as he tried to examine my face, but I tore away from him and unknotted my grappling hook. "We need to split up. I'm going to search for Mav, you see what we hit. Stay on your guard in case one of those zealot fuckers tries a sneak attack."

I didn't have high hopes of finding Maverick. How could he have possibly survived barely hanging onto the highest point of the ship?

It would be a miracle.

Then again, he'd survived a scorned dragon, so just maybe—

"Di?"

I blinked, wondering if I'd hit my head and was just hearing voices, but there it was again.

"Diana!"

I turned toward the call and found Maverick, crawling out from beneath an overturned lifeboat. Pale, shaken, but alive.

"Mav!" I rushed toward him and gave his shoulder a squeeze. "You've got nine lives, haven't you?"

I wanted to ask how he'd managed but there was no time.

"I've got to go with Raven and see what we hit. Stay here and keep watch. Call out if you see anyone trying to board the ship."

The madness in the eyes of some of the Vanators was growing, and something told me they wouldn't hesitate to take on a suicide mission if it meant furthering their cause. Not with Lilis pushing them.

I turned and rushed across the deck to the starboard side of the ship and realized quickly, even in the dim light of what was still visible of the moon, that I was going uphill. A sandbar maybe? Or—

"Rocks," Raven said grimly. "Just a massive pile of boulders jutting out of the sea. We are lucky the wave hit us when it did and not when we were even closer or we'd all be mincemeat."

He didn't say it but I knew it anyway. We weren't as bad off as mincemeat, but we weren't much better. With our ship battered, and fully stuck on the rocks, and only the three of us onboard, we were unlikely to be able to get ourselves unstuck. Our only hope was that the schooner had survived the tidal wave...

Raven's features shone suddenly in sharp relief and then went dark again.

"Wait...What is that?"

It happened again, and we both turned toward the source of the blinking light.

Hope grabbed me by the lady balls and hung on tight. "I-is that a fucking lighthouse?"

"I think it is," Raven marveled with a glimmer of a smile.

I stared at it, trying to calculate the distance in my mind. I might not be a strong swimmer, but I was strong enough for that distance. If the schooner hadn't made it, we'd swim.

"You can do it. I'll be there to help you."

"Not possible, since you'll be the one hauling Mav on your back."

Raven's head whipped toward me. "Not happening."

"Raven, he was injured and under the weather already. He's been knocked around, and despite having some sort of...gift, he's not as strong as us."

His steely expression didn't change.

"If you don't, I will. And I don't think I can manage..."

"But you'd die trying for that piece of shit, right?"

I didn't reply. I didn't have to.

"What kind of hold does this asshole have over you, Frostbite?" He let out a harsh laugh and shook his head. "You know what, forget I asked. I'll carry your boyfriend to shore if he can't manage to do it himself. But only because we need him to find Jade. After that, though, he's on his own. If I'm going to play the role of someone's daddy, it's going to be yours. Now let's move out now, before that bloodthirsty bitch regroups and comes back for another round."

I was still smarting–and a little flustered–from his comment a few minutes later when we noticed the small skiff floating in the bay. Shocked into silence, all we could do was stare.

I shook my head, stunned. "How could it possibly have survived the wave?"

It was beaten up and had been yanked from its moorings, but it was in what looked like one piece and bobbing on the waves just a few yards away.

"Grab some supplies from the galley; I'll be back in a minute," Raven said with a glance in my direction.

"I know how to steer one of those if I can be of some help..." Mav's voice trailed off as Raven turned his attention towards him.

Raven closed the distance between them and made the most of his height advantage, hulking over the smaller man as he glowered down at him. "I don't like you, and I certainly don't trust you, so I'm going to need you to keep your trap shut and only speak when spoken to until the burning desire to disembowel you passes. Are we clear?"

A challenge lit Mav's multi-colored eyes, and I very nearly slapped my hand over his mouth. There was still a hint of that cocky, young traveling thief inside him, and it would be true to form for him to let it show at the worst possible time.

He must've sensed my warning, or maybe he just wised up, because instead of taking the bait that Raven had laid for him, he took a step back and raised both hands in mock surrender.

"Sure, whatever you say, man. I'm just here to right some wrongs and help out where I can. You want to be the guy in charge, I'm happy to let you do it."

Reasonably confident they weren't going to kill one another, I headed off to the ship's galley. It hadn't fared as well as the schooner–though we at least didn't seem to be taking on water from a hull breach or anything catastrophic like that. Even so, it took a while to find food that hadn't been destroyed by seawater that had flooded in. Once I'd found a cupboard that had been relatively untouched, I made short work of packing a couple of rucksacks with supplies. A bag of blood for Raven and some canned goods that had survived, but all our jugs of water had been crushed. We'd have to make do and find something on the island.

When I got back to the main deck, Raven was already there, still soaked to the bone and sitting ready to row in the skiff.

He tipped his head toward me. "I can see the wheels turning. What's the plan?"

Dawn was breaking, but dark storm clouds still swirled overhead, and the seas churned like a brew about to bubble over.

"I say we head for the lighthouse and see if they can help us. Maybe they have a tugboat or a ship that can leverage us from the rocks."

Both men nodded, and I settled into my seat, trying not to think of how bad this would go if Lilis got her second wind before we hit shore.

"Don't you think it's weird that there's a massive crop of boulders right in front of the lighthouse?"

Raven sent a quelling look over his shoulder at Mav, who instantly locked his lips with an imaginary key and then threw it overboard before mouthing, "Sorry."

It *was* a little strange to have the lighthouse drawing ships to the boulders. But that couldn't be right. Could it?

Despite being close to my heat, I was soaked to the bone and freezing as the winds buffeted us. I was exhausted, sore from head to toe after the thrashing we'd taken, and worried about my friends, leaving me not at my best.

"Keep an eye out for any sign of the Vanators," Raven called over his shoulder.

I kept my gaze trained on the horizon, but even as the sun rose, there was no sign of our quarry.

Myrr's wizened face popped into my mind and I shoved it away before I could imagine her getting sucked into a maelstrom with a scream.

"If some of those Vanators are being controlled by Lilis, surely she'd have made sure they were safe. Maybe that's why they were brought here."

Mav chuckled. "Yes, because she seems like such a fair and reasonable deity so far."

A projectile from the front of the tiny boat flew past me, hitting Mav square between the eyes before clattering to the deck.

"Gods, man. What the fuck?" he grunted, rubbing at his forehead which was already getting red.

I looked down to see Raven's dagger and shot to my feet with a gasp.

"You could've killed him," I said, making my way to stand beside him and yanking on his arm until he faced me.

"Would that have shut him up?" he deadpanned.

"This needs to stop. Today. Now," I snarled, at my wits end with Raven. "And you said it yourself. We need Mav. At least until we find Jade. Not to mention, our friends are in danger. I'm not going to sit around and watch the two of you compare dick sizes. Again."

"Don't be such a killjoy. I know how to throw a knife, Frostbite. It hit him hilt first. If I wanted to kill him, he'd be dead."

I let out a grumble of frustration and turned to go back to my seat.

"But for the record," he called softly, "If we *were* measuring dicks, there'd be no comparing."

Idiot.

As irritated as I was with him, though, my wolf picked up her head and sniffed the air with a low growl of need.

Traitor.

But a good reminder that I needed to avoid small spaces with this man in my current condition, and I added it to the bottom of my ever-expanding To Do list:

#1. Save friends.

#2. Try not to get murdered by a psycho bitch goddess in the process.

#3. Keep Raven from killing Maverick.

#4. Stop thinking about how badly you want Raven's mouth on your...everything...

How sad was it that the last thing on my list might be the hardest of all?

CHAPTER 4

Raven

By the time we made it to shore, the red sun of dawn was just coming into view on the horizon, and I pulled my hood up a bit higher on pure instinct. The dagger protected me from the sun, but old habits died hard.

"I think she'll be alright here unless we get another huge storm."

I had just finished pulling the small skiff onto the beach, hiding it hastily behind a sand dune near a copse of gnarled mangrove trees. From there, the forest only deepened, and the beach gave way to a dense jungle with no sign of a trail.

Diana strode back toward the beach, staring at the spot where it met the morning tide. The deep sense of anxiety rolling off her kept me from laying into Maverick yet again for putting us in this circumstance in the first place.

It was his fault our three friends had been taken—he hadn't even had the sense to sound an alarm.

Diana jabbed her finger toward a spot along the shoreline, and I strode down the beach to meet her.

Chunks of wood, frayed rope, and a lifejacket that was torn in half washed up and down the shoreline.

"Must be from the Vanators' ship," she said, shaking her head as she stared at the remnants of a boat wreck. Based on the paint color and the freshness of the wreck, I agreed.

Irritation spiked through me as Maverick's voice broke the silence, "That damn witch stranded us. At least the Vanators won't be able to leave, either."

Diana glanced at him. "Do you think our friends could've survived?"

"They're probably fine," Maverick said with a weak smile.

You better hope so.

I bit back my reply as my fangs found my tongue. It only took a quick scan of the ocean to make out dozens more pieces of wood that hadn't yet floated to shore. When I met Diana's gaze, I knew I had to give it to her straight.

"Nicholas is strong. Assuming he didn't go down with the ship, he could've easily made it to shore. Hopefully he would've managed to keep his sun shield dagger you had made for him. And Kevin is strong as an ox. As for Myrr..."

I didn't need to say the words. She was ancient and

frail, despite her bold attitude and crazy behavior. It was unlikely she survived.

"Maybe she saw this coming and managed to avert it or something, maybe Nicholas helped her to shore–" she broke off, bowing her head.

I dropped an arm over her wordlessly as the scent of her skin and hair flooded my senses in a wave. I forced down the growing lust within me with every fiber of my being.

Not the time, Raven.

"If they're here, we will find them. You have my word on that."

When she pulled back a moment later, her face had been transformed. The troubled, distraught Diana was gone, leaving Diana, Queen of the Werewolves, in her place.

"Yes," she said with a sniff. "Yes. We'll start by combing the beach for signs of survivors, we can track them from there." She reached for the hem of her sand and sea sodden shirt and the lust surged once again as she pulled it up and off in a single motion, leaving her in just her pants and black camisole that left her smooth, golden midriff exposed.

My fangs ached, and blood thrummed hotly through my veins as I looked her up and down. I could just reach out and–

"Eyes on mine, Raven," she said, scowling as she tied the shirt around her hips. "You'll have plenty of time to gawk later."

"Don't threaten me with a good time," I replied, turning to lead the way down the beach.

The three of us combed the area methodically, splitting up to cover more ground, but there seemed to be no sign of life anywhere. I sniffed the air, searching for blood, people, anything...

Mav's obnoxious voice split the air once again, this time from a few dozen feet away. "Over here. Signs of travel."

I spun toward him, fangs aching in an entirely different way, but I kept myself in check. He stood on the edge of the forest, jabbing his finger at a spot in the sand just where it met the beach. "The tracks aren't clear, but I'm certain someone passed through here."

I growled as I looked down, "Where?"

Mav squatted down to point to a few small divots in the sand, then stepped toward the forest. "Signs of entry here, too." He gestured to a cluster of flattened grass and bent pieces of brush. "Hard to be sure, but it looks like they might be trying to conceal their passage..."

A part of me wanted to argue, but, looking at it more closely, it was starting to seem like he might be onto something. Someone had survived the shipwreck.

"The question is, are they friend or foe," I said, craning my neck to stare deeper into the forest.

"We pursue, but stay on alert for Vanators." Diana gestured into the forest and took the lead herself.

"Let me take point," Mav cut in, entering the forest

ahead of her. "I should be able to track them, unless they suddenly get a lot better at hiding their movements."

I wanted to point out that Diana was more than capable, seeing as she was a damn werewolf, but I bit my tongue. She was safer between us than out in front. Let Maverick take whatever hits came at us first.

"We should mark our way back," Diana said, grabbing a large stick and poking the ground in front of us with it. "So we can–"

"Go to the lighthouse? Yes, maybe we can try to find a way out of here. Maybe someone's manning it," I didn't realize I'd finished her sentence. I was more focused on what was ahead of us. The forest was looking more and more like an untamed jungle, which could hide all sorts of beasts.

To his credit, Mav kept us at a good pace. Apparently, his ankle injury had mysteriously healed itself in his sudden need to impress Diana. As much as it killed me to admit, he was actually good at tracking. We had to stop to find their path a few times but never had to double back, and Diana didn't have to shift to scent them with her keener wolf's nose.

As we walked, the rainforest only got more and more dense. Vines hung from massive treetops, and the canopy was even thicker than I'd thought. Birds and exotic insects flitted all around, and the forest floor was thick with mushrooms and underbrush. But the fact that we could be ambushed by Vanators at any moment made it a lot harder to appreciate the wild beauty of the place.

"Do you have any sense of how many people we're trailing?" Diana cut in, the first time she'd spoken in nearly an hour. An intoxicating rush surged through me when the curve of her breasts heaved up and down as she sighed, bare skin tantalizing me as she glanced around the jungle. The light sheen of sweat covering her made it possible for me to scent the heat on her even more.

And it was slowly killing me.

"Hard to say," Mav answered. "More than one, for sure. Maybe it's just Nicholas, Myrr, and the dog. Maybe it's the Vanators. It would make sense for either party to cover their path. The former would want to hide from the Vanators. The latter from us."

I tore my attention away from Diana's half-naked body, looking to the forest around us instead. "Nick could get Myrr through this, provided he wasn't too badly injured."

Diana strode past me, a curious expression on her face as she jabbed her finger upward. "Are those... oranges?"

I whirled, a jolt of surprise spiking through me as I caught sight of them. Sure enough, there it was: a white-flowered tree studded with brilliant orange-red citrus.

Diana strode up to it, grabbing one and peeling the skin off of it hurriedly. Bright, crimson flesh poked through, like that of a blood orange, and she sank her teeth into it with a delighted sigh. "So good."

I shrugged, shaking off a massive spider web as I pulled another from the tree. "We should save a few of them for later, in case we end up getting stuck here for a while."

"Ack," Diana sucked at her lip, frowning sourly. Seeing me looking at her, she added, "Orange juice, right into the cut on my lip."

I stared hungrily at her, eyeing the cut. "You know... it looks superficial enough that I can probably fix it with a single flick of my tongue." I looked further down her body, wondering if I couldn't find a few more spots to give the same treatment. "You don't want to get an infection."

She shot me a dead-eyed stare. "I'll take my chances with gangrene."

I ignored the muffled laugh coming from my right. I'd have plenty of time to gut that bastard when this was all over, assuming we made it off this island in one piece.

I glanced onward, wondering how far we were from our quarry. The blood hunger had begun to pulse deep inside me, and I hoped the sole bag we had with us would be enough to get us through. I turned, fixing my eyes on Mav as I mentally amended that. Technically, I had *two* blood bags, if push came to shove...

A gentle sound pricked at my ears as I turned, one that broke my chain of thought entirely. "There's water up ahead. *Running* water."

That brought both of them to their feet in an instant, and Diana trudged toward me. "We should get the salt off of us and get a drink while we can. My waterskin is almost empty."

Mav crouched, looking at a section of trampled flowers. "The path does seem to lead the way you're saying. Maybe we're in luck."

Luck was indeed with us. A white, picturesque waterfall, like something out of a postcard, came into view before long.

"What're the chances?" Diana said, chuckling as she stepped hurriedly toward it, pulling off her waterlogged boots before moving to her pants.

Blood rushed to my cock as her hips came into view, and my fangs pulsed, yearning for that neck. The feeling was poisoned, though, as I noticed that Mav had also stopped in his tracks just to my right.

Every bone in my body was screaming at me to leap on him. To grab him and beat him until he realized that she was mine. She'd *always* been mine...

"We'll need to start a fire at some point," Diana called, pulling my attention back to her. "We can't walk in wet shoes all day like this, or we're asking for trouble. We have to dry them."

I strode to the water, tearing off my own clothing. "We should be fine until we set up camp for the night, though it will be difficult to start a fire in these conditions."

"We should start grabbing any dry sticks or tinder we come across," Mav agreed, wading into the water.

Satisfied that I'd gotten all the salt off, I strode out of the water first, grabbing my clothes before heading to the beach-like patch of sand on the far side of the stream.

Feeling the beginnings of hunger-borne weakness setting in, I tore the blood bag from my pocket and sank my teeth into it.

The rush shot through me like a jolt of electricity, consuming my entire body in an instant. Strength and vigor surged back in waves, and I let out a contented sigh as I drained it, doing my best, as always, not to compare it to the taste of Diana's blood. The satisfaction waned as she came into view, still half-naked and dripping from her time in the stream.

I turned away, determined not to ruin a perfectly good meal by comparison to an even better one. My eyes fixed on a small copse of white-blossomed trees and shook my head in amazement. More oranges. We really had been lucky to land on such an island. If push came to shove, we could survive here for quite some time. It wouldn't be comfortable for me to go long without blood, but the miniature paradise had everything else we needed.

Mav hobbled over to us, and I was forced to reconsider. He still looked pretty green around the gills, and his gait had worsened during our trek. An infection could eat right through him in this state. I cursed inwardly. Regardless of how I felt about him, he was still our only shot at finding Jade. If we didn't want to leave it to chance, we were on a timer.

There was nothing for it, though. He'd be safer with us than without us, and we had to keep moving.

Was that–?

My eyes fixed in on a small patch of dirt I'd been gazing at, and I dashed toward it wordlessly. Sure enough, a small, charred log came into view, surrounded by a rough circle of stones. Not fresh, by the smell of it, but someone had camped here. And it wasn't the lone person or small group we'd been following. This firepit was old, days at least.

A half dozen distinct prints led away from the firepit, and not like the shallow, well-disguised ones we'd been following. Deep, full-on boot prints that led into the forest beyond.

"Couldn't have been from the Vanator ship. Too old," Diana said, echoing my thoughts.

I stood, nodding. "We should keep following the other path if we can find it."

"Mav is trying to pick back up on it now."

It only took a few minutes for us to get back onto the path, and I felt the bite of anticipation as we strode back into the forest. Whoever it was we were following, I just hoped we'd catch up to them quickly, before I ended up having to carry Mav's weak ass yet again.

"Strange," he mumbled, slowing to a near stop just a few minutes from the stream.

"What?" I strode up to him, glancing at the small clearing he was looking at.

"It's almost like some kind of game trail." He stepped off the trail to examine it more closely, taking a long moment before adding, "There's been some new growth since it was last used."

I glanced around, more curious than worried. What-ever the beast was, it had more to fear from us than we had from it. No animal alive was taking down a party with a vampire *and* a werewolf.

Maverick shrugged, sparing a final glance at the game trail before getting back to tracking. A loud *twang* split the air, and I moved on pure instinct, yanking him into the air by his shirt as a spear shot through the space where his stomach had been a moment earlier.

He winced as I dropped him back to the ground, hand reaching toward his leg, but he voiced no complaint.

"What the fuck was that?" he demanded instead, staring wide-eyed at the ground he'd just been standing on.

"Be careful where you walk," I said, irritation burning hot at having been forced to save him yet again. "There are traps set."

"Maybe the Vanators know we're trailing them." Diana stepped forward, catching the spear on the next backswing. The thin vine it was attached to stretched far into the canopy above, and it had clearly been rigged to fire with some kind of tripwire.

I examined the spear closely. "I'm not so sure that's who set these." The trap was crude in a way that didn't seem very Vanator-like. Why had the spear swung so low to the ground? Even if Maverick had been struck there was a very real chance he would've lived, at least for a few days. Why not rig it to swing at chest height? And, though we *were* in a rainforest, the wood of the spear was extremely wet and waterlogged.

A sign of age?

Diana shrugged. "Regardless, we need to keep moving, let's just stay on guard."

I nodded, shifting my focus to the sounds all around us as we continued walking. Small, climbing creatures rustled the canopy overhead, and frogs chirped all around, but I did my best to ignore all that, listening for human sounds.

None came.

Maverick stopped suddenly in his tracks just a few minutes later. "What the–"

I stepped up next to him, feeling a rush as a subtle scent pricked at my nose.

Blood.

Our trail came to an abrupt end, marked by the huge, muddy pit that'd opened right into the forest floor. The rocks that lined the bottom were streaked in red, and a single line of blood led out of the trap like someone had managed to climb out.

Diana appeared at my side, glancing all around us as she spoke, "Pitfall. At least one survivor."

I nodded, leaning over to get a better look inside. Who the hell lined a pitfall with rocks, rather than sharpened spikes or something else like that? Maybe someone short on time?

I crouched down even lower, pulling a deep whiff from the pit. "Well, I can tell you this much: it's all human blood. No vampires involved." It was good news since it meant that Nicholas hadn't been down there, but my uneasiness deepened nonetheless.

There was only one trail out of the pit, but there was too much blood down there for them to be the only one who'd fallen. "Be on guard. Something happened to the others who fell. And the blood is quite fresh."

I followed the trail at a half-jog, eager to get to the bottom of who it had come from. Though the blood droplets grew further and further apart as we went, I was able to use my nose to keep track of it. And, before long, I was picking up on the smell of the human himself. He smelled familiar, the faint whisper reminding me of the scents on our boat after we'd had Nicholas, Myrr and Kevin snatched.

"Vanator. Be careful," I whispered, gesturing toward Diana as I padded softly toward the massive, dead tree the scent was coming from.

I unsheathed my sword silently, holding it in front of me as I crept around the tree, preparing to lunge at the first sign of movement. A caged rat was often the deadliest, and the Vanators were strong enough in normal circumstances, never mind now that they had Lilis' power aiding them. The last thing I wanted was to be caught with our guards down.

As I approached the other side of the trunk, I leaped forward in a flash, ready to gut the man waiting for me on the other side. Rather than waiting in ambush, the

Vanator was crouched down inside the hollowed-out tree trunk, his face sheet-white as he stared up at me.

"St-stop," he whispered, holding up a quivering hand. "Please."

"Where are our friends?" Diana asked, stepping up to my side.

The terrified Vanator sank down even further, and whispered a plea. "Don't. Make. Any. Noise."

I opened my mouth to press further, but he cut me off with a gesture, jabbing his finger out and to the right.

Was it a bear or something? How had our crack-shot tracker Maverick missed those fucking signs of a beast large enough to terrify the Vanator?

I turned, following the Vanator's finger, and a cold chill ran through me as I caught sight of what he was pointing at.

A spider the size of a cargo van stood across the swampy ground, massive, spindly legs working in tandem with its silk as it wove a cocoon around what appeared to be a person.

Suddenly, the creature paused in its work. I froze, stock still as it turned. The morning sun backlit its profile and I was finally able to see it in all its terrible glory. Fangs the size of lopping shears dripped with saliva, but far more horrifying?

Its human face.

CHAPTER 5

Diana

"Don't move." I kept my tone low, and even despite the way my body was flooding with adrenaline. "Not a muscle."

Raven was absolutely still in the way that only vampires can pull off...As if he'd turned into a statue. Maverick's breathing was on the harsher side, but he didn't move either.

The Vanator that was in hiding, though?

He leaped from his hiding place and bolted to the left, stumbling over a line of webbing that criss-crossed the ground.

The massive spider didn't lunge after him. He spun and pointed his three-foot-long spinnerets, then shot a blast of sticky web that caught the running man in mid-stride.

I felt more than saw Maverick twitch.

"Don't move!" I hissed.

As its newest victim hit the ground, the spider crea-ture let out a high pitched, wet whistle that sent shivers through me. But it never looked at its freshly caught pretty. It stayed focused on the task at hand.

To finish mummifying the wriggling prey before him.

"Fucking hell," I whispered, taking a closer look at the man struggling. Every feature was etched with raw terror, and I had to look away.

"Its back is turned," Raven murmured, his voice barely audible. "This is our chance. Move slow. Steady. Don't touch anything you don't have to."

In absolute horror, we kept our eyes locked on the beast as we stepped backward, carefully placing our feet one after another. The Vanator thrashed and fought the web, but he only succeeded in getting his legs more tangled as the spider creature absently dragged him closer.

The Vanator rolled, and his desperate gaze locked on mine.

"Help me, please!" He clawed at the ground, digging a furrow in his wake even as the monstrous spider reeled him in.

I didn't realize I'd stopped moving until a set of hands summarily yanked me behind a trio of trees.

"You can't save him, Frostbite." Raven held tight to my forearm, squeezing me gently.

How well he could read me.

"But Myrr...Nicholas...Kevin..." How would we find

out where they were? If they were still alive? Surely, this Vanator had seen them, he had to know if they were alive. And even if he didn't, I couldn't deny that, despite him being our mortal enemy, the thought of looking on while that creature sucked him dry made me ill. Maybe losing my father had made me soft, but–

I shook my head, trying to get my mind wrapped around what we'd just witnessed. The spider creature was easily twenty feet across, and that was without its twelve-inch round legs stretched all the way out. Its body was covered in generous spikes, and the mandibles attached to its oversized human head and mouth were razor sharp...

I shuddered and hugged my arms around my body. Even my wolf cringed at the idea of fighting that monstrosity.

But fight it I would if that was how we got our friends back. I wouldn't lose them to this beast.

"Even if they did make it, how the hell are we going to save them when that's on the island, hunting us?" Mav whispered. "And what the hell *is* it, anyway?"

The sound of branches creaking and rustling leaves had my blood going cold. Raven motioned for us to flatten ourselves, and we all reacted the same way, lying low under the brush around the base of the tree. He pointed toward the canopy of the trees overhead.

I looked up to see the spider creature carefully working its way through the upper branches of the trees, dragging two well-wrapped bodies. There was nothing of their faces; they were covered in webbing, so there was no way to tell if they were male, female, Vanator, or one of our friends. Worse? They were both still wriggling to free themselves.

Still alive. Totally aware that they were about to be... *eaten* alive.

Bile rose up from my belly, whispering at the back of my throat and reminding me that had almost been us. If we hadn't stumbled on the Vanator hiding, we'd have never seen that fucking spider. It had been right there, and it had no scent. Nothing telling us it was even hunting us until it had moved, emerging from the natural camouflage of the forest and the patterns on its body.

The sound of the spider traveling above us faded into nothing and even then, we didn't move for another five minutes.

"I think it has poor vision." Raven sat up first. "Did you see how milky the eyes were?"

Maverick leaned against the tree. "Then how did it get that Vanator so fast? Luck?"

"Vibration." I pointed at the webbing over our heads and in places in the bush. "The Vanator running away created a vibration as he hit the webbing. Look at all these strands...they're connected to that fucking thing."

His eyes widened. "There's no way we can survive this, Di. We don't have any real weapons; we don't even have a good escape if we get its attention and have to run for it."

"Correction," Raven snorted. "*You* might not survive this." I shot him a look and he shrugged. "I'm not lying, am I?"

"Not the time."

Maverick though didn't seem fussed by Raven's assessment. "How do we know that's the only monster on the island? There could be other things that we can't fight."

"I doubt it," I said, refusing to even allow myself to go down that road. "That creature is very obviously the top of the food chain."

"Why do you say that?" Maverick frowned. "How could you know? We've only been here for a few hours."

I looked around at the space we were in, thinking about how we'd arrived on the island, and what we'd seen so far.

"Give me a moment."

Raven's eyes were on me, I could feel the weight of his gaze but I just closed my eyes and worked through everything. Lilis had used the storm to push us here. The lighthouse with rocks all around it. The sheer amount of naturally growing food that was on the island...food that would sustain most humans and many, many supernatural types.

The webbing.

The creature with the bad vision.

"It's all a trap." I opened my eyes as it came together. "Like an angler fish."

"A what?" Maverick shook his head. "How is this like a fish?"

Raven let out a sharp hiss. "Fuck. The lighthouse to draw us in? Thinking it's safe, only to be smashed on the rocks?"

I nodded. "No choice but to come here. And then once we do, look at all the food we've found. Oranges. I saw berry bushes back there, avocado and guava trees, and—"

"I saw coconuts," Raven said.

Maverick frowned. "Okay, so there's lots of food available. It's a jungle. Are you surprised?"

I stared at Raven as more puzzle pieces clicked into place. "Avocado and guava are high in protein. Avocados are loaded with fat." But it was more than that, and I knew why Raven had locked onto the coconuts. "Young coconuts can be used in a pinch for a vampire, it's not quite the same as blood," I said quietly, "But they would keep a vampire from dying. They might last weeks on just coconut water."

Assuming they either had a protective device like Raven and Nicholas, or they managed to hide from the sun during the day.

I could see that Maverick wasn't quite getting it. Raven on the other hand...

"We're in someone's private buffet," Raven marveled. "And they've provided food and nourishment to fatten us up and keep us alive while they hunt us down."

Maverick paled. "You...you're just being a dick again."

Raven snorted. "If I was being a dick, I'd say they were just hunting humans and then I'd grab a strand of that web and shake it to call the big bastard back. But it's obvious they—whether it's just that monster or someone else—are prepared for others too."

The quiet of a horrible understanding descended on us, with just the call of a bird here and there to break the silence. They weren't prey for the spider creature—they were too small. But they probably made great additional protein sources along with the variety of fruits and plants.

"So, what do we do?" Maverick asked, breaking the uneasy silence.

I had an idea forming. One that was leaping off what both Mav and Raven had pointed out. We didn't know who—or what—else might be on this island. "The lighthouse. There has to be someone manning it. There is no way that the spider creature is climbing up there, and making sure the flames stay lit."

Raven slowly nodded. "So we go talk to them. See if we can find out more about this place, using someone who lives here with the beast? Good call, Frostbite."

"And we can go back to the beach." Maverick nodded. "Stay out of the jungle and away from these webs."

I scrunched up my face. "No. The lighthouse was to the northwest edge of the island. It's not far from us if we bushwack. Straight west I'd say. If we go back the way we came it will take hours that our friends likely don't have."

Maverick stood up and offered his hand to me. "I don't want you to get hurt, Diana. Going through the jungle is more dangerous. How many times are we going to run into more webbing? We won't be any good to Myrr and Nick by getting caught ourselves."

His words tugged at me and I took his offered hand. Part of me knew he wasn't wrong, the other part—

"Well, there is the finest crock of cowardly bullshit I've heard in a long time," Raven drawled. "I think I've finally settled on your nickname. Chickenshit."

I closed my eyes because I didn't want Maverick to see that I understood he was scared. I didn't think he was a coward, but...

"You agree with him?" Maverick dropped my hand, and the warmth of his fingers was a tiny loss.

I opened my eyes and let out a sigh. "Mav, no. I know you're looking out for—"

"Himself," Raven grunted. "Always. And don't forget it."

I pushed myself to stand as Raven continued.

"I'll lead the way. I think I can manage not to stumble on a web."

Without waiting to see if we followed, Raven headed straight west. The spider had gone east, which would give us some distance. But I also knew it would take us further from our three missing friends.

I motioned for Maverick to follow Raven.

"You first. I'm not staring at the back of that asshole the whole way." Maverick waited with his arms crossed.

Which left me to take the middle spot. Again.

Raven was as good as his word, working us through the jungle, avoiding every web. Even those I wouldn't have seen. Aside from that, we were all left with our thoughts as we traveled in silence. Hours passed, the rest of the day slid by as we wove our way through.

Plenty of time to think of all the things we'd gotten wrong and how they had gotten us here. Plenty of time to blame myself for leaving the ship to go find Raven back at the Wild Queen Casino. I'd allowed him to distract me, and Nicholas, Myrr, and Kevin were paying the price.

We had to get them back, no matter what it took. I had to believe they were all still alive. There was no other option for me in my mind.

Hours into the walk, Raven put his hand out toward me, stopping me.

"Watch this on the right," he said. "It's another pit."

He skirted to the left of a pile of leaves and loose branches. Through the top of the carefully woven mat, I could see heavy boulders at the bottom. Not spikes. Things to incapacitate, maybe break a leg or knock you out, but not kill. Wouldn't want all that good blood going to waste.

"Fuck." Maverick whispered behind me, no doubt coming to the same conclusion I had.

I didn't disagree with him. Fuck indeed.

After that, the three of us continued to walk in silence, which gave me far too much time alone in my head. Far too much time to second guess every decision. Maybe Mav was right. Maybe we *should* just go. Not because I wanted to leave our friends behind, but because the chances of them being alive were slim, and I had two more people to consider. Was I leading them to their demise as well? And what of restoring the Veil? The tens of thousands who would die as the Territories continued to collapse?

The fate of the world depended on me making the right choice. The hard choice. The tightness in my throat had nothing to do with the heat, or my need for water, and everything to do with a decision that was looming.

When I thought the hike would never end, we finally found the edge of the jungle and were looking out across the sand and directly at the lighthouse.

I drew a deep breath and let it go, long and slow, noting that Raven and Maverick both did the same. As if we could finally relax to some degree. The strain of watching every step, every place we moved our bodies was draining to say the least.

The sun was setting on the far side of the lighthouse, but even so, the sky was lit with purples, pinks and oranges, turning the white-stoned lighthouse into a kaleidoscope of colors.

"We should rest," Maverick said. "Get some of the jungle food and then head to the lighthouse at sunrise."

Again, I heard what he was saying and understood

the caution behind it. But we didn't have time. The quicker we got answers, the better.

I checked out the bushes and fruit trees closest to the beach. Nothing here was covered with webs that I could see. "Ok, grab something to eat."

Raven turned and raised an eyebrow. "You want to wait?"

"No, but we can't do this on no energy." I was starving and the guava I'd grabbed was perfectly ripe. I bit into it, and grabbed a bundle of bananas off a low hanging branch. I tossed two to Maverick. "Eat up."

"Di…"

Raven stepped between us. "She's made her choice. You agreed to follow her, Chickenshit. Follow her or fuck off and stop trying to make it like you care, and that it's not just your own skin you're trying to protect."

Maverick surprised me. He stepped up to Raven, throat working as he met the vampire's furious gaze. "I would die for her."

"Why don't you just do that, then?" Raven growled.

Gods be damned…how did I end up with these two vying for my attention?

Movement caught the corner of my eye. "Put your dicks away. The lighthouse…there's someone in there."

Staring at the top of the lighthouse, I watched through a large, picture window as a figure crossed the room. A limping gait, someone on two legs.

Someone who was not a spider and not a monster. Perfect.

Time to get some fucking answers.

CHAPTER 6

Raven

I took the lead toward the lighthouse, much as I wanted to shove Maverick out front like the cannon fodder he was, the last thing I needed was him tripping some booby trap and getting us all caught.

I'd seen more than the two I'd pointed out to Diana. There had been strands of webbing above our heads, some attached to what looked like chunks of metal.

Fucking dinner bells by what I could see.

This place was giving me the serious heebie jeebies. Because as we'd walked, I'd remembered stories my old master in Seattle had told me. While I was hoping I was wrong, it was feeling more and more like this was it—this was Ludumin Island. Stories of Ludumin were that it was caught between the human realms and the Alpha Territories. A place that some fools thought to prove themselves when it was first discovered because of the terrors that lived here.

Very quickly, they'd stopped going on purpose and the island had fallen into myth and legends, as if it truly were its own realm, caught outside all others.

We walked toward the lighthouse and I slowed my steps so I fell in beside Diana. She wasn't going to like what I was about to suggest, but I had to try.

"I think I know of this place."

"What?" She grabbed my arm stopping me. "Why didn't you say anything?"

I shook my head. "I didn't put it together until we were in the jungle, and then I wanted to stay quiet. But there's an island that is known to be somewhere off the coast of the Alpha Territories, closest to the demons. Ludumin Island." I stared at her. "'Game Over' in Latin."

Her frosty blue eyes were wide. "And? What else do you know about it?"

"There isn't much outside the name. People don't come back from here, Frostbite. It's why it's a legend and not written up in some book with maps and directions." I looked over my shoulder to the jungle. Somewhere in there were our friends. And as much as I didn't have many, I counted Nicholas and that cantankerous old oracle Myrr as two of them. And that goofy hell-hound had started to grow on me.

More than that, though, was the fear that Diana would be hurt if we stayed. Taken by that fucking spider thing. Or something else. Something worse...I knew her well enough to know that she would stay and fight to the bitter end. "I think maybe you should go. Take the chickenshit and start the search for Jade. I'll stay behind and get Nicholas, Myrr, and Kevin, then we'll catch up."

Her eyes never left mine as she let out a snort. "You aren't serious."

Much as I hated to send her away, especially with Maverick, it was more important that she stay safe. Alive. No matter the cost. "I am."

"He's right," Maverick interjected and it took all I had in me to not smash his face in. "You are the one we need to keep alive, Diana. I hate to agree with him, but we should go."

Her face hardened, frosted blue eyes flashing. "I am not leaving my friends in danger. And that includes the two of you...for now. But you're going to want to stop treating me like I'm a dainty fucking princess. I'm a queen, boys, a *warrior* queen. Try to remember that before you suggest something that stupid again."

She shoved past me, anger radiating off her as surely as if she'd swallowed a piece of the setting sun.

"Good job," Maverick muttered as he passed me. I snapped a fist out and nailed him in the shoulder, sending him reeling across the sand a good ten feet. Not hard enough to break anything, just hard enough to make the point that I didn't appreciate him speaking.

Or breathing.

Or existing.

Diana made it to the base of the lighthouse ahead of me and she ran her hands over the exterior. "It's made of smooth marble and I don't see any doorways or even any cracks to suggest a secret entrance anywhere."

I put my hands on the stone and helped her search. "How would they get up and down?"

She shook her head and kept looking. "I don't know. Rapunzel style with a rope maybe? One they could pull back up so the creatures of the island couldn't reach them?"

The sun disappeared and the soft blue of the early night fell. I'll admit, it eased something in me. Staying out in the sun, even with the dagger at my side, felt... vulnerable in a way I didn't like.

We made our way around the base of the lighthouse at least ten times before we stopped.

Maverick stood with his hands on his hips. He huffed a laugh and put one hand to the base.

"Maybe it's a magic doorway. You know, open sesame?" A groan of stone on stone made him jump back. "Holy shit, it worked!"

Indeed, the lucky little chickenshit had figured it out.

"Good job, Mav." Diana smiled, patting him on the shoulder. He took the opportunity to grab her hand and give it a squeeze.

I struggled to breathe normally, to not launch myself at the two of them and tear him limb from limb for touching what was mine.

What I *did* do was push between them, so I went through the doorway first. "Night vision eyes in the lead," I said.

Then I reached back and took Diana's hand before she could protest and dragged her along with me. Maverick muttered something that sounded like 'dick' under his breath and then he followed us in.

The doorway behind us slid closed, but by the light of the stars filtering in for that brief moment, I'd gotten a layout of the room. Circular, there were stairs on the far side that curled up and toward the top of the lighthouse. Lacing my fingers with Diana's I held tight to her as I stepped slowly across the room, all my senses on high alert.

The scent of a human caught me off guard. I'd fully expected our lighthouse keeper to be something else. Fae. Demon. Shifter. Not human.

The first few steps were taken in utter darkness. But by the time we were halfway to the top, there was a light filtering down from above.

Diana's hold on me tightened and I tucked her close to my back, relishing in the closeness of my mate. She might not ever accept me as such, but I would take whatever moments I could get of her touch.

As we neared the top the sounds of movement filtered down along with the light.

A man was humming a soft tune, words caught here and there. The sound of footsteps, a limp, a heavy sigh. The creak of wood and the clink of utensils against a plate.

"Gods be praised, I suppose," he grumbled, "I'm still alive. Despite all the efforts made to the contrary."

I lifted my eyebrows and glanced over my shoulder at Diana. I mouthed *human*. She nodded and I reluctantly let go of her hand, untangling my fingers from hers.

Creeping up the last of the stairs, I kept my head down so I was out of sight but could take in a bit of the upper room. It was half the circumference of the rest of the lighthouse. To the left was a bed.

"I know that someone is here," the man said. "I have no weapons, and I'm old as I want to be. Likely will die soon anyway so...come on up."

He could have a weapon pointed at where my head was, and even I couldn't replace a head blown apart by a high-powered boom.

It left me with one option. I turned on the speed and was through the opening and standing in front of the man between one blink and the next.

He was probably in his late seventies, with a swath of thick, silver hair. He was tall, and slim, and his clothes had been patched a great deal. His shorts had obviously been pants at one point, the ragged, uneven edges clear even under the table. His shirt was threadbare and stained, one sleeve missing totally.

He sat at a small wooden table, unflinching despite my sudden appearance. A plate covered in a variety of fruits and nuts, a glass of chilled wine by the smell of it. He motioned at the chair across from him.

"Have a seat. Did Akmon send you to replace me?"

I blinked. "What?"

"Ah. Well, I guess not then." He speared a few

chunks of fruit and stuffed them into his mouth. "Do you know what I'd give for a loaf of bread? You'd think I'd not miss it after all these years, but I still crave it."

I didn't sit down. I didn't call Diana up. I wasn't sure what this man was about. "Who are you?"

"Ah, right, very rude of me. I don't talk to anyone but myself, so it's not often I have to reintroduce me to me." He sat back and took me in. "Name is Theodore. But call me Theo."

"Hello, Theo." I nodded. "And who is Akmon?"

He leaned forward. "It's been a spell, but shouldn't you give me your name before asking more questions? I could be wrong, like I said it's been a long while since I spoke to anyone but myself."

Diana shuffled as if she'd come up the stairs and I motioned for her to wait. I wasn't sure just what this fellow was playing at. Truly out of his mind, or just trying to fool me? I wasn't sure which.

"Raven. That's my name. Now tell me who is this Akmon?"

"You probably saw him out there. Giant big spider? Huge human body attached to the top, like Andre the Giant? I loved that wrestler. He was great. Do you think he's still alive now?" Theo leaned forward, excitement lighting his features. "I'll admit, it's been a while since I've had the guava wine go bad on me, this is a really good hallucination."

Shit.

Well, if that was the case. I grabbed the second chair and sat down. "Tell me about Akmon."

Theo leaned back with a sigh and took another swig of his guava wine. He never offered any to me, but why would you offer wine to a hallucination? And I wasn't about to dissuade him from that notion. "Well, what is there to tell? He likes to chase his prey, really loves to hunt and he loves to keep them alive as long as he can. I mean, it makes sense if you think about it."

"Does it?" I raised my eyebrows. The more I could get out of this guy, the better. "Why does it make sense?"

"Because we don't get a lot of shipwrecks anymore. So he—Akmon that is—has to keep his food prisoners alive for longer. That's why he made sure to plant more and more fruit trees." He waved his hands, his movements slow like he was moving underwater. "You know, he said he likes the taste of them better once they've been eating nothing but fruit for a few weeks."

I played along. "Right, well that makes sense I suppose. I have a preference for certain food types too."

"You like bread?"

"I like my food...frosty." I smiled as Diana huffed from the stairs.

"You won't get that here," Theo said. "Too hot."

"Fair enough. This Akmon here, you talk to him? Any tricks to staying alive out there? Better yet, where does he keep his prey, so I can avoid that?"

Theo frowned and looked into his cup. "You know,

my hallucinations don't usually ask me so many questions."

I shrugged. "I'm special. The guava wine is really off this time. Bat shit fell into it."

Diana hissed and I wasn't sure if she was trying not to laugh, or she was trying to get me to shut up. Either way, it made me smile.

She made me smile.

"Ah, frick, that makes sense." Theo sighed. "Yeah, well, his pit is on the east side of the island. Not far from the big waterfalls. And as for surviving...most people don't. I can't help you there."

Apparently, I wasn't moving fast enough with my questions.

Diana stepped up into the room. "We need your help. Anything you can tell us about Akmon. Anything at all."

Theo's eyes went to her, blurry and unfocused. I opened my mouth to tell her to get back down in the stairwell, when a splat on the window turned my head.

"Damn," Theo whispered. "I really don't like it when Akmon visits."

The entire window was covered in web.

Diana

I cocked my head as I tried to track the monster's movements by the clickety-clack of his spindly legs against the stone exterior of the lighthouse. He seemed to be making his way around to the side now.

"What the fuck is he doing?" I muttered. As if I wasn't feeling my adrenaline spike and my heart pick up speed at the thought of the spider creature climbing the lighthouse.

"Well," Theo closed one eye in thought, assessing the situation in his bleary-minded state, "My guess is he doesn't want you all to leave, but he's got a couple victims still out in the rainforest for tonight's hunt that he has to deal with before he gets to you."

"Hunt?" Mav said, his voice rising an octave. "He's already got plenty of food. We watched him wrapping up some poor bastard like a mummy. And there were others..."

Theo scratched at his stubbled face. "Yah, well, 'the hunt' and 'food' are two different things, aren't they?"

That explained all the traps out there meant to maim and not kill.

I hated that, as an apex predator myself on both sides of the family, I knew exactly what he meant. Meat was delicious, to be sure. But as much as it hurt my soul to admit it, outsmarting prey and running down your dinner felt different. Primal. Sort of like how I felt when Raven touched me...

Another splat sounded across the room, and a second window went dark. I cleared my throat. "He's going to trap us here, hunt down the others remaining free on the island, and then come back to kill all of us. That's what you're saying?"

Theo shrugged and looked away, refusing to meet my gaze. "Well, not all of us..."

It took me a second to remember this innocent-looking old man was anything but.

"You're the key to the whole operation, aren't you? Akmon uses you to lure the ships in because he can't run the lights without you. And you do it for him."

The disgust must've been evident in my voice, because Theo flinched.

"Give me one reason not to do this world a favor and gut you here and now?" Raven snarled, stepping closer.

I moved between them but Theo waved me off with a sniffle. "You think you're telling me something I don't know? I don't want to be here any more than you do. I just did what I had to do to survive. Man, you guys are pretty mean for hallucinations..."

I drew back and slapped his face, hard enough to leave an instant red mark.

"Shit's sake, what the hell did you do that for?"

"Not a hallucination."

He blinked at me and suddenly his bleary eyes went clear.

"You...you guys are real?"

"We are," Mav said with a curt nod.

Theo lunged toward me and grabbed my hand. It was only my glare at Raven that saved the poor old man from a blade to the gullet.

"You have to help me. I have to get out of here. I'll help you guys. I'll tell you exactly what to do and we can escape together. Do you have some way off the island?"

"We have a skiff and, potentially, if we can unwedge it and hope that we can repair anything that's busted, a ship stuck on the rocks."

Hope lit his bloodshot eyes. "Okay. Here's what we need to do. One of us," he shot a look around the room, his gaze finally sticking on Raven, "Preferably the big guy, needs to get outside before Akmon covers all the windows—"

Splat.

I whipped around to see window number three covered in wet silk. By my count, that left three more.

"You've got to hurry," Theo pleaded, turning his attention to Raven. "That stuff is like steel. If you're on the outside, once he leaves, you can cut it away with a blade. But from the inside, pushing will only make it stronger."

"Raven isn't like...other men," I said, choosing my words carefully. The last thing poor old Theo needed was to hear that he was in a room full of monsters just as dangerous as his arachnid master.

"I don't care what type of male he is. You know the demons come here and trade with Akmon for his silk to make their shields with? It's nearly as strong as fae-made armor."

Okay, so Theo wasn't completely in the dark.

"We can't take a chance on waiting," I said, the decision already made in my mind. "If Akmon wants a worthy kill, then Nicholas is surely one of the intended victims of this bloodsport. He might need our help. And if not, then all three of them might still be alive in the spider's lair. We need a man on the outside to check the lair for survivors and then come back and let the others out of the lighthouse to help Nick."

"You think I'm leaving you here alone when that thing is right outside? With only these two to protect you?" Raven snapped, his eyes wide with disbelief. "You must've hit more than your lip during that storm, Frost-bite. No chance."

"Not you," I agreed with a nod.

Raven paused with a frown. "Well, chickenshit here sure won't do it. And even if he did agree, he's too slow—"

I saw it the second it hit him.

"Oh, get the fuck out of here. Nope." He stalked away, raking both hands through his black hair. "You think you're going out there alone?"

"Di, you can't do that," Mav said, shaking his head furiously. "Did you see that thing? It makes Sal look like a pussycat. What if it sees you and decides you're the most interesting game to hunt instead?"

"I'll shift. We aren't in the Human Realm anymore. Not technically. My wolf is fast as lightning and strong enough to handle herself. I hate to keep reminding you both, but you swore fealty. To me." I stood as tall as I could, trying to seem regal in my torn, filthy clothes and belly exposed. "We all know what's at stake here. And we all know that the only one of us that isn't expendable right now is Maverick. And because of that, I need the male I trust most in this world to protect him." The words were manipulative to be sure, but also uncomfortably true in a way I didn't want to explore. "You three will stay here. I will sneak out and head for the lair."

I stepped forward to take Raven's face in my hands.

"If I'm not back in two hours, you will tear the fucking roof off this place if you have to. And you will get Mav back to the Territories even if it means you must swim there with him on your back. For the good of my people and yours. That is an order, soldier. Am I understood?"

Splat.

"We're out of time." It was a whisper that felt oddly

like a prophecy, and I tried not to shudder at the sense of doom that closed over me as I said it.

"Please, Frostbite. Don't do this."

Because it might be the last time, I ever saw him, I did something reckless. Something a queen would never do. I rolled onto my tiptoes and mashed my lips against his. The cut there stung, but I didn't care. I just held tight as his hands instantly dropped to my hips and yanked me closer.

"Uh..."

"Oh, my..." Theo whispered.

The embrace was over in a flash, but the glow that came from it, the sudden spark and sense of purpose lingered. I had to believe I'd make it back, because the two of us weren't done. Not yet.

"Good luck," I called over my shoulder as I rushed across the room. I could hear Akmon already tapping away at the window to the west, so I veered toward the east.

"You two. Start banging on the walls," Raven was saying to the others.

I let out a low sigh of relief. He would hate every second of it, but he was going to do as I asked and make some vibrations as cover for me while he was at it.

"Watch out for traps," Raven hissed, with a warning glare in my direction. His words were innocuous enough, but his expression said something else entirely.

You better live, or I'm going to fucking kill you for this.

My last thought as I slipped out the window I'd jimmied open?

If we lived through this, I was going to fuck his brains out.

Once I cleared the sill, I stood frozen outside the window, fear making my palms go damp. I'd fought a lot of creatures in my day, but this one...the thought of its creepy-ass human face staring into mine as those massive fangs dug into me and sucked me dry drew a deep fear up from my belly. The only thing that could be worse was if it wrapped me up tight and left me there to await my fate while the panic of claustrophobia swallowed me whole.

But then I thought of my father and all he'd done to save our people before he died.

And Lochlin, and Sienna, and Dom, and Will, and Bee, and the Duchess...all those who were depending on us.

The countless people relying on me—on us—to get this right. Success was the only option. I leapt out and landed lightly at the base of the lighthouse on the far side from where Akmon was.

I crept down the sand, staying close to the edge of the water, the waves covering any sound I made.

I glanced back once to see Akmon on top of the lighthouse, contrasted against the light of the stars and three quarter moon.

Letting out a slow breath, I kept moving east— toward Akmon's lair. If I could make it to the treeline without him hearing me or sensing my vibrations, I'd be golden. Once I was in the rainforest and in wolf form, it was a rare creature that could catch me, and Akmon was far too large and unwieldy to manage it.

I hoped.

Getting there was painstaking, though. As much as I wanted to sprint the short distance, I had to watch for every piece of driftwood, every washed-up piece of ship-wreck, to make sure I didn't accidentally call attention to myself.

When I finally made it to the treeline, I was bathed in cold sweat from head to toe. I took another quick look back. Akmon was still on top of the lighthouse, and I could hear the banging of Raven and Maverick inside, keeping the beast's attention.

Even so, there was no time to rest. I closed my eyes and centered on the ember inside me, calling to my wolf. She came like she'd been primed and at the ready, chomping at the bit, making the transition from two to four legs swiftly.

It was such a relief to stretch and uncoil my muscles that I barely noticed the pain that usually came along with the process as my haunches snapped into place, and my fangs poked through my gums. It took everything I had to hold in my howl.

Must find friends. Must hurry.

I loped off, nose pressed tight to the soft forest floor. The smells hit me like a sucker punch so much, all at once. Hibiscus, moss, damp leaves and the almost rotting sweetness of overripe fruit. There too, though, under it all, was the scent of humans. Vanators? Or others?

I paused at one intersection, sure that I smelled a human child...but it was there and gone before I could be sure, and I did not have the luxury of time on my side.

I lengthened my gait, keeping my eyes peeled for signs of more boobytraps. I saw four as I made my way across the length of the island.

Pits and snares for the most part.

On four legs, I covered the distance in the jungle from one side of the island to the other easily and many of the traps went over my head. Literally. They were designed for bi-pedal creatures. Not those of us on four legs.

As I got closer to the eastern edge, I could hear the roar of waves against a shoreline and caught a whiff of the clean scent of fresh water. My hackles rose as I ran faster, a new, faint scent calling to me.

A strange mix of mothballs and roasted chicken...

Myrr.

My heart hammered against my ribs as I stretched into a full sprint. She was alive, she had to be. And if she'd made it there was no way I was going to believe that Nicholas and Kevin hadn't.

As I worked my way through a thick patch of bush, I paused with just my nose poking out.

Ahead of me was a pair of waterfalls and a massive, gaping hole in the side of a rock just to the left of the larger of the two falls.

Akmon's lair. I knew, because as I drew in a deep breath the scent of rotting meat, fresh death and spider venom gagged me. As my human mind recalled the neat little body packages he'd wrapped up for later, my wolf mind snarled. At least she wasn't scared.

I crept closer, using every one of my senses to ensure I wasn't about to be skewered by a swinging spear or crushed under an avalanche of rocks.

Surprisingly enough, I made it to the cave entrance without incident. Strange, but then again, maybe not. What creature would be stupid enough to come here on purpose, never mind venture inside? Akmon would not be expecting anyone he didn't bring here himself.

"Hello?"

My ears perked at the rusty sound of Myrr's voice. Not only was she here, she *was* alive. I bounded forward like a pup, tossing my head with joy.

"Ha, is that you, girlie? I was wondering when you'd get here." I searched for my friend in the shadowy cave and stopped short when I finally saw her hanging against the wall, wrapped in silk from the neck down, only her head free. "Nice set up he's got, eh?"

I had so many questions, but they'd have to wait. I padded toward her, on high alert as I rose up on my back legs and began to carefully tear at her bindings.

"I sort of wanted to stay a little longer because he was feeding me these amazing bananas before he left, and I saw what looked like a fruit salad," the old Oracle said. "They were the best I've ever had. Huge, and so sweet..."

I growled, letting my lips tremble for maximum effect, and she stopped talking. It took longer than I wanted it to, but soon enough, she was free and, on her feet, again. I tipped my head toward the cave entrance, and she shook her head.

"Not yet. Kevin's back there and wrapped up too, worse than me since he wouldn't stop barking and biting."

My hell-hound *had* survived! It was a banner day, and I wasn't about to squander the luck the universe had doled out. It was almost too good to be true.

I nodded and the pair of us made for a cavern off to the right but a pained scream in the distance stopped me in my tracks. A voice my wolf ears knew well. It was one of ours, and he was being hurt.

Myrr met my gaze with a grim stare, and my stomach bottomed out.

Nicholas.

CHAPTER 8

Raven

Pain arced through my body as I jammed my shoulder into the web-covered window for the dozenth time.

"Son of a bitch!"

A chunk of glass was still poking out of my left shoulder, but it was the last thing on my mind. I ripped it free and threw it aside.

I'd tried the door downstairs in the hope that Akmon had missed it, but it was sealed shut and even less likely than the windows to be broken through.

"Find something to give me some leverage instead of standing there gawking at me," I barked, hot fury rolling through me as I turned to Theo.

"S-sorry." His eyes widened in fear, and he stumbled right into action.

It had only been fifteen minutes since Diana's departure, and nearly five since I'd heard any sign of Akmon.

I tore my sword from my belt, thrusting it into the center of the web with everything I had. My arms screamed as they thudded dully into the stuff, sending agonizing vibrations all the way up to my elbows. I stared, dumbfounded, at my sword as I yanked it free.

Faced with the strength of the web, the metal of the blade itself had given way first, the tip of it bending downward like a bent finger. I hurled it aside in a rage, sending it clattering against the stony wall, "Fuck!"

Theo let out a little yelp, wincing in fear as I turned, but I strode right past him, heading for the stairs. "Keep looking for something to give me leverage."

Mav had disappeared elsewhere into the lighthouse, no doubt doing the same, and I was thankful that he wasn't within reach. Because, with the way I felt right now, I wasn't sure I could guarantee his safety if he was any closer to me.

Had Diana managed to avoid all the creature's traps? Had Akmon seen her making a run for the jungle? And if she had made it away from the beach, would she be able to find her way to Nicholas and the others, assuming they were even still alive? A big part of me hoped she wouldn't find them.

Because when Akmon got back to his lair, if she was there rescuing the others, she would be forced to stand and fight rather than run like she should. And trying to protect three others, while fighting, was a good way to get killed.

"Fealty," I spat, fingers digging into my palms.

Fuck fealty.

And fuck the Territories and everyone in them except Diana. If she got mad at me for busting out of this place and following her before her stupid two-hour time limit, that was fine. Her fucking kiss had short circuited my brain...the taste of her blood off the cut on her lips, the way her body had molded to mine.

If not for that, I'd have been out a window fourteen minutes ago.

I would do what I had to do, so long as she lived.

I surged up the countless stone steps that wound their way up the lighthouse, leaping onto the top floor a few moments later. The entire perimeter of the room was encased in glass, and in the center, a massive, unlit lightbulb.

Thing about those windows? No webs covered them. I leapt up and hung from the rafters there with ease so I could look out the window to see what I was dealing with.

I sucked in a deep breath as I stared down into the churning white caps below. The lighthouse was easily twenty stories tall, but it was a fall I could manage...

Assuming I hit the water and missed the outcropping of rocks that poked through the roiling water every few yards or so.

I let out a mad chuckle, exhilaration overtaking the fear. I lifted my fist, preparing to ram it through the glass, anticipation thrumming hot through my veins.

I'm coming, Frostbite.

"Fucking hell, Raven!"

I wheeled around, fist at the ready, to find Maverick stepping out of what looked to be a low-tech elevator, almost like a dumbwaiter but for people.

"What the hell do you think you're doing? Do you think you're going to be able to help her if your brains are splattered down below?" He let out a huff of disgust that almost had me launching that fist after all, but then he held up a hand. "Wait! Look, I have an idea. Come downstairs with me. It will take two minutes of your time. If you don't think it's solid, you can come back and...do whatever the hell you were planning to do here." He tossed a dismissive wave toward the glass then motioned for me to join him in the dumbwaiter.

I opened my mouth to argue that there was no time for stupid ideas, but the torch he held gave me pause. "Is the webbing flammable?"

"Not as is, but I have something in mind."

I crossed the room and stepped through the door, a mix of anger and hope rushing through me. When we reached the ground floor, Theo was waiting.

"Any luck?"

Mav stepped out and scanned the room for a brief second, his eyes settling on something near the desk at the room's edge. He surged toward it, with a glance at Theo. "Is this your guava wine?"

The older man nodded, cocking his head. His face lit up with realization a moment later, "Hot damn, that might actually work! If I wasn't drunk, I'd help–"

I bowled right past Maverick, hefting the keg and bringing it to the window I'd managed to smash earlier. The alcohol pricked at my nose as I doused the web in the stuff. It was *strong*, more like liquor than wine. And that was exactly what we needed.

Mav set his makeshift torch to it a moment later, and my whole body hummed with tension as I stared at the flames.

Come on. Come on...

It felt like an hour before it took, but it was probably only seconds before the web was ablaze with bluish fire. And it didn't just burn, it completely vaporized the stuff.

"Yes!" Mav shouted.

But I didn't stick around for the celebration. I bolted through the open window the moment the web gave way, ignoring the stinging lick of flames. I hit the sand, using my momentum to roll so I could leap back to my feet without slowing down. I turned.

I hated to give the guy any credit at all, but for Diana...

"We have a better chance of saving her with both of us there." Besides, I might need some bait to lure Akmon away from her. I fully expected the coward to try to convince me to wait like Diana had asked. And I wasn't sure what would happen if he did.

Fear flashed in his eyes, but his head dipped into a nod. "Agree."

He followed just behind me, leaping out a window no mere human would jump from, and, to my surprise,

Theo pulled up the rear, letting himself out the door at the base of the lighthouse. I shook my head, holding up a hand. "You won't be able to keep up."

"So be it." His bleary eyes were clear as a bell in the moonlight now, and gleaming with determination. "This is my only chance to get off this damned island, and I'm not going to miss it. Even if it kills me."

I glanced at Mav, then nodded. I was the fastest of the three of us by far and carrying him wouldn't slow me down much. More importantly, the old man's knowledge of the spider could come in handy.

His eyes widened in fear as I lunged, but I had him by his midsection before he could resist, throwing him over my shoulder.

"Let's go," I spat, breaking into a full-on sprint.

Mav rushed after me, his strange, suspicious magic no one could really identify allowing him to *almost* keep up. And he'd have to do just that, because I wasn't about to slow down for anything—not with Diana's life on the line. We covered ground fast, avoiding pitfalls and trip wires, and it wasn't long before a familiar scent pricked at my nose.

Diana. Or, her wolf, to be more precise.

Traversing the length of the island was faster at the speed we were going, but it still took time. Time that I felt ticking by far too fast.

The sound of water caught my ears just as Theo spoke.

"That's his lair. Right ahead," he gasped.

I tossed him unceremoniously to the ground and moved closer to the cave entrance, every muscle tensed for battle, ears straining to hear something–anything– over the rush of water from the twin falls.

I took in the condition of the forest from the opposite direction we'd come in, and knew that Akmon *had* returned, there was no question of that. He'd torn ass to get here, trampling trees and underbrush the whole way. Mav wasn't far behind, but there was no time to wait. All that mattered now was getting to my fated mate.

I couldn't wait for him. "Stay here."

Not that I thought Theo would follow me in.

A riot of sensations flooded my enhanced senses at once as I entered the dank cave. The smells of Diana, Nicholas, Myrr, Kevin, and countless others. The sound of a body struggling uselessly against impossibly strong silk, thumping and bumping against the cave walls.

But that wasn't what had my attention.

The enormous spider was just yards ahead, those milky eyes fixed directly on me. Body tensed and ready to spring.

The only way to her, is through that thing.

I let out a battle cry as I hurled myself at the monster, blood thrumming hot. I'd experienced it many times before, almost always when fighting werewolves, or other vampires, but there was something different this time. I wasn't fighting for myself, or some aloof monarch in a high tower somewhere. I was fighting for Diana.

My heart.

One of the beast's enormous arms snapped toward me like a switchblade, and the realization hit me as I dropped to the sandy ground and slid under it. For the first time since I could remember, it really felt like I was the underdog—that I might not survive this. It was a strange sensation, and one I didn't enjoy at all.

Time to turn the tide.

I whipped my dagger from my belt, slamming it into Akmon's chest and sidestepping his next attack in a single motion.

Green blood coated the tip of the blade, but it hadn't been nearly deep enough. Maybe if I still had my sword… I shoved the thought down, leaping sideways in time to see a ball of web blast through the spot where I'd been standing.

I surged forward for another attack, but I had my work cut out for me to dodge as he lunged to meet me, massive pincers snapping closed where I should've been. A loud thud hit the beast a moment later, and I roared in pure elation as Diana's wolf form came into view, spitting a hunk of the monster's flesh from her mouth.

She was alive.

Footsteps sounded from all around, but there was no time to look at them. I dashed forward, kicking off as the monster's milky gaze shifted to Diana. He turned back to me just in time, and shooting pain coursed through me as he caught me in the side with a swipe of his spindly leg.

He was on me in an instant, following up with a flurry of attacks that few could have blocked. Fortunately for me, I was one of the few fast enough. I rolled under his body when the opportunity came, slicing at his belly in a counterattack of my own. My eyes flitted to my stomach for just a moment, and I cursed. He'd cut me badly, and the same could hardly be said the other way. The tiny dagger was a ridiculous weapon against such a monster, but I'd have to make it work.

I'd make it a death by a thousand cuts if I had to. And I'd make sure the blow he'd landed on me had been his last. I sliced off the tip of his leg on his next attack, falling into the groove of the battle as Diana fell in beside me. A burst of web surged toward her, with Akmon's pincer-like jaws just behind, but I was on him before the attack could be realized, jabbing my blade into one of his eyes.

A horrible scream that fell somewhere between a Hunter and a banshee split the air, and I winced as one of his legs smacked into Diana's jaw. She flew across the room as if hit by a cannon, bouncing off the wall and hitting the ground with a thud.

My vision went crimson, and I leapt forward in a rage, exchanging a dozen blows with the monster in a matter of seconds. His legs, jaws, and spinneret all worked in practiced harmony, never giving me the opportunity to land a clean attack. But, if I was anything, I was fast. And that fucker couldn't see me.

I parried or dodged every strike, landing minor cuts and scratches every time I could. I just had to find my moment to finish him off–

A rock smacked into the side of Akmon's deformed, human head, stunning him for the briefest of moments as he turned to see a defiant-looking Theo at the mouth of the cave. I took advantage and lunged, curving mid-air to dodge an attack from one of Akmon's legs and jammed my dagger directly into his neck. I roared victoriously, but he wasn't done yet.

His mandibles shot toward my arm, and I released my dagger just in time to keep my arm attached to my body, then rolled to the ground. Diana was at my side but looked shaky.

"Careful," I shouted, dodging under a combination attack of the monster's web and legs.

Judging by the amount of blood gushing from the wound on his neck, it was only a matter of time. But that was a fact I could hardly make use of, given Diana's condition.

I slammed my foot into an unsteady-looking leg, grinning as it snapped beneath my boot. The monster reeled, letting out a high-pitched screech, but didn't go down. Diana snapped with her jaws, and swiped at it with her claws, and I let out a growl as its eyes flitted toward her. The spider struck at the cave's ceiling, whirling backward to blast a massive gob of web at her in the same motion. Rocks and stalactites rained down on her, but I had no time to see if they'd hit.

I pushed off with everything I had, getting to eye-level with the creature just as a form appeared behind him. The spider screeched in pain as something hit, and I seized the opportunity, gripping my dagger from where it had lodged into his collarbone, and shoving my other arm into his chest as I dragged the blade in a circular motion.

Stinking, green blood oozed coating me in sickening spurts as I decapitated him, in tune with the final few beats of the dying monster's heart. Mav came into view at the monster's back, yanking his sword free of its spinneret.

I whirled toward Diana, sprinting to the pile of rubble blocking my view. "Diana!"

One of the rocks rumbled, then rolled aside, revealing her wolf form. The fur faded slowly from her skin, as she shifted back to two feet, and my heart skipped a beat. Was she hurt or worse?

Her chest heaved as she pushed herself unsteadily to her feet. She let out a weak chuckle, shaking her head at me. "God damn you're a mess."

I looked her up and down, ignoring the thick green blood that was now all over my body. I whipped off my shirt and gave it to her. "Are you hurt?"

"I've been better, but I'm okay." Her brows knit with worry as she glanced at my stomach, tucking my ripped shirt around her. It dangled to the tops of her thighs. "Definitely better than you."

"It'll heal before long. We just need to get the hell out of here," I said, finally getting a chance to take in the surroundings. The cave was enormous, with a half dozen mossy, dripping passages leading in all different directions. "Did you find the others?" I winced at the smell of spider entrails as I sniffed the air.

"Myrr's fine. I tucked her away when Akmon brought Nicholas back. He's hurt, but he'll live, if we can get some blood into him." Diana turned to face Maverick and Theo. "You two, wait here and keep watch for any Vanators while we get the others."

I followed as she led the way toward the nearest passage. She was a bit shaky on her feet, but werewolves were a sturdy lot, and, miraculously, it seemed like mostly minor cuts and bruises were all she had been dealt.

"It was good timing you showing up when you did, vampire," a familiar, raspy voice called.

A loud, chewing sound hit my ears, and I couldn't help but laugh. "Even at a time like this, she eats."

"Her powers make it easy to be calm, I think. I'll wager she already knew we were going to win," Diana reasoned with a weary smile as Myrr and Nicholas came into view a moment later.

Myrr was setting a banana peel atop a pile of a dozen others, and she turned to greet us with a nod. She took a bite before speaking, "Can't we just stay here for a bit longer? The spider's dead anyways, and there's so much good food here."

Diana rolled her eyes, gesturing roughly for the older woman to rise. "We're leaving immediately. There could still be more Vanators here, and we need to get off this island before they find us. We're battle-scarred as it is, and we need the head start on getting to Jade before more come looking for us."

A shape poked out from behind a nearby rock, and I stepped to get between it and Diana before realizing what it was. Despite her words a moment earlier, Diana dropped to her knees as a massive beast loped into view.

"Kevin!"

The hell-hound's ears perked, and he leaped from side to side in between taking licks at her palms. He rolled over as Diana petted him, and she set upon him for a belly rub.

Myrr glanced over at her. "He's a smart one. Tried to fight off the spider at first, but then gave in and stayed very still, so as not to draw attention to himself. He managed to get free when he scented Diana, but the fighting was over."

"Definitely smarter than he looks," Nicholas agreed.

I turned away from the reunion, shooting a glance his way.

He raised a hand in greeting, grinning as he met my gaze. His other hand was pressed against the large gash on his side. "Wish I got to see how you guys killed that fucker. Speaking of which, you've got a little..." he gestured to his cheek.

The adrenaline flooded out of me in an instant, and I found myself laughing with relief as I wiped a chunk of spider meat from my jaw. "Man, it's good to see that you're alive."

His eyes bulged as he looked around to confirm that I

was, indeed, talking to him. "Coming from you that may as well be an 'I love you buddy'. Are you getting soft on me, Raven?"

"Nah," I said as I reached down to help him off the ground. "I just don't want to be the only vampire in this ragtag crew. Right now, we're the majority. I want to keep it that way."

Despite my words, though, I couldn't deny that my heart felt a little less heavy seeing his grinning—if pale—face. "We'll get some blood into you soon. Can you walk?"

He accepted my hand, pulling himself to his feet. "I should be good, as long as we don't have to run anywhere. Myrr...helped me in that department."

Myrr rose as well, and a jolt of surprise shot through me as I glanced at her. There was a large, reddened bite mark on her wrist. Nicholas had drank from her, and recently.

"Bleh." She waved me off as she caught my gaze. "I'm drier than a bale of old hay. Didn't seem to do much good."

"It did a lot," Nicholas cut in. "Even if it did taste like dirty socks."

She let out a cackle, gave him a light shove, and then went in for another bite of her banana. "If he could have used one of the Vanators that would have been better, but they all died. On their own, like they did when you caught them before. Their mistress don't like them getting caught."

I looked at Diana and she tipped her head. I could almost hear her thinking that if Lilis had taken her wrath on her own men, then we really needed to get the fuck out of here.

"You guys about ready to head out?" Maverick called. "Probably best if we go before Lilis gets her second wind."

Again, I had to agree with the shitbird. And no doubt, Diana did too.

"Hop to it, all," she said as she strode past us, Kevin in tow as she led the way toward the cave's exit. "We're headed for the beach and whatever boat is still floating."

"Back to being bossy, as usual," Myrr muttered, stuffing a few choice fruits into her shirt before following.

We made our way out as a unit, finding a victorious-looking Theo staring up at the sky right outside the mouth of the cave.

"Last look at the most beautiful stars in the world," he said with a happy sigh. "Now let's get off this damned island."

"I'm with you, my friend. But your rescue comes with a price. These two need to borrow your wrist," Diana said, waggling a hand between me and Nicholas. "They both need to heal if we want to get back to the beach and unwedge our ship from the rocks."

"My name is Nicholas, and I do apologize for requiring a favor so soon after meeting you, but I'm in a pinch." Nicholas managed a sheepish smile as he gestured to the crimson stain spreading across his white shirt. "I won't take too much, don't worry."

Theo went a little green around the gills, then reluctantly tipped his head. "I do owe you...and all the others I may have led astray."

He held out his arm and squeezed his eyes closed. "Go."

Nicholas made short work of it, piercing the man's skin with one fang and then drinking deeply before releasing him.

"Th-that's it? I thought it'd hurt a lot more."

"That's it. Thank you." Nicholas hesitated before continuing. "And I'm sorry for what you've suffered."

Theo froze and stared at the vampire for a long moment. "You saw...in my head?"

Nicholas nodded.

The old man seemed to absorb that quickly. "Thank you. It's been difficult, but I'm ready to move on."

I had questions. How long had he been here? Did he have anyone to go home to? But I opted to save them for another time, instead, taking hold of his arm. I took a few, hard pulls from his wrist, suppressing the rush of hunger that gripped me. When I pulled back, I could already feel the surge of power rushing through my body.

I was about to thank him as well, when he let out a gasp. "And who is this magnificent creature?"

We all looked around in confusion until it became clear that his attention was fully focused on Myrr.

"Name's Myrr." She cocked her head and sized him

up with a glance. "And while I prefer my men a little prettier than you, I like the hobo look. Like you woke up today and said, 'I don't care what anyone thinks of me.' Refreshing. I do that too sometimes."

"Or maybe he woke up as the prisoner in a fucking spider's lair and fashion wasn't high on his priority list," I muttered to Diana under my breath.

She swallowed a laugh that made me feel even better than the fresh infusion of blood. If she was still able to laugh after all we'd been through...gods she was amazing. So, fucking resilient.

"We'll see. Maybe I'll let you make me dinner sometime if you play your cards right," Myrr continued.

I had to admire both of them. Myrr for the confidence when she looked rather like a goblin herself, and Theo for shooting his shot, and seeing Myrr's inner beauty. Though even that was questionable.

More likely she was the first woman in his age range he'd seen in who knew how many decades...

Either way that and the fact that none of us were dead lifted my mood.

For the next few hours, we trekked through the forest, making our way to the beach in good time despite the two older humans slowing us down. We had to take a lot of breaks, which allowed Myrr and the others to grab more fruit.

We were nearing dawn when we popped out of the treeline, and I gestured down the beach a piece. "That's where we hid the skiff. I'll drag it down to the shore and–"

An ominous crackling sounded at our backs. Soft at first but growing louder with every second. Then the creak of wood being torn, followed by what could only be a huge tree crashing to the ground.

I whirled, unable to make anything out in the dark, dense brush. "What the fuck was that?"

Theo dropped to his knees; eyes wide with panic. "Oh boy. This is bad. Worse than bad."

Diana made her way to my side. "Lilis?"

"Could be. Maybe she's creating some kind of earth-quake or—"

Theo was already rising shakily to his feet. "That's no earthquake. That's Bathsheba."

"Who?" the rest of us demanded in unison.

His wrinkled throat worked as he swallowed hard. "Bathsheba. She only rises twice a year. She shouldn't be here, she's months early from rising, but she must've sensed Akmon's death."

"How big is she?" Diana asked.

Another tree fell in the distance, closer this time. Then, a horrible screech filled the air, drowning out Theo's reply, but I saw my answer soon enough. The ground beneath us shook as a cluster of trees crumbled near the edge of the forest twenty yards away from us, and the first of Bathshe-ba's legs made contact where the beach met the jungle.

Kevin whimpered as the spider stepped onto the

sand, her dozens of bright red eyes fixing directly on us as she advanced. A woman's torso and head protruded from the top of her thorax, barely visible on her enormous frame. Standing a solid thirty feet tall, she made Akmon look like something you might find in your cellar.

There was only one thing we could do.

"Run."

CHAPTER 9

Diana

"Forget the skiff! Straight to the ship!" Raven hollered. "We've got the old ones. Go!"

I whirled, adrenaline already surging through my veins as I broke into a full-on sprint toward the ocean. It only took a few moments to realize that the beach was much bigger than it had been when we arrived.

Low tide. What a reason to be killed.

Fear made my legs churn faster even as the ground shook and rumbled beneath me. Behind me.

More beach meant less swimming, which was great... if we made it to the water at all. Even now, I could see our ship by the light of the moon. But low tide would make it that much harder to unwedge the boat from the rocks.

One problem at a time.

Not that far...just keep going.

There was another roar, and I didn't dare to turn

around for another look. Akmon had been a dangerous enemy, but we'd faced plenty of those before. We'd survived, but it had taken all of us, and even I knew we'd gotten lucky.

Bathsheba went far beyond that.

She was a thing of nightmares.

Raven and Nicholas were fast, strong, and lethal, and I was no slouch myself. But this bitch was the size of a building. And best as I could tell, she didn't have milky eyes. She was staring us the fuck down.

"Take her." Raven appeared at my side for the briefest of moments, with Myrr thrown over his shoulder like a sack of potatoes. "I'm going ahead to try to dislodge the boat. Don't stop moving."

"Got it." I shouldered Myrr's slight frame, completely ignoring my instincts as I looked over my shoulder.

Bathsheba was just a few dozen feet away now, her hundred crimson eyes and bladed legs glimmering in the moonlight. Short sharp hairs covered every inch of her building-sized abdomen and thorax, except the horrifying human torso sticking out of the top. More corpse than woman, the bones of her human body jutted out at odd angles, and her lopsided face was contorted into something that resembled a smile.

My wolf howled for me to shift, to run as fast as I possibly could until I was far away from here, but I repressed it. Inhaling deeply, I glanced at the others, taking stock of the situation. Kevin was at my heels, Mav was close behind, with Nicholas and Theo bringing up the rear. Raven would be at the boat any second now. Running ahead would only serve to split us up because we weren't getting out of here until that boat got moving.

And if it didn't?

I shuddered, trying not to think about what she'd do to us if she caught up. At least it would be quick...I hoped.

My heart skipped a beat as a blur of white zipped over my head, smashing into the beach just ahead of me with a force that left a small crater in the ground.

I blinked just in time to avoid the scattered sand, zigzagging around the glob of steaming web.

"Try to dodge the web as you run," I shouted, wincing at the huge ball of web hurtling straight toward my face as I turned to see when the next was coming.

I tossed Myrr to the side and dove face-first into the sand, rolling awkwardly to my feet as the web splashed harmlessly into the ocean just a few feet away now.

"I can swim real good," Myrr said, hobbling into the shallow water.

Raven was already at the ship and had climbed onto the rocks. I could hear him grunting as he heaved with everything he had to free it. With the water low...would even his strength be enough?

Water splashed against my cheeks as I dove forward, sending up a silent prayer to the Goddess that we'd live to see another day. Seeing that the others were still following just behind, I pumped with everything I had, swimming faster than I'd known I could.

And, when I heard the series of booming splashes at our backs, I kicked it up even further. We would not die today.

I kept my eyes ahead and watched Raven, praying under my breath. He was pressed up against the ship's hull, every muscle in his body tensed as he pushed off against one of the rocks. The ship creaked audibly as he heaved, and my breath caught in my throat as I watched.

Come on. You can do it.

He pulled back, pausing for just a second, then slammed his feet outward once again, roaring with pain as bones and sinew were pressed to their very limits. His muscles strained from the exertion, and the ship moved almost imperceptibly. The shift in tides had definitely dislodged the boat somewhat, but it was so heavy, even for a vampire with supernatural strength like Raven. I cursed, already thinking of alternative options. If the ship wouldn't move then–

A low, cracking sound split the air, and the boat floated gently away from the rocks it'd been trapped in. Raven had torn a one-foot hole in the side, but it was above water level and still seaworthy. The ship rolled forward on the calm sea to meet us, and Raven's arm was in my face before I knew it. I waved it away, gesturing for the others to board first.

I winced as a net of web smacked into the hull just inches to my right but there was no time to waste. I hoisted Theo up to Nick, and only then accepted Raven's hand now that everyone else was on board. His strong hand gripped mine like a vise, and he yanked me up with ease. Worry flashed across his face as he glanced behind me, but he dashed toward the helm rather than speaking.

We weren't out of danger yet.

"We need to make it to deeper waters as soon as possible," I called, heaving the anchor back onto our ship as the engine whirred to a start.

Bathsheba was closing in on us fast, but a wave of hope washed over me as our boat slid into motion. On our ship, we at least had a fighting chance. Mav's crossbow twanged to my right, and I was in motion before the arrow had even struck, racing to the storage room. I dove to my knees, tearing open three large weapon chests before catching sight of the wooden grip of another one of our crossbows.

I pulled it free, finding two more just beneath it, then sprinted back to the deck. I turned, tossing one to Nicholas.

Fear snaked up my spine as I kneeled to load up the other. The spider had closed nearly half the distance in such a short amount of time. At this rate, we weren't going to make it out of her reach. I fired off a quick shot, aimed right at the human head on the monster's torso.

She dipped under it, sending ripples through the water that reached all the way to our ship. "Fuck."

She had ridiculously fast reaction time, as if the

monster needed any other advantages, on top of no weakness that I could see. I yanked back the string, jamming another bolt into place and taking aim as she rose. Only a couple of tries left.

"Wait for it..." Raven's steadying voice came from my right, and I turned to see him staring down the bolt of another crossbow

Bathsheba lurched forward, massive legs kicking off the ground in a shocking burst of speed. My breath caught, and time seemed to slow as her sword-length mandibles shot toward me, her massive, hairy body following just behind.

"Now."

I found her head again in an instant in the adrenaline-fueled haze, letting the bolt fly. I raised my arms in terror as it whooshed through the air, hoping it struck true in time to stop her.

Our boat rocked as she lurched suddenly sideways, and the bolt sunk into her thorax rather than her brain. Two more crossbows twanged before I had time to load again, one on either side, and my heart froze in my chest as I stared after them.

Her gnarled, human arm shot upward in a blur, tearing the first projectile right out of the sky, but the second was just behind it. Her head whipped backward, exploding in a cloud of green mist as it struck true, and waves surged around her as she scrambled for footing.

Mav let out a whistle from my left. "Got her."

Her screeching roar brought me to my knees, rattling

me through my bones, and I forced another bolt into the crossbow as she steadied herself, but it was too late. In a desperate heave, she flung her enormous body the last bit of the way, smashing clumsily into our ship, flailing in the water.

The crossbow clattered across the deck and the air whooshed from my lungs as I was catapulted headfirst into the remnants of the mast. I was still seeing stars when a massive, bladed leg appeared just above me, and I scrambled to move out of the way, panic driving me. But it was no use. My arms floundered, hardly responding to my brain's commands. Shock from the fall? I couldn't say, but one thing was certain.

I was going to die today, after all.

Something big blocked my view of the early morning sky and I blinked to see Raven's broad, muscular back. Dagger raised, he let out a roar as he prepared to meet the coming attack. Mav flashed into view from the side, an ax whirling as he leaped at the spider's tree-sized leg. He hewed clean through it, leaving the severed tip of Bathsheba's leg twitching and writhing on the deck, green blood oozing from the severed limb.

My ears rang as the stump of that same limb smashed into the boat a moment later. I reached for the mast, willing my jelly-like arms with everything I had to grip tight, knowing all the while how futile it was. Bathsheba could sink our boat with a single strike. I could only assume she liked to play with her food, but I was sick of the games.

Sick of being terrified.

So, I craned my head back, opened my eyes, and stared defiantly into hers as she loomed over me.

I'll meet you on the other side soon, father.

Her mandibles click-clacked and her red eyes gleamed with something like glee as she swooped forward to strike, only to stop short.

The next few moments went by in a haze. There was a loud splash, followed by an enormous crash like two trains colliding, and a massive, green and gray blur. I hunched over, covering my head as the ship rocked and rolled and what sounded like a deluge of hail clattered against the deck.

"Holy hell did you see that?" Theo shouted.

I forced my eyes open just in time to see Sal diving back into the ocean with Bathsheba's head in her mouth. A quick look at Bathsheba told the rest of the story. Her entire upper half was missing, human torso, pincers, and all. And the rest of her went crashing into the sea.

Dead. Torn in half with a single bite from Sal.

The dragon had returned to us, and just in the nick of time. She'd saved us all.

Theo backed up against the stairway, eyes fixed on her. "What the fuck was that?"

"I'll tell you what happened." Myrr broke into a fit of cackles, smacking the side of her leg with a wizened hand. "That spider thought she was tough. Then she met Sal. Ain't nothing meaner and faster than a dragon, boy. Not even a big ass spider like Bathsheba."

Kevin let out a single bark, apparently thinking better of it when the sea-dragon leaned forward, pushing her head over the railing of our ship as she swam alongside us. I strode up to her, laying my hand on her nose. Despite the excitement of the moment, I couldn't help but frown at the melancholy energy radiating out of her even now. She'd never forget what happened to her George. But her sadness was tinged with warmth, this time. She hadn't just stumbled upon us. She'd sensed the danger we were in and had wanted to help us.

"Thank you."

A soft rumbling came from her throat in response. Something like a cat purring?

A wave of putrid air hit me in the face like a punch as she belched loudly, licking at her lips with her massive tongue. So... definitely not a purr, more like indigestion. I chuckled, patting her cheek a final time before she pulled away, filling my mind with a final, parting thought.

No, Wolf Queen. Thank you.

CHAPTER 10

Diana

We drifted along the sea in shell-shocked silence for a few minutes, until the stress and adrenaline of the past few days poured out of me in a rush, and I broke into a semi-hysterical laugh. "You seriously couldn't make this up if you tried. No one would believe you."

A warm hand fell on my shoulder, and I turned to see Raven standing behind me with a look of concern on his face. "You okay? You took a pretty hard fall."

I shrugged, not quite able to bring myself to push away his hand. "I felt a bit loopy for a second there but I'm pretty sure I was just stunned. I'll be sore tomorrow, but I should be fine. I'm just laughing because how do you defeat the biggest spider you have ever seen, only to be attacked by a spider twenty times bigger, and have it get eaten by your not-really-a-pet dragon? It sounds insane."

He flashed an uncharacteristic smile. "It'll be a hell of a story for when we're done with all this."

"Still not sure why we were in such a rush to leave," Myrr grumbled, yanking a bag of nuts out of a nearby chest. She frowned disdainfully as it hit her tongue, but continued chewing, nonetheless.

I rolled my eyes. "He was just trying to fatten you up to eat you, you know."

"Would've crossed that bridge when we got to it."

Theo chuckled, stepping over to her and extending his hand for a nut. "I do appreciate a woman with a healthy appetite."

"Hers might be a bit more than healthy," Nicholas said, blocking an elbow-jab from the Oracle.

"We should really get to work." I glanced around, surveying the damage that'd been done to the massive ship. From the broken mast and ruined stairway to the holes that had been punched into the side, it looked like we'd survived a hurricane. And, in a way, we had survived much worse. Kevin's massive tongue slapped up against my cheek, and I leaned into him, exhaustion sucking the last dregs of energy from my body.

Using the glob of spider webbing, we patched up the hole that Raven had put in the boat tearing it from the rocks. Like Theo had said, the stuff was hard and as we manipulated it, it hardened like steel over the breach in the hull.

"That's the most urgent thing," Raven said. "The rest can wait."

Exhaustion rippled through me, and I didn't have anything left to argue. There was water that needed to be pumped out, food stores to account for, water to replenish. Maybe more repairs that we couldn't see yet?

I ran a hand through my hair. "I guess we can save it until tomorrow. Let's get some sleep and get this all taken care of when we wake up."

Nicholas breathed a sigh of relief, already heading toward the cabin. "Now that's an order I'm happy to follow."

I nudged Kevin. "You can go too, buddy. You earned your rest."

He eyed Raven for a long moment, then leaned forward to give his hand a lick. Raven pulled away from Kevin's tongue, giving him a scratch behind the ear instead. "Eck. Hell-hound breath sure is something, huh?"

I shrugged, unable to stop myself from smiling. They were right. Kevin was smart. He had seen the way Raven had jumped in front of me, and it felt like this was his way of thanking him. I was certain of it. "We'll have to ask Gabe about some fresher breath options next time we see him."

Theo and Myrr lingered on deck, looking out across the water. Strangely they did suit one another. I opened my mouth to say so to Raven.

"How will we find Jade?" Raven asked quietly, tipping his head to look up at the sky and the distant pricks of light above us. "Where do we go next?"

I followed his gaze as a star shot across the horizon, flaring brilliant and then disappearing. "I don't know. Mav thought he might be able to find her."

Raven turned to look at me, and I thought he'd be angry that I'd brought Maverick up. But his eyes were not angry, not one bit. "I know you want to believe him, Frostbite. I just don't want you to get hurt by him. Not again."

I had to look away from the sincerity in his face. Because I didn't doubt he meant what he said, but I also couldn't help but want to believe in Mav.

"Perhaps you should make a wish," Raven smiled and handed me a coin.

I laughed. "A wish?"

"A prayer to whatever gods might listen?" He shrugged. "What is there to lose?"

I took the coin warmed by his hand and rolled it across my fingers. I recognized the stamp of the Wild Queen on it, a crown on one side.

I flipped it in the air once and caught it. Perhaps... perhaps it wouldn't hurt. I pressed my lips to the coin, to the side the crown was embedded in. "To whoever might be listening while we float under the stars, please guide us to Jade."

I held the coin a moment longer and then flipped it out into the ocean. There was no splash, no sign that it hit the water. We leaned over the edge to see a burst of light flow up and around the bottom of the boat.

"Strange," Raven murmured. "Maybe you have a little magic after all?"

"Me? No, that was probably just—"

"Are you okay?" Theo said.

We turned as he reached out, missing Myrr as she went to her knees. Her upper body stiffened, and she turned to look at me, her voice deepening to an impossible timber.

"*The one you seek is in the desert sands, brave the fire of the blasted lands.*"

Myrr gasped and thumped a fist against her chest. "Damn heartburn!"

My body froze as the words hummed in the air. Blasted lands. That was Demon Territory.

"Did we just get help?" Raven shook his head. "Damn, all this time..."

"Come on, Myrr," Theo helped her stand. "You should go lie down."

"Bah, I'm not that tired." She yawned so loud her jaw cracked, and I took note that she didn't argue with Theo, letting him take her arm.

"That's the same voice...the one who's spoken through Myrr before," I said. "I think he wants to help us."

Raven sighed. "I hope so. Because Demon Territory is a shit place to die if the voice is sending us in the wrong direction."

But at least we had a direction. Hell, we were alive, *and* we had a direction.

Raven stared wordlessly into the distance. The pinprick of light from the lighthouse was still visible, likely just hours away from being extinguished forever. Not that it mattered much anymore. Now that the monsters had been vanquished, the island was the paradise it had masqueraded as for all this time.

I stiffened as I had a thought. "You know...back at the lighthouse, you disobeyed a direct order."

"And I'd do it again to save you. When are you going to get it? You are my reason, Diana. I will always disobey if it means protecting you."

I scowled, twisting away from him. "You need to stop saying things like that. You're a distraction neither of us can afford. This," I gestured to him and then myself, "doesn't work."

My thoughts about fucking him senseless hadn't left me. I was just more...aware now that we were back on the boat. Headed into danger again, and I couldn't afford to indulge this connection between us.

"Seems to me that we keep running into problems because it works a little too well."

The heat in his gaze sent a shiver rolling through me and I had to look away as he continued.

"I don't get it, Diana..."

I was filthy, and exhausted, and my whole body hurt, but I couldn't deny it. His voice was like a wash of silk over me, and I had to squeeze my thighs together to stay the rush of warmth that pooled there. I couldn't stop thinking about his mouth on me, back at the Wild Queen Casino that night...

"We're on this earth, for who knows how much longer. And we have so many other beasts to fight." He paused to swipe a curl away from my cheek. "Why fight this, too?"

I pinched my eyes closed against the onslaught of sensations, turning my back to him. He was close enough that I could feel his chest against my back...his breath feathering the nape of my neck...that hot mouth just inches away.

"Especially when we both know how good it will feel." His lips found the side of my neck, a lingering soft kiss, heat racing through me.

I couldn't help it. I backed into him with my hips, grinding my ass against him with a low groan. I struggled to think, to find a way to make this not what he wanted it to be.

To make it safe for my heart.

"If we do this for real this time, I need you to know that I'm not giving in to you, Raven. I'm giving in to *me*. It isn't going to turn out the way you're hoping. I have too many people counting on me to focus on my own needs long term. This is for tonight and tonight only. Say you agree."

His fingers closed over my waist and then slid lower to grip my hips as he pressed the hard length of his cock against me. "If you still feel that way in the morning, I won't fight you. But all is fair in love and war, Frostbite.

And tonight, I'm going to do anything I can to change your mind."

Those questing hands abandoned their post on my hips and slid around, over my belly and upward under his shirt I still wore, to cover my breasts. My nipples peaked instantly, and I swallowed a gasp. Holy hell, my reaction to this male—my wolf's reaction to this male—was terrifying.

But I didn't have the strength to deny myself what I needed so badly. Even if I was lying to myself that one night would be enough.

"Take me to bed, Raven."

He let out a snarl, and a second later, my feet whooshed out from under me as he swept me into his arms. We crossed the deck and made it down to my quarters with dizzying speed. And when he finally set me down on my feet, I had to hold onto his shoulders for purchase. Fine by me.

I leaned in and plastered myself against him, but he held me at arm's length and stared down at me, the tips of his fangs gleaming in the darkness.

"You have cuts, and bruises. Let me take care of you first."

I almost fought him on it because that was too tender. Too much. But as he made his way to the bathtub and turned on the water, a sigh exploded from my lips. Maybe just for tonight, I could be soft. Let someone else take the wheel so I could rejuvenate and come back even stronger tomorrow.

I stripped off my shirt—his shirt really—silently, letting it fall to my feet. He watched, motionless, turquoise eyes drinking me in. His hands balled into fists at his side, and I knew he was fighting the urge to touch me. The knowledge gave me peace, because at least I wasn't alone. Naked in front of him, the sound of his breath sawing in and out of his lungs...a song that had my clit throbbing.

My wolf let out a low growl as she began to pace, waiting...anticipating the satisfaction that only Raven could offer.

I turned, giving him my back, as I stepped into the massive copper tub. The hot water pooled around my calves, and I lowered myself to sit. The heat instantly soothed my aching muscles but did nothing to cool the fire in my belly.

"Close your eyes," Raven murmured from behind me.

I did as he asked and let myself slide deeper into the tub with a sigh. I heard him moving around, felt his breath on my neck as he settled to kneel beside the tub.

"I'm going to wash your hair now."

With that warning, he poured warm water over my head, taking care to avoid my face and eyes. Gentle hands stroked my hair, and I bit back a groan. How could something so simple...so small feel so good? But nothing could've prepared me for the tenderness of his touch as he massaged shampoo into my hair.

By the time he'd rinsed the conditioner out a short

while later, tears were streaming down my cheeks, unchecked.

"Did I get suds in your eyes?"

No. I'm a fucking hot mess of hormones and feelings, and you're making me question everything in my life.

"Yes," I lied. "But it's okay, though."

I was still trying to get my stupid emotions under control when he held out a massive bath towel for me a short time later.

"Thank you," I managed, stepping out of the tub and into his arms as he wrapped the towel around me.

He took the ends of the nubby cloth and gently dried my hair. "I could do this every night for the next thousand years, and you'd never have to thank me."

"Stop." I bit my lip hard as I drew back to stare at him. It was making me want something I could never have. Something we could never have. Even if I wanted to...I was a queen of the werewolves. He was a vampire. There was nothing we could have together.

It was the reason why Lycan had never been able to take Evangeline as his mate.

"If we're going to do this tonight, you need to stop with all that. You have to. You know we could never be."

His slow nod and sad smile made me want to take it back. But I never had the chance.

"I'm yours to command, Frostbite," he murmured. And then his mouth met mine. The second our lips collided, my wolf let out a howl, and I plastered myself against him.

This was what we needed right now. All three of us.

I barely registered it when he lifted me into his arms and carried me across the room. The sweep of his tongue against mine, his scent...the heat of his skin like some sort of intoxicating potion made just to bewitch me.

He laid me down on top of the downy blankets and began to strip off his clothes. I was frozen in place, my eyes eating up each inch of skin he revealed. Those ropy, muscled shoulders...his flat stomach with that dark trail of hair leading lower. The hollow just above his lean hips that begged for my tongue.

"Fucking hell. Just seeing your face like that could bring a man to his knees," he hissed, kicking off his pants and climbing onto the bed beside me.

"I've already had you on your knees," I reminded him with a soft laugh as I pressed him onto his back. "And soon I'll return the favor. But first..."

I dipped my head low and reached for his cock with a swallowed gasp. Long, thick, and pulsing in time with the beat of his heart. The pressure between my thighs became unbearable, but I didn't give into the need. Not until I tasted him the way he'd tasted me.

I batted the swollen head of his cock with the tip of my tongue. So smooth, like velvet. I was so taken with it, I barely heard Raven's growl from above.

"Enjoy the teasing while you can, Frostbite, because I'm on a short leash."

Despite the gruff warning, I was undeterred. I closed my lips over his thick head and sucked hard.

"Fuck me."

But the words fell on deaf ears as he flexed his hips in a silent demand for more.

Satisfaction sizzled through me, leaving behind a livewire of sensation. My nipples stiffened as I rubbed against the soft blankets. My pussy ached as I shifted to grind against his thigh. And all the while I bathed him with my tongue. Licking, sucking, pulling even as my hands clutched at his hips, pulling him closer.

"That's enough. Fucking hells, Diana. I'm going to come in your mouth if you don't stop immediately."

But that only made me work him harder. I wanted it. I needed to taste him, salty sweet on my tongue. To watch him as he jerked and flexed, to watch him lose control.

I moaned and sucked him deeper.

"Fuck!" He stilled, gasping...Just a hint of his silky seed leaking out. "Enough!"

The room spun as his hands closed over my waist and he lifted me over him onto my knees. My whole body shook, already tightening and releasing in anticipation of his cock inside me.

"I can't take it any longer. I need to be inside you. I need to feel—"

But the words died on his lips, ending in a snarl as I lifted high and got centered. I should have taken him by inches. Slowly. Gently. Instead, I plunged onto his swollen cock like it was my lifeline. And damned if it didn't feel like that...

I gasped, the world spinning around me.

Every nerve in my body screamed with delight as he filled me to bursting. Neither of us moved, but we didn't have to. His cock kicked and danced inside me, sending a wave of searing pleasure rolling over me.

"Raven, I'm going to come," I whispered, half stunned by the realization. Were we such a perfect fit? What would happen if he *did* move?

But the answers no longer mattered as he bent at the waist to sit up, and nipped at my aching nipple.

"Raven!"

Just like that, I came in a rush of heat and wet and howls and cries. I might have screamed his name, I don't even know. Animalistic noises spilled out of both of us.

My pussy clenched tighter around his unforgiving length, squeezing and releasing in exquisite time.

Through the haze, I could feel the edge of his fangs scraping against my nipple and it only made me come harder. Giving into the need, I swirled my hips against him, grinding that tight bundle of nerves against him even as his cock plowed deep.

"That's it, Frostbite. Take yours."

It was only when the last shudder passed over me that I opened my eyes to find him staring at my face in wonder.

"And I thought you couldn't get more beautiful."

I was still gasping as he rolled his hips beneath me, using my hips to guide me slowly up and down his full length.

"Can you come for me again, love?" he whispered as he worked me over that long, thick cock in slow, steady strokes. "Can I watch your face when you get there and break apart?"

I whimpered my response because I couldn't form words. I could only feel. The rhythm of our bodies moving as one. The way he filled me as no other, like a hand in a glove. The tension as it grew tighter and tighter. And then—

"Fuck!" he growled the word even as I gasped his name.

"Raven!"

His fingers gripped my hips tight, sealing himself inside me as I exploded around him. A shower of starlight burst behind my closed lids and he was only seconds behind. Every part of me relished his low growls as his cock spurted inside me, the movement only drawing out my own climax.

For a long moment, we stayed that way. Bodies twitching. Hearts pounding in the aftermath of more pleasure than I'd ever known.

Once my heart had slowed its wild gallop, I slid off him with a groan, landing next to him in a boneless heap. How could every nerve ending in my body be alight, while every muscle felt like melted chocolate? I wanted to ask if he knew.

And how he could possibly fit me so well...

And why his scent made my she-wolf purr like a fucking cat...

I wanted to ask him a lot of things, but my eyelids fluttered as exhaustion closed over me. I vaguely sensed him tucking me against his side and whispering into my hair.

"Sleep, Frostbite."

So sleep, I did.

When I awoke, the very first rays of dawn had broken through. I'd probably only been out for a few hours, but it had been the most restful sleep I could recall in years.

I scrubbed the grit from my eyes and searched the room, finally catching sight of Raven's naked, muscular back. He was standing on the balcony, looking out over the sea. My heart gave a heavy thump in my chest and I couldn't muster the will to drive it away.

It seemed insane. I'd spent decades hating vampires and everything they stood for after what Edmund did to me, now I suddenly had a whole host of them in my affections. Dominic, Will, the Duchess, and now Raven and even Nicholas. As much as I'd tried to shield myself from Raven, he'd somehow managed to break down the walls between us. And the further I allowed him in, the more I wondered if he wasn't right. What was I even fighting for?

What if there was a world where we could actually restore the Veil and be together?

No. That was a fool's belief. We restored the Veil, and I would go back to being Queen of the Werewolf Territory, and he would go back to Seattle.

My people would never allow me to take him as a consort, never mind anything more permanent.

I swallowed the knot in my throat and pushed myself from the bed, pausing to don a t-shirt and underwear before joining him on the balcony in the cool morning air.

He turned as I slid the door open, a sexy smile spreading across his face. He was naked but for a pair of briefs, and seeing his beautifully contoured muscles and lean belly made me want to—

The sound of seagulls in the distance had me turning my attention to the ocean. It was a cacophony. I'd never heard so many at once. Maybe a bloated whale carcass had floated to the surface? "What is that?"

We both leaned over the railing, trying to get a better view. A few moments later, I caught sight of something bobbing in the water ahead. Then several somethings...

"Raven, is that what I think it is..."

Horror stole my voice as what I was seeing finally began to make sense.

It was the four-foot wide, iridescent tail of a fish. Only I knew it wasn't from a fish, because beside it floated the decapitated head of a mermaid. Her long black hair splayed around her like the tentacles of a jelly-fish, sightless eyes wide with unseeing terror.

"Ah, gods be damned!" Raven hissed.

I tore myself away from the gruesome sight and turned my attention ahead to where Raven had his gaze locked. It was a sight that would be seared in my mind for all eternity. As far as the eye could see, bobbing on the crimson sea, were mermaids, torn to pieces. Hundreds of them.

But it was the green hair floating around a mermaid that was face down that had me coming apart. The green hair on a child that did not deserve this horrific death.

The scream that echoed in my head sounded like it had come from a wounded animal, but I knew it was my own.

"Xefia! No!"

CHAPTER 11

Raven

My fingertips bit into my palm as I stepped back into the ship's galley. Diana was exactly as she had been when I'd left to correct the ship's course. Curled up in a blanket in the corner, that same, broken expression on her face that made my chest ache. Maverick took an untouched cup of tea from her trembling hands and set it on a nearby table.

I couldn't fault her for her reaction. It'd been a task just to wrap my own head around it. I'd seen battlefields with less gore, less blood.

I set the bowl of bread rolls I'd warmed next to Diana wordlessly, but even Myrr didn't reach for them.

I cursed myself inwardly for not noticing the scene first and finding some way to shield Diana from seeing something so awful. A broken sob cut through the silence, and I dropped to the seat beside her, knowing there was nothing I could say or do to mend such a wound and fucking hating every second of it.

She had dove into the sea instantly when it had become clear what we were looking at. Floundering through the bodies...so many bodies...screaming Xefia's name as she searched the faces of the dead. The first child with green hair we'd seen hadn't been her.

I'd followed an instant behind to join the search for the girl mermaid or any other survivors but to no avail. Diana would probably still be searching now if I hadn't dragged her back. Whatever evil Lilis had unleashed had killed hundreds of them, from grown men and women to children. And the carnage had been brutal. Limbs and severed tails in a sea of crimson. The chances of Xefia surviving the onslaught were slim to none.

The laughter that had floated through the air as we'd searched had solidified the truth.

Lilis had done this.

A wave of revulsion rolled through me as a memory flashed through my mind's eye, just before I'd dragged Diana from the water.

The tiniest tail, so fucking small and helpless...

The mangled body of the infant mermaid it had belonged to.

"Ah, gods, the fucking babe..." I ground my teeth together to keep from roaring.

I cursed myself as Diana lurched to her feet, cupping her hand over her mouth until she reached the sink to retch. I moved to follow, but she waved me off, pausing to rinse out her mouth before trudging right back to her nest of blankets.

"And I thought the spiders were bad," Theo said, staring straight upward into the ceiling above.

Kevin padded over to Diana as she sat, curling up against her leg. Her hand shifted to his head, and she reached toward the tea with the other.

"I dreamt it, but I didn't know...I thought it was just a nightmare," Nicholas murmured.

My mind refocused in an instant, and I fixed my eyes on him, but Diana was first to speak. "You what?"

"I saw it. The bodies–" he broke off and cleared his throat, his eyes looking as haunted as I felt. "I saw it exactly as it was. I woke up when I heard Diana screaming."

Myrr eyed him, raising an eyebrow. "Even I didn't see it coming..."

As if his powers around reading people's minds hadn't been creepy enough when he'd just been able to see into people's pasts. Now he was seeing the future, too? The realization struck me like a blow to the head. "Fucking hell. Probably from drinking Myrr's blood."

He nodded, "One could assume. Still...strange. And unnerving, even for me."

It was amazing, truth be told, but of little help here. The Oracle couldn't force a vision, and Nicholas' had been far too late to help Xefia and her people. On a regular day, Nicholas' revelation would've prompted dozens of questions. Would his visions of the future be permanent? Could we use it somehow to find Jade or help our case?

But today was not a regular day.

Maverick cut in next, sliding a hand through his hair. "Diana… If we stay here much longer, we're going to be in the drink beside them. We're low on water, food, everything. I know you're grief-stricken, but—"

"Grief-stricken?" She sucked in a breath, then tossed the blanket aside, shoving herself to her feet. Her hair was a mass of dark curls, her eyes full of wild fury, like some avenging angel. "The bitch who did this should be so lucky. You know what I am, Mav? I'm *done.*"

I watched as the sadness melted away under the growing flames of her rage.

"Lilis has pushed me too far." She strode toward the door, tearing it open and sticking her head outside. "Do you hear me, bitch?" she bellowed. "We're going to foil your psychotic plans and restore the Veil. Then, I'm going to find you. And when I do, know this: I will make you pay for all the pain you've caused. You will find *no mercy in me!*"

Her words were carried off by the winds and the room held its breath as we waited for Lilis' reply. But none came.

Diana slammed the door shut before whirling to face us. Her eyes were bright with determination despite the tears streaking down her cheeks. She'd never looked more beautiful as she pushed past me marching to the center of the room. Heartsick, vulnerable Diana had disappeared, leaving Queen Frostbite in her place.

"Let's get this ship patched up and make haste to the Demon Territory. Theo, I'd love to take you somewhere safe in the Human Realm before we go, but I don't even know if we'd make it given how quickly things have escalated..."

Theo blew out a weary sigh. "I've been part of this twisted, middle ground since the Veil fell. I don't fit in the Human Realm any longer. I know too much. I don't even know what a normal life looks like anymore." He shook his head slowly. "I'm exactly where I'm supposed to be. I think."

She gave him a quick nod. "We'll revisit that down the line, but for now, we're in agreement. Raven and Nicholas, you two focus on the rest of the damage caused by Bathsheba and check the hole from when you dislodged the boat. The rest of us will right the mess around us and take stock of our supplies."

I nodded in agreement, gesturing for Nicholas to follow. It was a relief that she'd managed to shelve her sadness for a time, but seeing the stonewall protecting her firmly back in place was like a kick to the groin.

One step forward last night, and two steps back today. And rightfully so. Her loyalty and commitment to those she cared about were unmatched. But it also meant that she would have one, and only one, focus right now. Necessary or not, it stung that she could cut the cord between us so easily. All I could do was help her on her mission and hope she would find her way back to me again when it was over.

The final fixes to the ship went more quickly than I'd expected, and we were on our way before the sun was high in the sky. By the time it was beginning to set once more, we were already docking in a port on the far edges of the Demon Territory.

I was the first to step off the ship, and a wingless demon came up to meet me almost immediately. He took a heavy pull off a squat stub of a cigar, blowing the acrid smoke directly into my face as he spoke. "This way, this way."

My muscles tensed, but Diana's hand on my shoulder stopped me before I could react. "Yes of course, we will follow you," she cut in, pushing to the front of our group.

I kept my eyes on the dozen or so dock workers as we passed. Kevin whimpered, pulling closer to Diana as we approached the large Cerberus style three-headed dog they were using to haul materials. The more humanoid demons carried barrels of supplies into a nearby ship, glancing curiously over at us every few seconds.

"Think they know who we are?" Nicholas whispered, turning toward me.

"Doubt it. I just think we probably look like some sort of circus. We're going to get strange looks." A werewolf leading a group of vampires, humans, and a hellhound was a rare sight. The territories didn't work together, not ever as far as I remembered.

The vampires and the werewolves were two of the worst as far as rivals went for supplies and land. To see us all together would be a sight for sure.

"Just follow the hallway all the way to the end." The creature that'd greeted us yawned, baring a mouthful of rotten teeth as he shoved open the door to the huge building positioned at the end of the dock. A sign emblazoned with the word 'Customs' written in gaudy, gold lettering hung above the doorway.

I looked around as I followed Diana. Demons were the most varied of any of the supernatural creatures, lower classes without wings, higher classes with wings. And the caste system also dictated how well they lived. They'd been stuck in the dark ages for a long time, but clearly had decided to get with the times as this little customs setup felt rather familiar...

"Hell of a lot different from the last time I came here," I muttered.

"You're telling me," Maverick cut in, glancing all around.

I suppressed the spike of irritation that came whenever he spoke, eyeing the security checkpoint ahead. The wiry demon running the show had exposed, dagger-like teeth that would've been terrifying if not for his turtleneck shirt and the thick-framed glasses perched on his nose. A cluster of burly, warrior-types stood on either side, awaiting his command.

The thin one with the glasses waved us forward with

raised eyebrows. "And what brings you to the Demon Territories?"

"We have business with Malach," Diana answered.

He swallowed a chuckle as he scribbled something down on his clipboard. "Right. So, I doubt he'll actually meet with you, but that's not my problem, is it? Let's get you checked in. Who wants to go first?"

Theo stepped forward first, and a few of the sturdy, soldier types stepped closer to keep watch on the proceedings. "State your name and species."

Theo did so, and he scribbled it down.

"Any weapons or contraband?"

"No." The demon got to searching. A quick pat down focused on the upper back, and a trip through an x-ray machine, and Theo was waved through.

More lenient than I'd expected, which was a relief. I'd been given more grief from TSA agents flying from Seattle to LAX.

Myrr stepped up next.

"Name and species," glasses droned in his nasally voice.

She scowled. "Myrr, the Oracle."

He penned her in, without even blinking. "Any contraband?"

She folded her arms over her chest and shook her head. "Nope."

He patted her down for only a second before pulling back, gesturing for one of the thicker, taller agents. "This woman has something—"

Myrr pulled what looked like an entire, cured ham haunch from the front of her loose-fitting shirt. "Is this really what we're doing here? Denying an old woman her food?"

Glasses gestured for a large trash bin to the side. "I'm afraid you won't be able to pass with it. We can't bring in any fruits or meats from other territories. Too much potential for agricultural contamination or disease."

Her eyes lit up with disbelief. "Agricultural contamination? The whole place is a fucking desert!"

"And still..." Glasses took hold of the ham hock, but Myrr, held on tight. They got into a full-on tug-of-war as she lifted one leg to use the turnstile for leverage. I kept my gaze trained on the closest guard, ready in case he started feeling aggressive, but, thankfully, it didn't take long for Glasses to best the old Oracle.

She jabbed her greasy finger into his chest. "Bully for you! Well guess what? You're going to die 93 days from today, and I'm not going to tell you how. But I *can* tell you that it won't be pleasant. You'll scream like a pig."

He sputtered, wide-eyed, and then waved her away, turning to the nearest of the sturdier demons.

"Finish checking her over and strip her of any other contraband."

"We're letting her through after she wrestled you over meat?"

"If she really is the Oracle, Malach'd never let me hear the end of it if I turned her away." He turned back toward us, shooting us a sour look. "Next."

Mav stepped up. "Maverick Wilder. Human."

"Are you?" Glasses eyed him closely, pulling on a new pair of gloves to replace the ones that'd been soiled by Myrr's ham. "You do *look* human..." He paused to stare long and hard at Maverick's mismatched eyes, but then shrugged. "Any contraband?"

"None."

Glasses patted him down before ushering him into the x-ray machine. Still looking unsatisfied, he turned to the demon who'd just finished checking Myrr. "Bring Rathmon, we'll need to check this one a little more closely. Something's...off."

I couldn't agree more. But I could see Diana getting restless. We'd known that Maverick had gained some sort of longevity and strength from either his time with the demons or some other misdeed, but we hadn't been able to suss out the nature of it fully yet. I, for one, was riveted to the action and wondered dispassionately if they would relieve him of his head for his false declaration.

More than half-hoping they would.

The hell-hound they brought over a moment later put even Kevin to shame, though cross-eyed Kevin didn't seem to know it. His rumbling growl rolled through the room, and I eyed the larger hound closely, wondering if I was going to have to intervene.

"That's enough of this. We need to get on our way now," Diana said from the sidelines. "I'd hoped not to call attention to us, but I am Diana, Queen of the Werewolves and the caretaker of the Southern Alpha Territory, and I vouch for him. Malach will understand. Can you please get this charade over with?"

My fangs sliced into my inner lip. Vouching for a fucking thief?

Glasses' eyes widened, looking like he'd been struck as he eyed her up and down. "M–my apologies, Your Majesty. We didn't know–"

A low rumbling echoed all around us, shaking the walls of the small space. My hand found the hilt of my sun-dagger on instinct.

"What's going on?" I demanded, but the answer came before Glasses could speak.

A troupe of crimson-winged demons descended on us from above. Moving at alarming speeds, each one was larger than the last. And every one of them looked like a true warrior. From their lithe, muscular builds, to the regimented way they flew in formation, it was immediately obvious that they weren't to be toyed with.

"Easy, Raven," Diana said, and I let my hand fall to my side. "They're the King's Guard. They will bring us to Malach."

Three sets of hands gripped me at once, and, as they yanked my hands behind my back, I couldn't help but wonder if we'd just made a huge mistake. We'd get our audience with Malach, but it was far from the cordial welcome we'd been expecting.

CHAPTER 12

Diana

I swallowed hard, juicing my tongue for the last bit of saliva as the wagon slowed to a halt. It'd been at least half a day since our passage through customs, and the harsh, desert environment had not been kind. The wood at my butt and back was soaked through with sweat, and I winced with every passing breath.

It wouldn't be long before there would be no more sweat—we hadn't had a drop to drink since we'd come off our ship.

The wooden door swung open, revealing one of the King's Guard. "Out."

My muscles ached as I pushed myself up, moving to do as he'd asked. I dropped my feet to the sandy ground and met his gaze, putting on the most Queenlike expression I could manage, given the circumstances. "We go no further before you bring us water." I gestured to Myrr.

"She's an old woman. You can't expect her to continue like this."

He sneered. "We'll let Malach decide whether you're worth wasting water on, she-wolf."

Raven was upon him before he could move, fingers digging into the wrist of the other man's sword-arm. "Water, now."

The demon moved to strike him, but the largest of our captors stopped him with a hand. "Stand down, Balgor, and go fetch a waterskin. He said to bring them in alive."

Alive? The word stopped me short. Had there even been a question of whether we'd have been brought in any other way? While I wouldn't call us friendly, we'd shared an uneasy alliance with the demons in the past as we shared a portion of our borders. What had changed? Surely, Malach knew the political ramifications of murdering a neighboring territory's queen. Especially when she had clearly come in peace. Killing me here would mean certain war with my people, to say nothing of what Will and Dominic would do if Nicholas and Raven were executed...

The younger demon wrenched free of Raven's grip, scowling. "Better to pour it into the sand than waste it on these wingless rats."

"Their fate is for *Malach* to decide, not you. And my intervention is the only reason you're still alive to say such things. That vampire is not to be trifled with—he'd kill you before you could draw your weapon."

Balgor spared a final, angry glance for Raven, then stalked off to do as ordered.

"I apologize for the boy. We'll get you watered before your audience with our King, I had forgotten how spongy you non-demons are. Gotta get the water on the regular or you just dry up."

I dipped my head in thanks. Not exactly the red carpet, but it was something. And things would turn around once we got to see Malach. Like most demons, he always looked out for number one, and it was in his best interest now more than ever to be on the good side of the newly formed alliance between werewolves and vampires.

Myrr slid out of the cart, assisted by Nicholas, and glanced at the imposing demon before whispering, "Have him grab us a bite to eat, too, while you're at it."

Kevin crept out of the cart last, and his tongue lolled out of his mouth as he pulled in a deep whiff of the desert air. He managed fine in most climates, but this was what he'd really been bred for—this was his homeland. I glanced around, really taking in my new surroundings for the first time. Carrion feeders and hawks flew overhead in the distance, watching the miles of pristine desert for rabbits and snakes, dead or alive, and a few scattered dunes of sand were the only things blocking the view all the way to the horizon.

The true marvel, though, was the giant palace that stood a few hundred yards ahead. We'd always met on neutral ground, and despite having seen pictures of it in books, I was still taken aback by the size. Named The

Spire, it was a narrow spike of a structure, hundreds of meters high, like a huge, onyx finger stretching into the sky. And there wasn't a single plant anywhere near the tower, not even a cactus. The surrounding lands had been blighted by its presence, it was said. Miles of ashy black sand stretched all around it in a uniform circle, growing by a few dozen feet with each passing year.

By the time we were ready to move, the dry itch in the back of my throat was gone. The Spire was a strange mix of modern amenities and fiery, hellish imagery.

As we entered through the tall narrow doors that mimicked The Spire, I took in the paintings covering the walls. As terrifying as they were beautiful, I found myself staring at them, when I knew I should be watching the demon soldiers that patrolled every inch of the building.

"Few have seen what you are about to," the chief Guard commented, pressing the pendant he wore on his neck against a bare section of the marble wall. A glimpse of it showed the pendant to be an engraved image of flames and a skull with wings stretching out from the sides. Nice.

The wall slid open, revealing an elevator, and the guards hurried us into it. I glanced upward, wondering what floor of the massive tower the King lived on. "Does Malach know we're here yet?"

"I sent word a short while ago, he's expecting you."

The elevator slammed shut behind us, and Theo cleared his throat as he eyed the painting on the wall next to him—a pair of men stretched out on a table as a torturer cut their limbs off. It was only upon staring at it that I realized why it bothered me so. When I blinked, the torturers had moved a little. As if the scene were really happening somewhere.

"I'm starting to miss the lighthouse."

"I know, and I'm so sorry," I said.

"I wouldn't change it. Better to live with all I got for whatever I got left."

The old man's words were a small comfort.

Kevin shifted nervously at my side as the floor began to rumble, and, rather than shooting upward, the elevator began to descend. A basement?

Or a dungeon...

"Where are we going?"

"The seventh level," the demon said simply.

A light flashed ahead, and I staggered back as I realized that the wall on the far side of the elevator was actually a window. Gouts of fire spurted through the air all around, the only source of light in the massive chamber. A dozen times as wide as The Spire, a full-on town came into view.

Screams of agony cut through the air every few seconds, and the hairs on my arm stood on end as I stared at the scene below. Armies of lesser demons labored in groups, tilling fields of strange moss and digging into the walls on all sides. Our elevator hurtled downward, moving far too fast to take it all in, but a smaller, second layer opened right after, only slightly less horrible than the first. And on it went. The buildings grew nicer and more modern in each layer than the last, and the workers gradually disappeared, giving way to slick buildings and houses.

By the time we reached the seventh level, we were in what looked like a demonic version of an idyllic town. A few dozen mansions, complete with fountains of lava, were visible in the light of the massive pillar of flame that stood at the town's center. Here and there I saw pools of blackness that I couldn't decide if it was water, or bottomless pits.

Despite having read about this place during my education to become queen, I still found myself shocked at the inequity of it all...

"Who gets to live down this far?" Raven asked, gesturing toward the massive homes.

"First caste only."

The elevator screeched to a halt, and he sucked in a deep breath as he gestured for us to leave through the door.

He led us down a wide path that was edged with dark blue flowers that seemed to be bleeding out their pollen. At the end of the path was the only castle in the seventh level.

The main doors were wide open, guarded on either side by a pair of winged demons. They didn't look at us as our guide hurried us through and to another smaller door.

A moment later, we entered a chamber the size of my own Great Hall before coming to a halt. One guard stayed for each of us, while the remainder split off to enter the throne room. Every wall was a full-scale mural. Angels died in droves by the hands of monsters summoned by demon princes, and every brushstroke was perfect in its horrific beauty.

Mav shuddered. "I don't miss this place one bit."

The screech of a single horn cut through the silence, beckoning us onward, and my breath caught in my throat as I stepped forward. Luckily, Malach didn't keep us waiting long; a pair of twin doors behind the throne slid open, revealing the King himself.

His hair was white, streaked with brilliant red as if he'd bathed in blood. I'd have expected him to be tanned from exposure to the sun, but he was pale, as if he hadn't been above ground for years.

His eyes were white, but there was a distinct red line around the iris.

Fire and ice.

A chill swept through me despite the heat of the room as I looked up at him. Flames licked at the arms of his jet-black throne, and a statue of an Angel was fixed, upside-down, to the wall just behind him, her radiant crown sitting just above his own.

After another few strides, I had to amend that assessment.

Not a statue.

A *corpse.*

Aliyah, first queen of the Angels, nailed to the wall

like a piece of taxidermy. I shuddered, fixing my gaze on the man beneath her.

"King Malach," I said, dropping to a knee.

He stared at me for a long while, and his voice wavered slightly as he spoke. "Bring her closer, Algrin."

A quick jolt of surprise shot through me as the Guard Captain's hand fell to my shoulder. General Algrin was a famous war hero among demons, and I'd heard many stories of his exploits. But the thought didn't hold my attention for long as I got a better look at the King I'd come all this way to see.

A king whose help I needed to find the girl.

Malach's bluish skin had gone almost white, and his skin sagged like a too-large suit. A whisper of a smile passed over his lips as he locked eyes with me.

"What brings you to this place, Wolf?"

The condescension in his voice was thick, and his lack of using my title was a slap to the face.

Raven struggled to my right, trying to move toward me, but he relented as I raised a hand. The time for fighting had passed. Only diplomacy would work now.

"We come as representatives of the Vampire and Werewolf alliance, and we come seeking knowledge, as well as passage through your lands."

He leaned back in his throne, pressing a bony fist to his cheek as he croaked, "Knowledge of what?"

"Perhaps a more private conversation would be better, I–"

"*Speak.*" The word echoed through the throne room a dozen times before stopping, booming in a way that I'd never have expected from a man who was head of state. Not even in my few dealings with him had he ever been rude.

Something was wrong.

Very wrong.

My fingernails dug into my palm, and I forced a Queenly confidence into my voice as I replied. "We're searching for a woman who passed through here. She is integral if we ever hope to re-seal the Veil, and we have reason to believe that you'll be able to help us find her..."

He went silent for a long moment, writhing uncomfortably in his chair. When he finally spoke, his face was lit with rage and his voice had changed. "You would disturb me over fairytales and rumors? Bring me their heads."

My wolf rushed to the surface, as I reeled at how quickly this had gone downhill, but I tamped my wild side down as I noticed the guard's unmoving hand on my shoulder. A demon to my right let out a yelp, and I turned to see Raven charging up to stand in front of me.

The rest of the King's Guard moved as if to advance on the vampire, but Algrin held up a hand, stopping them in their tracks.

"Your Majesty," he started, stepping out from behind me. "If it is truly your will, it shall be done, but I wish to remind you that The Oracle is among their party. Not to mention we risk war with *two* kingdoms if we proceed with this course of action."

"*Disobedience?* From my own general?" Malach stood, trembling with fury as he jabbed his finger directly at the man. "Bring. Me. Their. Heads."

"I— yes, Sir."

I eyed the opposition, calculating our odds. A guard for everyone in our party, plus a dozen or so more, every one of them a master warrior. I didn't like our chances, but it beat going down without a fight. Algrin advanced, shaking his head bitterly as he unsheathed his sword.

Kevin lunged toward him, but the demon that'd been assigned to him pinned him down before he could close the distance.

A wracking cough split the room, bringing the demons to a halt. I glanced back to see Malach's pain-wracked gaze as he dug his fingers into his temples. His words were labored and slow, but his voice had lost the chilly bite it'd had since we'd entered the room.

"Get them out of here, Algrin. *Hurry!*"

Algrin nodded, thrusting his sword back into its sheath as he hurried toward me, grabbing me under the arm. "We need to go, now."

I stumbled along with him, completely bewildered as I gestured for Raven to follow. Malach broke into another fit of coughs, followed by an enraged, shrill scream. I spared a final glance for him as we left the room as he punched himself in the side of the head with a closed fist.

"Out, damn you, out of my head! OOOOOUT YOU BITCH!"

I skidded to a stop as the truth hit me–I was not the bitch he was trying to command.

Lilis had managed to possess the Demon King himself. We were only being released because she couldn't maintain control long enough to have us killed. I turned to Raven, seeing that he'd come to the same realization I had.

As much as we needed to go, a part of me wanted to wolf out and leap on Malach to tear his–or her–heart out. But he was nothing more than a puppet. Her messenger. He was no more responsible for his actions than the Vanators had been.

I forced the bloodlust down and let Raven and Algrin drag me along. The trip to the surface passed in the blink of an eye, and my heart was thumping just as fast by the end of our trip as it had been when we'd started running.

The Spire's front door swung open, and I was surprised to see the demons slow to a halt as I dashed toward the black sand outside. "Are you coming?"

Algrin shook his head, a stony look of pure determination on his face. "Our King needs us now more than ever. If he changes his mind again, he might send warriors after you. We need to be here to stop him. We can't have him plunging our people into a war we cannot win."

"You could be killed," Nicholas said.

"That's a risk I'm willing to take." His gaze shifted to me. "I had no idea he was that far gone. We were stationed at the harbor for the last week, his condition worsened in the short time we were away from his side."

I stepped out onto the sandy ground, feeling a strange sympathy for the Demon General, despite the fact he'd been ready to gut me just a few minutes earlier. "It's not just a condition; he's being controlled by an evil force. The goddess Lilis."

He blanched and then nodded. "That helps. I will try to find a way to keep him deeply sedated and go speak to our Void Bishop. We might be able to protect him now that we know what ails him." He lifted a hand. "Good luck."

Myrr, Nicholas, and the others joined us outside, and he let the door close behind them.

I groaned as I stared out at the endless sea of sand, a dry breeze catching my lip. "We move west back toward the ship," I announced, using the position of the rising sun as a makeshift compass. Despite knowing that Jade was somewhere out here, we had no way to pinpoint her. "We have no supplies and need to head toward home to regroup."

And so, we walked, mile upon mile. Black sand gave way to white, and the sun reached its zenith, but there wasn't a drop of water to be found. Nicholas and Raven began to slow, their sun protection daggers being stretched to the limit, and Mav and I had to take turns carrying Myrr after only a few miles of travel.

I stared upward, eyeing the peak of the dune that was only a few yards away, repositioning Myrr on my shoulders. I stopped to breathe, then forced out the final few steps. An ember of hope burned hot within me as I reached the top but was quickly smothered. The whipping sand made it hard to tell, but there wasn't a town or water source in sight. I dropped to the ground, setting Myrr down beside me as gently as I could manage.

How far inland had we come in the wagons? Easily eight or nine hours, being pulled at a steady pace. On foot, it could take a day or more.

I glanced at the others, shame washing over me in waves. Willingly or not, I had led them to this. Even poor, old Theo. Their blood would be on my hands when we all died out here. Kevin lapped at my hand, looking curious. His tongue still had the last remnants of moisture on it, as he was only just beginning to feel the effects of the desert.

"You might make it if you go alone, let Kevin carry you," Raven rasped as he settled beside me. He pulled his hood up further, turning his head away from the sun. "Leave us."

I was about to waste the last of my energy on slapping him when I turned and saw his face. Blisters had begun to form on his cheeks and lips, and his skin was red and raw. I felt for my wolf, reaching with everything I had.

If I can just shift, maybe I can run ahead and find some water.

My wolf was there, but out of reach. I'd need far more strength if I wanted to pull something like that off.

Raven eyed Mav, fangs protruding ever so slightly, then exhaled sharply, glancing back into the distance.

How much further could we even make it? I pulled up an arm to shield my eyes as a particularly strong wind gusted through. "Sandstorm?"

"In fifty yards you will find your salvation."

"D-did you hear that?" I stumbled awkwardly to my feet, gritting my teeth as I threw Myrr over my shoulder.

Mav hobbled to my side. "Hear what?"

Probably just the first hallucination of the many to come. But, if there was even the tiniest chance that I was wrong, I had to keep moving. Xefia's smiling face appeared in my mind, and I forced myself onward. I was going to make Lilis *pay* for what she'd done. And I couldn't do that if I died here. Raven and Nicholas swayed, and staggered just behind us, half-walking and half-sliding down the dune. Theo had yet to rise.

"One more try," I called. "Come on, Theo, you can do it."

He grunted, pinching his cheeks. He let out a moan as he pushed himself to his feet before wobbling violently, almost flying face-first down the dune. Then, he caught himself and straightened. "One more try. I can do one more try."

Each step was agony, and every muscle in my body screamed for me to lay down and let death take me rather than take part in this useless struggle. My father, Lycan, wouldn't have given up. And it would've caused him so much pain to see me give up at a time like this. I slipped, nearly falling, and ended up sliding the last dozen feet down the dune.

The wind was moving even faster down here, bordering on a true sandstorm. How much further could fifty yards be? I sucked in a ragged breath, unsure how many more steps I had in me. Ten? Fifteen?

I took another step forward, worried that I'd stop moving entirely if I didn't, and nearly walked face-first into a piece of orange cloth. I pulled back, dumfounded, then stepped a few feet to the side.

Not just an orange cloth.

A tent.

It had blended in with the sand, impossible to see in the wind. And, hidden behind it, there was a pool of water, surrounded by a cluster of shrubs and small trees. I croaked out a laugh, reaching for the cloth. This was one cruel hallucination.

My heart skipped a beat as my hand brushed against it, and I staggered forward the last few steps, eyes fixed on the pool of water.

A tall man with long, white hair and striking, golden eyes stepped out of the tent, right into my field of view.

"Welcome, Wolf Queen."

Then everything went black.

CHAPTER 13

Raven

A splash cut through the silent dark, and my eyes shot open. A large, cloth canopy hung over me where the sweltering sun should have been, and my back was pressed up against the cushion of a chaise lounge.

Somehow, I was still alive. Or maybe I was dead, and this was the other side of death? I wasn't sure I'd be one who ended up in a heaven....

I turned, seeing the large pitcher at my side, water droplets sliding down the sides of it, mesmerizing me. Condensation clung to the glass too, citrus and ice floating inside in equal proportions.

Was this...real? A hallucination of the desert?

I took a deep breath and the smell of ice-cold water called to me, a siren song.

I grabbed the cup and brought it to my lips, gulping the liquid down. Not sweet enough to be lemonade or juice, too sweet to be water, more refreshing than anything I'd ever drank.

Perhaps that was my state of mind, to be fair which could focus on nothing but quenching the burning thirst in me.

The liquid wasn't blood, but it was damned close. The flavor and consistency of it was so very close to blood, but cold without being coagulated.

Some sort of magic to be sure, but I couldn't care in that moment—I'd have drunk it regardless of how much magic it contained.

As my body absorbed the drink, my memories came rushing back in, slamming into me like a ton of sand.

We'd been walking through a desert. Me and—

A rush of panic shot through me, and I jumped to my feet, dropping the pitcher and cup not caring that they spilled. "Diana?!"

"Raven. We're all here." Her voice reached me first, soothing me like the drink had soothed my throat.

Her long, dark hair came into view as she sat up and turned, flashing me a worried smile as she rose from the cushion she'd been seated on. I dropped back against the lounge, relief flooding through me as she approached.

"Welcome back, pal," Myrr said, opening her mouth to accept a grape from Theo's outstretched hand.

"Are we dead?"

"Not yet." Myrr chuckled as she chewed her grape open mouthed.

A loud bark pierced the air, and I stared past Myrr,

Diana and Theo to see Nicholas cannonballing through the air, landing in a pool of crystalline blue water, Kevin following close behind him.

That was the noise that had woken me up. So different than the howling winds of the desert that I'd passed out hearing. The sound of sand filling my ears and heat baking my skin, crackling it like I'd been put into an oven.

Maverick waded through the pool, shielding his glass from the splash as he made his way closer to the edge.

After the hell of the desert, I might've thought we *were* in heaven, if I believed in such things. How had we survived? What the hell had happened?

Diana moved to my side and crouched next to my lounger, eyes widening as she looked me up and down. "How are your burns?"

"Pretty good, compared to how they felt before." I took a closer look at my hands to find the skin was totally normal, not a blister or red patch in sight. Not even a tender spot left to remind me how close I'd come to being cooked alive. Realization struck, and I fixed my gaze on Diana, my eyes straying to that flawless neck.

"Did you have me drink from you?" Blood rushed to my cock at the thought. I sucked on my cheek and tongue, trying to pull out any lingering taste as I cursed myself for being asleep when it had happened.

Her hand curled around the armrest. "No. I woke up a few hours ago. Myrr had gotten some of that water into you. The burns didn't go away instantly, but your breathing went back to normal. By the time I woke, I could tell you were going to be alright. Same for me."

"Magic water, huh?" I grabbed the pitcher of the stuff, taking a deep inhale from the top of it.

No scent of anything but the lemons. But the flavor said it was something else.

She looked around before leaning closer to whisper, "There is a man here, he has golden eyes. You will want to meet him."

I couldn't tell if she was worried, scared or excited. Maybe all three.

"You sure about that?"

"Yes, I am quite sure we all should meet." The warm voice was almost melodic, and I turned my head to see a smiling male walking towards us, hands lifted in a sign of peace. Tall, with features that in one breath made me think he was fae, and in the next demon, and the next vampire, then werewolf, then angel, even human. As if each step his face morphed a little, shifting so slightly that if I hadn't been watching closely, I might have missed the changes.

Undoubtedly, he was not like any of us, though. An energy of relaxation and contentment radiated from him, which made me instantly suspicious.

"You're no demon, so what are you?"

His smile was too easy, too kind. "My name is Nefir, and I can assure you that you are safe with me."

Despite my natural wariness, in a way, he had proven that—so far. We'd been unconscious and at his mercy for hours, yet here we all were. Alive, and better than when he'd found us out in the desert. Kevin charged up to him, tail wagging as he stared, entranced. The man patted him, but his eyes were fixed on Nicholas as he walked over, rubbing a towel over his shirtless chest.

Diana shifted her focus to the strange, golden-eyed man. "While we all appreciate what you've done, can you at least tell me why you're helping us?"

Nefir cocked his head in thought, as if considering it for the first time. "I'm not sure, I guess I find you interesting...unusual. You're all mortals despite your seeming longevity, yet you risk your lives struggling against a goddess. Frankly, I find it fascinating."

Diana frowned, and she slowly rose to stand. "How do you know about any of that? What do you know about Lilis?"

I stood next to her angling my body to get between them if need be.

He glanced from me to Diana and back again. "Lilis is my sister."

The words sucked all the air out of the space. Fuck. The ramifications were...immense.

I stared at him, my muscles tensing as I moved to pull Diana back, but he shook his head as he added, "I'm not on her side, to be clear. She's actually quite mad."

"So, you're a god, then?" Diana asked.

"That is one name by which we are known." There was a bit of dance in his step as he strode forward, seating himself on the nearest cushion with a satisfied sigh.

"Look, I'm not sure if giving you hope that you can best my sister is a kindness, but I'm intrigued enough to give you what little help I can, if that's the path you choose. Your little wish on a coin certainly was interesting enough..."

"A voice told us to come here. A voice we've heard before," Diana said. "Do you know Elhimna? I think it was him."

Nefir tipped his head. "I know him. But it was not him this time, it was me."

He was the reason we were here? The reason we'd come to the desert? Fuck, what if this was all a game to him and Jade wasn't here at all?

Diana moved to sit across from him, keeping her eyes fixed on him the entire time. "There is no choice. We must defeat her. All the realms are at risk."

Nefir frowned at that, cocking his head. "Why not find a remote place to live out your days in leisure, rather than all this? You can eat, drink" —his eyes strayed to Nicholas again— "fuck your days away."

Nicholas blushed and wrapped his towel around his shoulders.

"The Veil is torn," I cut in, snapping my fingers and drawing the *supposed* god's eyes back to me. "It's bad news for everyone, from those in the Alpha Territories to those in the human realm."

He nodded sagely. "Ah, the Veil... I had forgotten about that situation. It's been a few months since it fell now, yes?"

Irritation pricked at the edges of my consciousness, deafened by the aura of calm that surrounded him. "Try fifteen years ago."

"Hmmm." His forehead furrowed at that, but then he shrugged. "Time is a construct. But I suppose the Veil being down *will* make things somewhat difficult for everyone to survive. I still wonder why you don't spend this time trying to find a safe place for you and yours to relax, though."

Diana raised an exasperated hand to her temple. "And just wait for our demise? Allow everyone to suffer and die? No. Your sister has gone too far. I'm going to take her down if it's the last thing I do."

The god leaned forward, grinning as he locked his sparkling gold eyes on hers. "That's exactly the spirit that intrigues me so much about you lot. Fire. Determination against hopeless odds. It's the most entertainment I've had in years!"

I positioned myself between Diana and him, taking a seat on a nearby chair, his lackadaisical attitude rubbing me the wrong way. "Are you powerful enough to match her directly?"

He chuckled, taking a swig out of a flask that was tied to his belt. "Oh, I don't know about that. I'm not really a *fighting* god. I'm more of a 'relax and watch the world unfold' kind of god. But, if I had to guess, I'd assume she is the stronger of the two of us. She's had far more practice tapping into her power and pursuing violence. And I don't quite have the gut for it, you see."

I scowled, but Diana spoke before I could comment. "What do you know about her and her plan? What is her goal, just to...wipe us all out?"

Nefir was quiet a moment, his eyes thoughtful as he swirled his flask. "I know that there was a time when she was quite normal. Still willful and bold, but with none of this hatred she has in her now. I know not why–perhaps it was some falling out with our parents...they can be difficult–but at some point, things changed. She disappeared for a long while, and when she returned, she'd become unhinged. There was no talking to her, the family dinners were terrible..." He took another long pull from his flask. "I probably should've reached out, but I'd fallen madly in love with this handsome artist and his wife and matters of the heart must come first, you know. By the time that relationship had run its course, Lilis had hidden herself away again and concocted some plan to start fresh. Everything and everyone in our world except those she could indoctrinate to her new 'religion' were the scourge. I hoped it would fizzle out once she grew bored. Seems she's only gotten more bloodthirsty in my years away."

I tried to hide the disgust over his apathy. Surely, having a god on our side would even the playing field a bit, but with the way our new ally was behaving, I wasn't sure that was the case at all. "Is she truly invincible or does she have a weakness we can exploit?"

"She's quite powerful, but there *are* limits, as I'm sure you've seen." He swirled his hand and an image of

Malach appeared, made out of sand at his feet. "It takes a lot of strength to pull something like she has with the demon king, as strong-willed and independent as he is. I don't like your chances in a straight up fight, but if what you say about Elhimna speaking to you before...that is our father. Well, if that is true, then your best shot is to gather more people like that Sienna girl."

Diana shot a hand forward to grab his arm, accidentally knocking the flask out of his hand. "How do you know Sienna?"

He rolled his wrist, and another flask appeared in his palm. "I felt her when she unlocked her power. It doesn't compare to my sister's, but the threads of fate were re-woven, ever so slightly, in that moment. The strands of the Veil were scattered when it was shattered, and your Sienna carries one of them."

I looked at Diana and could see she understood as well. The gem we sought. Could it be a piece of the Veil itself?

Diana nodded, then leaned forward. "I believe that's exactly what we're looking to do. There's a girl we need to find. You know it...you sent us here."

Nefir yawned as if this whole conversation was suddenly too much for him. "Eat and drink your fill for tonight. It may be some time before you have another chance to rest. Tomorrow, I will lead you to what you seek and send you on your way from there. It is best that you do not stay in any one place too long. Lilis has eyes everywhere, but her powers wane as the time-of-day passes. She tends to be more active during the daylight hours, and...reinvigorates herself at night." He stood without waiting for a response and faded from our vision with a wave and a shimmer.

Maverick strode over, his teeth sinking into a crisp apple. "Well, that was fucking crazy."

And, for once, I agreed with him, even if he was a chickenshit.

Diana inhaled deeply, reaching for a nearby plate of fruit. "We're lucky to have his help, as strange as it—and he—might be. Let's take this time to get as rested as we can so we can put our best foot forward tomorrow and get him fully on our side. Who knows when we'll have another chance like this?"

I nodded, knowing full well that I wouldn't be doing any resting. He'd been good to us so far, but he was as unpredictable as he was cowardly, and that was a bad combination.

As far as I was concerned, none of these 'gods' or 'goddesses' could be trusted.

CHAPTER 14

Diana

The oasis soothed the ragged edges of my heart, and I didn't think it was just the water, food and safety. Those would have been enough to recharge me and the others, but it was more than that. There was something about this place that was magic incarnate, and I couldn't fight the desire to just...be. To exist only as myself and nothing more. Not a queen. Not a warrior, just me. Diana.

Which is why I found myself lying awake, in a tent made of silk, staring up at the sky through the place where the material connected. A small gap, but the stars peeked through, blinking and dancing in and out of sight.

Myrr slept soundly in the tent to my right, her snoring and snorting in her sleep perhaps a small part of why I couldn't sleep. Maverick chose a tent behind mine, his breathing soft and even. Nicholas and Theo were to my left.

Raven...Raven wasn't resting. He was somewhere in the oasis, keeping guard over all of us. Despite me telling him not to.

Out of all of us, he was the only one that still didn't trust Nefir even a little bit. I rolled to my side, the plush bedding below me cushioning my hips and shoulders like a lover's embrace.

A flash of Raven's arms around me had me squirming. "Don't think about that." I mouthed the words.

I needed to focus on what would come next. Finding Jade. Understanding that pieces of the Veil themselves had been ripped free and...placed? Embedded? In people?

That had my mind spinning back to when Nicholas had placed his hand on Maverick, and Mav's memories had lit up in front of us. How the explosion at Stonehenge had sent a shockwave through all...through all those little girls.

A chill swept through me, and I sat bolt upright. That was it. Nefir had pushed my mind in the right direction.

"You sneaky bastard."

In the air around me, I thought I heard the whimsical god laugh. Was he pleased I'd figured it out? Was this part of the entertainment he sought?

Everyone else was asleep, but I had to say this out loud...share my revelation with someone.

I was on my feet and pushing through the silk tent flap in a flash.

I took a deep breath, scenting the air. Raven had passed by not that long ago; I'd heard him pacing. But he had moved away and hadn't circled back.

Following my nose and the scent of the vampire who made my blood burn hot, I tracked him through the oasis, down to the edge of the crystalline pool.

He stood, outlined by the light of the three-quarter moon. Raven cut an imposing figure with his wide shoulders and lean, muscular frame, but he didn't intimidate me. I'd felt those muscles under my hands, traced the scars and lines of his limbs. I knew how gentle he could be, given the opportunity. I sucked in a sharp breath and tried to steady my libido. I was here to talk, not fuck.

He didn't even turn around. "You should be sleeping, Frostbite."

"Says the kettle to the pot." I made my way to stand next to him, staring out across the water. That was better than looking into those turquoise eyes in the moonlight. "I...I think I've sort of figured out what we are looking for."

I felt more than saw him turn to me and my skin prickled. "Tell me."

"The vision we saw out of Maverick's memories, Stonehenge exploding? There were little girls everywhere. Sienna was there, her hair was blonde, not red, but...she was there. And she has this power and connection to Lilis with that power." My words picked up speed as my thoughts tumbled from my lips, "And now we are hunting for another girl, Jade, who took a shard of the Veil from her sister, before she died. That same sister was there, with Maverick and Sienna at the sight of Stonehenge and the Veil shattering."

I did turn to look at him then, my excitement rising above my desire. He didn't ask any questions, patiently waiting for me to get it all out.

"They both carry a piece of the Veil itself. That is where the power Sienna has is coming from. It's why we have to find all of them and somehow...I don't know, use them to heal the Veil? Piece it back together?" I shrugged helplessly. "I don't know the rest, I just..."

Raven's eyes flickered and he closed them. Did he think I was a blathering fool right now? Was he going to argue or try to tell me that—

"Gods above, Diana. I think you've cracked it." He opened his eyes and stared down at me. "But why did Sienna survive then, and not Jade's sister? What's different about them?"

I frowned and shook my head. "I don't know."

Raven ran his hand through his hair. "We could have Nicholas pull up that idiot's memories again, see if we can slow it down and get some clues?"

"Don't call him an idiot," I said, half-heartedly. "He's saved us."

"And still, he left you. Only an idiot would walk away from you."

My heart squeezed, as if he'd reached in and grabbed

it with his words. "And you wouldn't leave me?" I asked, fully aware of the challenge in my voice.

Because truly...everyone left at some point. That was life, wasn't it?

He lifted a hand to my cheek, sweeping his thumb across my cheekbone. "Never."

I wanted to laugh at him. "You don't know that."

His smile was...sad? Why sad? "I do know it, with every breath I take, Diana, I know it. I will never leave you. You could command me away, you could tell me you hate me for a thousand years, and it would not change this truth. I will never leave you."

I turned into him, letting my body lead as I leaned against his chest, pressing my face against him, his words digging deep under my skin and settling somewhere around my heart region. "I don't want to believe you. I want you to be..."

"A liar?" His hands found their way to my lower back, tugging me closer. "You want me to lie to you and tell you I don't feel something for you that I've never felt before? That this thing between us isn't all consuming?"

I groaned, my eyes pricking at his words. This place was making me weak, the illusion of safety allowing me to think about things that had nothing to do with saving the world.

I should tell him to knock it off. To end the flow of pretty words. "Stop." It was all I could manage and even that was strangled.

"I will lie to you if you want me to, Frostbite." He

wrapped his arms around me fully, pressing me so tight to him that it felt as if I were bound in ropes to him. "I will tell you I feel nothing, that my every breath does not whisper your name, that my every heartbeat does not continue only because yours beats too. I can tell you all the lies you want."

A shudder slid through me, tears trickling down my cheeks, absorbing into his shirt. Because the sincerity in his words, the feeling in them, I couldn't escape or deny. But I would still try. I had to try, or I would lose myself in this.

"Raven, this isn't real. Nothing that has happened is anything more than lust."

"Of course not." He pressed his lips to the top of my head. "But if we are lying to each other tonight, then tell me one, Frostbite. Lie to me, just for tonight."

I slid my hand under the back of his shirt, desperately needing that connection to him, to know he was really here, and this was not another hallucination. I should have walked away, should have done a lot of things. But instead, I lied to him.

My words were shaky and low. "I...don't wish for a future with you, Raven. I don't dream of a time that this could be something more. I don't want to know what it would be like to wake next to you every morning...to have a life with you."

His arms tightened, and a sigh shuddered through him. "That's what I thought."

His lips found mine, dragging a moan from me as his

tongue swept across mine, gentle, insistent. Kissing me as if it would be our last, which had me gripping his shoulders. I didn't want this to be the last time I found myself in his arms.

No matter that I knew it could never be. The Werewolf Queen and a vampire were not a match made in heaven, nor hell. Evangeline and Lycan had understood that. It was why they had spent all those years apart. And when they finally had given in to their love?

Agony.

I tore my mouth from his. "I can't." My words caught on the edge of a sob as I pulled away. "I can't, Raven. I can't shatter what's left of my heart on you. I have too many people relying on me to be whole..."

Oh, the truth, gods be damned...it fell out of my mouth before I could catch it. Damn this place, this lull that had opened me up and tangled me between Raven's game of truth and lies.

But Raven, he was not like anyone else. He cupped my face. "For tonight, be as you wish it could be, Diana. None of us are guaranteed tomorrow, or to see this journey through. Regret is not something I want to die with."

I blinked up at him, his turquoise eyes serious as he waited for me to make a decision. There was no coercion. No pressure.

"What do you want, Diana?" The sound of my name on his lips...that was all it took. He said it with a reverence reserved for a goddess. As if...as if I were his entire world.

"You. I want you, Raven. For tonight, that is all there is."

He slid his hands down my arms, to tangle his fingers with mine. He lifted first one hand, then the other, kissing the backs of them, then without a word, tugged me toward the water. "Swim with me."

Swim with him.

I didn't like water. But any fear I had in the past wasn't there, because I was with him.

I lifted my hands over my head, and he silently peeled me out of the sheath dress, I barely blinked, and he was stripped out of his clothes and leading me into the water.

The coolness of the pool crept up my legs, making my skin pebble, caressing my limbs, creeping up my body.

Raven was waist deep when he paused and turned to me, his eyes skimming over me, his one hand still holding onto me. "Wait a minute." Untangling his fingers from mine, he turned and dove out into the water, disappearing under the surface.

I took a few steps, uncertainty rocking through me.

Water slid down his body, his dark hair mussed and a smile that was every bit boyish and rake, rolled into one. I walked out to meet him. "Showing off?"

"I was debating whether or not I had any control. I needed to cool off."

A laugh bubbled up in my chest. "A cold bath?"

His grin widened. "I cannot help what you do to me. If you knew how many times you made me hard in a day...just thinking about you, replaying every touch, every kiss..."

He reached out and ran a hand from my collarbone down over my breast, tugging on my nipple. I could have stepped closer to him, but the line between pleasure and pain was knife edge thin and it made me ache.

I couldn't reach him, he was too far away.

His eyes were on mine, the devil in them as he rolled and tugged on my nipple, then reached for the other, urging me toward him. A game of chicken, was it? My heart was light, the game making me flush in a way...how long had it been since I'd played?

I groaned and let one hand slide down between my legs as I watched him through hooded eyes. "I think you will break first."

His laugh was soft. "Oh, this is a game I like. Are you sure you would not rather have my mouth between your legs over your hand, skilled as it might be?"

His words caused a gush of heat rushing to my core. I slipped my fingers under the water and found my aching clit. "What are we playing for?"

Fangs flashed as his grin widened. "Ah, that is difficult. Hard." He dipped his chin, indicating his cock.

He tugged a little harder on my nipples, and I pressed two fingers to my clit, rubbing a slow lazy circle, imagining it was *his* mouth. *His* hand. I tipped my head back and let my breath come in little gasps in time with the pulses.

"Fuck, you win. You can have anything you want."

He was on me in a flash, his mouth on mine, his hand shoving mine out of the way as he plunged his fingers into my molten core.

Laughter shouldn't have been on my lips and yet, it was there. "Perhaps I'll let you win next time," I could barely say the words between the thick pressure of his fingers in me, his thumb driving a steady roll across my clit.

He huffed. "I may have to take a pity win, I do not think I could hold out against your little noises. They undo me, Frostbite."

With a swift move, he growled and lifted me, his vampiric strength on full display as he held my entire body up, so he did not have to bend down to take my nipples in his mouth, feasting on them, dragging them across his teeth, sucking them hard enough to have me arching.

Gasping I ground my pussy against his midsection, the waves of pleasure growing fast and hard.

Pleasure. Pain. Laughter. Trust. Safety. They were wrapped up in him, in me.

They were everything.

With another growl he lifted me higher, and I was balanced on his shoulders, his mouth buried in my pussy as he latched onto my clit. Sucking, teasing, dragging me closer to the crest, holding me there long enough that I didn't know if I could...

"Raven!"

Nothing but this moment mattered. Nothing but Raven and me, here. He let me fall and all but impaled me on his cock, catching me so that we were flush and together, the first thrust of his hip sending me over the edge.

My body spasmed and he held me there, his mouth covering mine as the scream of release erupted. I couldn't have contained it, didn't want to contain it.

Over and over, I rode the waves as Raven thrust deep into me, the water sloshing around us, the moon bright overhead and for just that moment...I was free.

CHAPTER 15

Raven

I stood at the entrance to Diana's tent watching her sleep. A soft smile on her lips, her hands curled tightly under her chin, dark hair spilling across the silk pillow. My heart–gods she was my heart–and for a few moments I'd felt her relax that ironclad hold she had on her control. I'd felt her let go of every expectation as I'd held her body high and feasted on her. Worshiping her as the queen she was—with or without a crown.

Something had shifted between us there, in the water. Or at least for me it had.

I didn't think I could fall tighter under her spell; I didn't think I could need her more. Yet now, the bond between us was stronger than I would have thought possible.

I could sense her even when I was apart from her. Walking around the perimeter of the oasis, I'd been able to pinpoint her no matter where I'd stood. Not that I was unhappy about this change, it would help me keep her safe. But it spoke to another level of our mate bond.

I rubbed a hand across my chest as if I could physically touch the strands of fate that had woven us together. From the moment I'd saved her the first time, to now, there was no doubt in my mind that we had always been meant to find our way to each other.

A birdsong in the oasis had me turning my head to the east, followed by several more as they began to call to the morning.

Only a few hours till the sun rose, and I wasn't tired at all—benefits to being an older vampire, I could go without sleep for ages. Not that I wouldn't have gained from a rest, but my mind wouldn't settle, so there was no point in trying.

Stepping back, feeling as if I were tearing myself apart to put distance between me and my Frostbite, I made my way to where the lounge chairs were set up, as if we were in an all-inclusive resort—a front for something more? Nothing could be this idyllic. Not in this world. Not in the demon realm. And certainly not from a god who shared blood with Lilis.

No one else had the same worries that I did, though. Everyone else slept as if we were truly safe.

Even fucking Kevin was sprawled across two of the loungers, his tongue lolling out so long it touched the ground. I reached down and scratched the top of his head.

"How are you not suspicious, with hackles raised right now, big guy?"

He let out a fart in response to my question, and I stepped away before the cloud of green toxicity could reach me.

Towels hung from low tree branches. The water sparkled and beckoned. Everything was seemingly calm, and yet...

I let out a slow breath and tuned into the world around me, feeling every breath of wind, every single grain of sand shifting around me.

Including the soft footstep of someone trying to sneak up on me. No scent. They didn't speak, I couldn't hear even a heartbeat.

I spun and grabbed a throat only to find myself staring down at Myrr. Her one eyebrow arched, and I immediately let go.

"Sorry, Oracle. I am on edge."

How did she sneak up on me? The old coot was stealthier than she let on.

"No shit, bloodsucker." She shuffled over to the lounger closest to me and plopped herself down, leaned back and closed her eyes. I listened. There was a heartbeat, and I could hear her breathing. There was a scent to her too, faint but there now that I'd caught her.

Maybe she had a few more tricks up her sleeve than we knew.

I looked back to see if her faithful hound had

followed her, but Theo remained absent from our impromptu meeting. "Myrr. It is hours yet before the sun rises. You should go back to bed."

She huffed. "Do you know anything about anything, boy?"

Boy. As if she were so much older than me. "I remember when you were first called as an Oracle."

Her eyes flashed open. "You were barely out of diapers you mouthy brat!"

I grinned and crouched beside her. "Fine. Have it your way. You can call me boy if you like."

"I will then, thank you very much." She closed her eyes, and her voice softened. "She is afraid, you know."

My belly clenched, understanding exactly what and who she was talking about. "I...I know."

"I hear her talking in her sleep about a boy who saved her. What if he was her mate? What if he's dead?" Myrr didn't so much as crack an eye, so I wasn't sure if she knew that boy was me. It was possible. She was, after all, the Oracle.

The urge to tell her nearly overwhelmed me. Not that Will—new King of the Vampires—would mind that I'd nearly killed his tyrannical elder brother, Edmund all those years ago. Hell, I'd probably get a medal and a promotion.

But I realized somewhere in the long journey here, between each touch, each merging of our bodies that I didn't want my Frostbite just because she was fated to me. I wanted her in every sense of the word: her mind, her soul, her heart and her body. They were equally beautiful to me in all their strength and compassion. Her intelligence and drive.

And I wanted her to want me the same way.

Not because of fate, or gratitude. But because...

"You want her to see you for who you are, huh?" Myrr flopped a hand toward me and patted me on my calf.

I drew back and glared at her. "Are you reading my mind, old woman?"

"Easy to read your mind, you're a man, the words are simple in that book. Besides, if you'd wanted to force it, you'd have simply told her that you were her fated mate. That the vampire blood still humming in her spoke to you, and boom, she'd probably agree to anything. Well, maybe not, she is the Werewolf Queen, so I suppose it's a secret fling? As long as she doesn't get caught. Because then her people would call for her head, wouldn't they?"

I didn't want to hear what I already knew. That Frostbite, even if she came to realize we were...more than fuck buddies...would know the truth I'd been avoiding. We could never be together. Not in the way that I wanted. Maybe we'd have a tryst here and there, but she could never rule the werewolves with a vampire as her consort...

As her mate.

We'd have to run away to the Human Realms and

there was no way Diana would turn her back on her people. Nor would I ask it of her.

Myrr sighed. "Love is a funny, fickle thing, Raven. But do you know what's even worse?"

"I don't want to know—"

"Fate. Fate is a real bitch if you don't do what she wants. I guess you have to pick your poison."

I stood. "I won't force anything, Myrr. Not on Diana. Not on anyone."

"No, no, you idiot, you don't force it! You lean into it! Lean into fate, let it take you where you need it to take you." She took another swing at me, catching me in the knee this time. "Idiot."

Much as I wanted to roll my eyes at her, she *was* the Oracle. Not that she had been giving me anything new, or even a prophecy to help point me in a direction.

"Myrr, go back to sleep."

She let out a deep, rattling snore in response. I shook my head, fully intending to go to Diana, and curl my body around her. Even if I didn't sleep, that was where I could relax the most. Where I could at least try to rest.

A gurgle from Myrr, as if she were choking, had me spinning back in her directions. Her eyes were open, staring blankly at the sky.

Her voice though, that was not her own. It was deep, a baritone that I recognized. The voice of Elhimna, an entity that had spoken through Myrr before, and who seemed to be on our side when it came to dealing with Lilis.

"Nefir will help you. It is the price he must pay for his sins. Remind him that the stars are always watching, and they know his heart." She took a long rattling breath. *"The Wolf Queen must die. It is one of many deaths that will save the realms."*

Myrr gasped and slammed a fist to her chest, her voice back to her own. "Damn heartburn!"

"No." I could do more than breathe the word.

"Yeah, it was all that citrus! It always does that to me, I should know better, but I love oranges," Myrr grumbled.

I dropped to my knees as if I'd been sliced through the hamstrings.

The Wolf Queen must die.

I grabbed my head with my hands as if I could stop from hearing the words. This could not be.

I couldn't lose her.

Lean into fate…is that what Myrr had meant? Lean into losing Diana?

Because I knew Diana, and she would *allow* herself to be killed to save the realm, to save her family and her people. She had a heart as fierce as any Hunter, with more compassion than she let on—her reaction to the death of all the mermaids, the sorrow and grief of all those lives lost and she didn't even know them. Her kindness to Maverick even though he'd abandoned her.

For her to know and understand that her death would save so many others? She'd jump in the fucking fire herself without question.

My guts clenched and I wasn't sure I could keep what little food was in my stomach.

I did the only thing I could to assure myself that my Frostbite was still here, that whatever death fate had planned for her, it had not yet arrived.

I made my way to her tent and let myself inside, slipping out of my shirt. I didn't want to wake her; I just needed her close. Needed to feel her body against mine as she took every single fucking breath, so I knew she was still with me. She was alive.

Lowering myself carefully next to her, I pulled her gently into my arms, cradling her body to mine, just breathing her in.

A soft sigh slid out of her as she snuggled in closer, her lips finding the spot above my heart and pressing there before she settled once more.

I closed my eyes and held her, my body shaking, a chill washing over me.

The image of her cold and still, her lips blue as they'd been turning under the water all those years ago...

No.

No matter what it took, I would not lose her. Nor was I going to tell her that her death was somehow required by fate. Myrr wouldn't remember the moment the god had spoken through her, so there was no one to speak the words but me.

I would keep it from Diana, and when the time came...I would bear the cost. The voice had said many deaths would be required—mine in place of Diana's. A deal with the gods, if need be. A life was a life. Surely mine would do.

I would *make* it do.

Her warmth seeped into me, chasing the chill away. And with my decision made regarding her fate and my own, I let my mind turn to other questions.

How many gods were we dealing with? A small part of me had thought Nefir and Elhimna perhaps would be the same entity. Nefir seemed the type to find it funny to go by multiple names and personalities but...this voice from Myrr debunked my theory.

I mulled over what Myrr had said, the other words that had come first. That Nefir was paying for some sins. Did that mean he'd helped Lilis at some point? Did that mean he was more dangerous than he was letting on? He was a god after all.

Diana shimmied in her sleep, her arms slipping around me. I kissed the top of her head, wishing we were somewhere else. Wishing I'd reconnected with her sooner...wishing I'd killed Edmund all those years ago, and Diana had never had to leave the Vampire Territories.

But then I would have been executed. And she still would never have known me.

"Fucking fate," I muttered, seeing that this path we'd both been walking was the only one where we even had a few moments together. This path that ended in disaster was the best we were going to get.

Diana slipped a hand over my waist in her sleep, slipping lower until she stroked my cock, drawing a low moan from my lips.

If this was it, then I'd best make the most of it.

"Frostbite," I growled her name as I tipped her chin up and kissed the pulse in her neck. "Are you awake?"

Diana

Raven's lips were at my throat, sliding across the flesh reminding me of just how good things could be between us, reminding me of how he'd held me up and feasted on my body as if it were the only thing in the world. My fingers were wrapped around his cock, and I squeezed as I dragged my hand up and down his hard length, knowing exactly how it would feel when he drove into me, hitting sweet spots only he seemed to be able to reach. Feeling the wetness flood between my legs, ready to take him in again. I threw my leg over his hip and scooted closer as he curled one hand over my ass cheek, his fingers sliding down to find their way around to dip into that warm, wet—

"You awake?" Myrr stuck her head into the tent, and I jerked away from Raven with a gasp, as if we were teenagers caught by a parent. I sat up, feeling the heat in my face and chest bloom as a blush whipped across my skin. Myrr just stood there, unblinking.

"Gods, Myrr!" I snapped at her, not sure if I was mad or embarrassed. Maybe a bit of both.

Raven rolled onto his belly and groaned. "Fucking Oracle."

She grinned and winked at me. "That fellow with the golden eyes is back. And he brought more food! Thought you'd want to talk to him. I mean, you could stay in here, but that might be considered rude."

As much as my skin and body were flush and craving attention from the vampire who lay in my bed, Nefir was the key to finding Jade. He'd sent us here to the desert, and I had to believe he would help us on our way.

"Yeah thanks, Myrr."

I yanked the silken sheath dress I'd worn the day before over my head and hurried from the tent, doing what I could to calm the need raging through me. One touch and my body had been ready for him.

Damn it.

Shake it off, woman. Focus.

The sun had barely risen in the east as I made my way across the open section of the oasis, where all the lounge chairs had been the day before. This morning there was a long table with enough seats for everyone, food weighing it down so heavily I was surprised that the wood was not groaning.

Nefir at the head of the table, dishing food onto his plate. Eggs, roast meat, steaming fresh flatbread, more dipping sauces than I could identify. Fruit of every kind —pomegranate, huge red berries, guava and enormous dragon fruit dominating those baskets. Yogurt, nuts, crepes stuffed with different jams and creams. Jugs of cold drinks, and several steaming carafes that beckoned to my sleep deprivation.

"Come, come eat! Then we will discuss whether I can help you further."

I gripped the back of the chair closest to me. "Wait, yesterday you said—"

He waved a fork at me, cutting me off. "Yesterday was yesterday. Today is literally a new day, and I am unsure if it is in my best interest. As entertaining as you all are, I must keep my loyalties to my family, you know. If not, there could be...unpleasant consequences."

Letting go of the chair, I stepped to the side and slid into the seat, disappointment and anger warring to lead the conversation. Which would help me best win him back over? I went with both.

"So you won't help us? Are you a liar then?"

One by one the others joined us, but I barely paid them any attention, my focus solely on Nefir. We needed him, and the fucker knew it. We had nothing to offer him either. No boon we could give, no treasure to trade. Nothing. Raven had been right to remain suspicious.

Kevin slipped up to my side and tucked his head under my hand, likely sensing my frustration and anxiety. I scratched him behind the ears, mind whirring as I tried to think of some way to persuade Nefir to support our cause.

Nicholas sat across from me and I tipped my head in Nefir's direction. I'd seen the way the god had ogled the young vampire. Maybe he could get close? Put his hand on Nefir and learn something that could help us?

Nicholas grimaced, but he stepped up to the conversation. "Why? What's changed from yesterday?"

Nefir gave the young vampire a slow smile, his eyes roving his body. "Well, you see we said *her* name too many times and she took notice. She sent me a message last night. That's not good for any of us."

Her.

Lilis.

"She *threatened* you?" I forced myself to put food on my plate. My mouth was dry as ash, but I knew I needed to replenish my reserves as much as I could while we were here. Because with or without Nefir's help, I was going to find Jade.

I dug into the food, eating quickly and I motioned for the others to do the same. Because it was highly likely that we would be striking out again back into the desert that had nearly killed us.

Nefir's smile seemed off as he looked back at me. "Something like that."

Raven approached the table, the last to join us. The scent of his desire washed over me first, and I wanted...oh damn it. I stared down at my plate, focussing on the food as I got my hormones better under control.

"Enjoy the water last night?" Nefir said with far too much innocence.

My head whipped up and I stared at him. He gave a slow wink, the insinuation clear.

He'd watched Raven and me in what had to be one of our most intimate moments. Not just because of the sex, but because of what we'd said. What had passed between us was not something to be mocked or shared with anyone but each other.

Apparently, I wasn't the only one who picked up on what Nefir was throwing down.

Raven was a blur as he went over the table and tackled Nefir out of his chair, pinning him to the ground.

"Holy shit!" Theo gasped. "What got into him?"

Mav groaned. "Now we're all going to get fried by a god because that macho prick can't keep his anger under wraps."

Myrr cackled. "Was only a matter of time, I saw that coming!"

I scrambled to get around the table as the others offered their thoughts on the situation. What I knew was that Mav was right. Raven had physically assaulted a god, seemingly without provocation. Surely, whatever rules of nature that bound them from killing us outright didn't apply here. Nefir could end us all.

He could end Raven.

"Stop! Raven, let him go!"

I reached them just as Raven spoke, snarling and low,

one hand wrapped around Nefir's neck, the other holding his dagger to the side of the god's head. "The stars are always watching you, you piece of shit, and they know your *filthy fucking heart*."

Nefir paled, his already pale skin going snow white. At first, I thought it was anger and then I realized it was something else.

Fear. His throat bobbed and he managed two words that meant nothing to me. "*Bessan fatin.*"

"Raven!" I grabbed him by the bicep and pulled him off Nefir. "Not worth it. We still need him."

He turned to me, turquoise eyes softening from the hardness he'd been giving to Nefir. "Yeah, yeah it is worth it. He fucking tried to make it foul. And it wasn't."

I swallowed hard; chest tight as I clung to his arm. "Nothing can change what it was. Not even a god."

Nefir dusted himself off and got to his feet as Raven gave him space. "Well, that changes things."

I did a double slow blink. "What do you mean?"

"Well it seems your blood...*sucker*...here had a chat with one of my parents last night. I owe...no, it does not matter why. *Bessan fatin.* It will be done. I will help you." He sighed and clapped his hands. The table and food disappeared, and I stumbled back as if I'd been shoved, a hot wind snapping around my body, tugging on my limbs.

I looked down. My sheath dress was gone. In its place was loose khaki pants, a white long-sleeved top, a thin white material that went around my head and around my neck in a long looping pattern.

Across from me, Theo pulled the bottom part of his head wrap up and easily covered his nose and eyes. "A keffiyeh. This will help in this heat and against the blowing sand."

Solid leather boots on my feet that rose well over my ankles. By the looks of things, everyone in our party had been outfitted the same—prepped to traverse a desert.

"Come. We cannot magic our way to the girl. My sister would sense it immediately. As it is she will be searching for you. And if she knows where the girl is, if the girl has used her power...well she could be waiting." He turned and the oasis slipped away on a spinning cloud of sand as if it never had been.

A dream within a dream. A place that had never truly existed.

I pulled my keffiyeh up over my mouth and nose and tugged the portion on my head low over my forehead. While I wouldn't say it was cool, it was a hell of a lot better than what we'd entered the desert wearing the first time.

Catching up to Nefir, I fell into step beside him, determined to make the best of the time we had with the god. "How far is she?"

"Maybe a day's walk. Could be less, could be more. I'm not sure." He looked straight ahead, all his charm and lightheartedness gone as if Raven had washed it all away with those few words.

The stars were watching. When I'd thrown the coin, I'd said, "To whoever might be listening while we float under the stars, please guide us..." Was that why he'd taken notice? I had a feeling it was, even if I didn't fully understand what it had to do with the stars. Maybe stars were another name for gods?

"Tell me about your sister, please. I have learned that it is better to know our enemy, to understand why they do what they do if you can. It's the only way to stop her." I looked sideways at him. Nefir's mouth was set in a grim line, not a smile in sight. Maybe I needed to start smaller. "At least tell us *how* she is watching us. You said because we used her name?"

Nefir led the way, heading northeast by what I could tell, though the desert was throwing me off.

I ignored the grumbles of Myrr behind us.

Raven fixed it. "Kevin, let her ride you. She's nothing but a bag of bones despite what she eats."

"Brat boy!" she snapped, but she stopped her pissing and moaning. A quick glance showed me that Kevin had indeed allowed the old Oracle a ride at Raven's request.

Through it all, I didn't feel Nefir so much as take a breath to answer me. When he finally did, it was slow and methodical as if he weighed every word.

"I will tell you what I can. As I said yesterday, I have been...away. I do not know all that has happened in my absence."

That wasn't quite what he said, but I wasn't going to

contradict him. Not if he was going to speak up about Lilis.

"She is vain. Saying her name calls her attention. As you've seen. She has the ability to see through those who have tied themselves to her. Binding their souls to her purpose. That could be a human, a demon...anyone who claims her as their goddess."

Mav joined us. "Does she leave a mark on them? Something we can identify easily?"

Of course, he hadn't been with us in the graveyard when we'd had to put George to rest. He hadn't seen the swirling, spiral tattoos with the spiked edges on the chest of the Vanators. Ice cold to the touch...

"Your Wolf Queen knows that mark. But it is always hidden. She does not announce herself. So unless you wish to strip everyone you meet, it is unlikely you will easily detect her worshippers."

Well at least that confirmed we'd been right about the Vanators.

His eyes never shifted from the horizon, and he walked with such purpose he seemed like a different god than the jovial free spirit we'd met just the day before.

I had to push him, to get him to tell us more. Because no matter what he'd said so far, there was no way he'd told us all of it. This was his sister...

"She wiped out hundreds of mermaids in the waters just off the shore of the demon territories. Female, male... children. Infants, Nefir. Their bodies were torn to pieces, it was no accident. Whatever she was before, whoever she was, she is a monster now. Please...please help us stop her."

"She was not always like this," he whispered. "She was kind, and just...always fair. She was always fair before. I don't..." He kept walking but he closed his eyes. "I can only tell you what I think drives her, because I do not know for sure. But to see her change like this? To see her as a monster that in the past she would have fought against? It can only mean one thing..."

We were at the top of a dune, and below us a barren plain spread out, the sand gone, just hard packed rock without a single living thing sprouting from it. Pockets of darkness, caverns that fell into the earth below were scattered as far as the eye could see, waiting to swallow us whole. In the distance were mountains that spewed gouts of fire and smoke. Of course, Jade would be all the way across this plain of death.

Myrr sighed as she sat swaying on Kevin's back. "This looks like less and less food."

The others joined us at the top of the dune. "Shit," Maverick grumbled. "We gotta cross that, don't we?"

I turned to the god who would help us, ignoring the others. One problem at a time. "Nefir, what do you *think* drives her? How can we stop her?"

His eyes were solemn as he took us in. "Revenge. Revenge is what drives her. And as to stopping her? I don't think you can."

CHAPTER 17

Raven

Diana's shoulders stiffened as Nefir dealt the emotional blow. Lilis likely could not be defeated. Far be it for me to contradict him and mention that the realms could be healed...if the Wolf Queen died.

I'd already decided...that wasn't going to happen.

"Don't underestimate her." I brushed past the god. He'd not fought me at all when I'd tackled him, and I could still feel the stillness of his blood. It hadn't moved or pulsed under my hand. He wasn't alive like we were.

"I wouldn't underestimate my sister either." Nefir slowed to a stop. "This is as far as I can go. The one you seek is at the base of the mountains."

Diana stepped out and in front of him. "How do we stop your sister? A weakness? Anything at all will help, Nefir."

I thought he wouldn't answer, that he'd just puff into smoke and disappear. And maybe he would have if I hadn't reminded him.

"The stars watch, motherfucker," I growled under my breath.

He stiffened and his energy spiked as if he were restraining himself from attacking me. I half wanted him to try.

"There are two things I can tell you. One, as gods we are bound by few static rules. The first is that, if a solemn vow is made by a god, it cannot be broken. Do not trust her unless she swears it on the stars." He lifted two fingers. "Second, while you don't have the power to stop her completely, she can be driven back...temporarily held at bay. But it requires both the heart to face her and the strength and bravery to risk it all." Nefir turned to look at Diana.

A chill swept through the air. "Like Sienna did," Diana breathed. "Sienna drove her away."

"Yes. Lilis is stronger now, so it won't likely be so easy this time, but it can be done." Nefir dipped his head, his eyes closing as his image began to fade. "I must go. Even the stars will not demand more of me."

A breath of hot wind gusted around us and Nefir completely disappeared, his body turning into grains of sand, blown apart by the wind.

"Well ain't that an exit!" Myrr dug her heels into Kevin's side as if he were a pony. Kevin grunted and obliged, bringing her close to Diana. "We find Jade, and she can drive the goddess away for a time. Sounds like a plan to me."

Maverick was quiet, his eyes searching the horizon. "I have a feeling it won't be that easy."

The others turned to him. "Why not?" I restrained myself from calling him chickenshit. With effort.

Perhaps it was the deepening connection to Diana, or maybe it was the knowledge that I would die and she would be alone...unless she still had Maverick. Fuck. I might as well have swallowed a pile of Kevin's shit for the nausea that rose at the thought of them together. Me dead and gone. Her needing comfort and turning to Maverick–

I spun on my heel to look at the distant mountains as Maverick spoke, my throat tight and my chest throbbing with a pain that I knew was coming.

"Nefir said...he said it required heart and bravery and the strength to risk it all. Only then could the goddess be driven away. I don't think Jade is capable of that. She's not bad, don't get me wrong, but she was just so afraid. How could she face a goddess and her fury?"

All good questions. "Won't find out unless we actually track her down." Look at me go, not spitting vitriol at him. Mostly it was a strange sense of impending doom I couldn't shake.

I started down the sand and rock slope, sinking in deep to the dune as I let gravity pull me forward. I couldn't look at him right then, couldn't look at what might be Diana's future.

But I loved her enough that I wanted her to find happiness once I was gone. If that meant Maverick... fuck...

I led the group, and Nicholas joined me. Diana was right behind me, with Myrr riding Kevin at her side.

Maverick and Theo pulled up the rear. Nicholas picked up his pace a little and I matched his speed until we had a good twenty feet between us and Diana.

"What's wrong? I can sense something..." he breathed the question for only the two of us to hear.

Did I tell him? Or did I let him see?

If I was going to die soon, did it matter if he saw what was in my head? Probably not, and whatever fear of his gift I had, faded under what I felt for Diana.

"Take a look if you want."

Nicholas startled, but he didn't ask if I was sure. Carefully he brushed his hand against the back of mine as we walked, so casually I doubted anyone noticed.

I let my mind stay open to the conversation with Myrr as she'd spoken for Elhimna.

Nicholas pulled back before he saw anything else. "Fuck."

"I see you grasp the situation," I drawled, hiding behind my court persona. "I will take her place, Nicholas. It will be up to you to see them back to her Keep."

"You would trust her with me." Not a question.

How did I say all the things that needed to be said

without alerting Diana that something was wrong? She would see our heads together and then she'd be asking questions, if she wasn't prepping to pepper us already.

"You swore allegiance to her, that is all you need to remember. And yes...I trust you." I glanced at him, then skirted around the first dark opening.

I paused at the mouth of the hole that spanned seven feet across, a gust of cooler wind spilled out. Cooler, but foul, as if a giant had belched straight up the pipe.

"Disgusting, and I'm riding a hell-hound who uses his farts for added propulsion, I'm sure!" Myrr and Diana joined us, Diana crowding close to my side. Kevin let out a long low whine, pacing around us, butting his big head against Diana's hip.

The urge to wrap an arm around her and just breathe her in was almost too much...but not here. Not now.

"What do you think made these holes?" Theo asked. "Like are they craters from asteroids?"

Maverick grunted. "Maybe giant worms? I heard talk of such things when I was here but I didn't put stock in it."

A rumble under the ground wobbled my knees. I grabbed Diana and pulled her back from the seemingly bottomless cavern. "Let's not find out."

The earth heaved and the edges of the cavern fell in as *something* moved within.

"Too late," Diana said. "Run."

Kevin took off first, Myrr clinging to his back. Of course the hell-hound was born in the demon realm, he likely had some experience with whatever it was that we were...I grabbed Diana's hand and started running as all the dark holes began to grumble.

The first creature to appear seemed to be long and tubular, that was my first glimpse.

"Gods, dumbass, why did you have to say giant worms!" I bellowed.

Only it wasn't a worm that crept out of the earth. Tentacles shot out, the tips of them split into three pieces that came together like a thumb and two fingers. If a thumb and two fingers could be covered in spikes. More and more of the long reaching tentacles erupted, and I didn't know if it was a single creature under the earth, or if there was a fucking nest of them.

It didn't matter.

"Faster, we gotta go faster!"

Maverick was dodging the flailing, grasping tentacles as was Kevin and Myrr but...

"Theo!" Myrr yelled.

Diana and I skidded to a stop. Behind us, Theo was literally limping along.

My Frostbite took a step, as if she'd turn around, and I tugged her back. "Go. I'll get him."

I could pack him no problem and still run at nearly full speed. As strong as Diana was, I didn't want her burdened at all.

Not with her life literally being foretold to end—I wasn't leaving anything to chance.

I bolted back to Theo, grabbed him and flung him

over my shoulder. The wind whooshed out of him, but he didn't complain. He was all bones and wiry old man muscle, which meant we both felt every bounce of him on my shoulder as I wove my way through the now field of waving tentacles.

I caught up with the others quickly, because they were slowing down. "Why are we not still running?"

"They aren't attacking us." Maverick grabbed his side as if he had a stitch. I'd give him something to heave about. "I think they're harmless."

"Chickenshit, we are in the middle of this plain, if they decide to attack, we're all in trouble." I didn't set Theo down. I looked to Diana who was nodding, but we'd held still too long.

The first tentacle shot toward Myrr and Kevin. The hell-hound dodged no problem, but the clack of the three-pronged pinchers, the grinding of the sharp points on one another, and the mouth that opened where the three pinchers connected...that was too close for comfort.

"Still think they're harmless?" I snapped at Maverick as we all took off running again.

Only now we weren't just dodging the thick bases of the tentacles. We were dodging every lightning-fast snap as they shot toward us.

The only weapon I had was my dagger that held the sun at bay, and I wasn't about to lose it in mid-day in the middle of a desert. Which left me running on defense.

Diana was just ahead of me, and I split my focus

between keeping her safe, and keeping myself from being snapped in half.

"Duck!" I yelled as a tentacle from behind her shot forward. She dropped to the ground, rolling and leaping back to her feet just out of range.

Maverick took a hit to the side from a sweeping tentacle, which sent him flying through the air.

Diana bolted forward and caught him as he landed, helping him stay on his fucking feet.

Nicholas stayed close to Diana and Maverick, and I brought up the rear.

Our group ran for what felt like hours, avoiding being cut in half, but barely.

The pinchers missed us, but not by much. Slices littered our bodies, arms and legs, the near misses many. But at least they were misses. We were going to make it.

"Almost there!" Myrr called back as she and Kevin charged past the last of the tentacles and wormholes.

Sweat and blood blurred my vision, but Diana, Nicholas and Maverick were clear of the monsters.

I stumbled past some invisible line that I felt more than saw, and dumped Theo off my shoulder.

"Thank you," he gasped the words as if he'd been the one running.

I grunted a response, unable to do more than that as I dropped to my knees, a buzzing running through my blood. My vision was blurring, and my breath came in gasps. No one else was reacting as I was to the...

"Venom." I gurgled.

Nicholas grabbed me and pulled me further away from the strike zone. "Shit, are you allergic to it?"

Allergic. To a fucking worm? I tried to say no, but my mouth and tongue were numb, and my muscles were spasming, contracting over and over out of control.

Diana dropped to my side, her fingers ghosting over my face. She was covered in blood too from the pincers. "You need to drink from me. No one else is having a reaction like this, so we have the antibodies. Nicholas, help me."

Nicholas lifted me up and grabbed my bottom jaw, prying it open even as it tried to clamp shut on its own, muscles seizing. No words, I couldn't say anything as Diana straddled me and tucked her neck close to my mouth.

Nicholas got the angle right and helped to sink my teeth into her. She could have offered me her wrist, but this was a sign of great trust. Her eyes closed and her chest rose and fell a little faster.

Fuck, this was not how I wanted to drink from her. Not like this. Not surrounded by people. With Maverick watching.

My teeth pierced through her skin, and her blood flooded my mouth; a heady rush of magic and frost, of the forests and wolf and that sweet essence that was purely Diana. The very core of her was my mate and that was something I couldn't even identify as a flavor. It just was.

A soft breath from Diana, as if she were fighting the

moan that wanted to roll through her, the pleasure that came with the bite. There were no new ties that locked into place, I felt no different than I had a moment before.

Because I was already bonded to her deeper than any simple blood bond could create.

I swallowed convulsively three times, drinking deep. My muscles relaxed and the reaction to the venom of the tentacled creatures faded. I couldn't lift my arms yet, and Nicholas' hands moved to pull us apart before I took too much. That was good.

"That's enough, he'll be okay now," Nicholas said.

Except...except he touched both of us at the same time, skin to skin.

A groan slid out of me as Nicholas, Diana and I were locked together, scenes playing out through my mind. The oasis. The words of Elhimna.

The world seemed to scatter around us, and I knew without a shadow of a doubt that we were catching a glimpse of our immediate future.

Diana flat on her back, blood spilling from her mouth. Her chest unmoving.

I jerked away from them both, a roar of pain erupting out of me. No, no it couldn't be so soon. Because even though I would throw myself on the sword for her, I knew the truth.

Prophecy would not be denied.

Diana caught my face with her hands, her warmth centering me, her icy blue eyes calm despite just seeing that she would die soon. "It will be okay, Raven. Trust me."

"It isn't you I don't trust, it is the monsters we face, it is the prophecies…" I pulled her into my arms and crushed her to my chest. As if I could just hold her there and make everything else go away. Because she'd seen the words of the god. She knew her death would help heal the realms now. Something I would have kept from her forever if I could have.

Nicholas shook, still on his knees. "I…I didn't know that could happen."

"None of us did. Chances are it couldn't have until you drank from Myrr," Diana said, still calm as if she hadn't just seen her death. "And I think we have time to figure out what it means. Prophecies rarely go the way they sound."

How could she think that? It wasn't exactly vague, but I wanted to believe her too much to argue.

She didn't try to wriggle free of my crushing hold. Slowly, I let go of her, though it was like tearing free from one of my own limbs.

"Well, fun as that is, I smell food and I'm hungry," Myrr announced. "And I see smoke up that way so let's go get us some eats! Maybe they will have a big old welcome feast? That would be nice. It's been a trying day."

A trying day.

Theo laughed. "Well, that's the truth, my beauty."

I didn't care where Maverick was. Part of me was hoping he'd fallen into one of the creature's gullets.

Diana's eyes didn't leave mine. "It will be okay, Raven. We will figure it all out. I swear it."

My body sung with the blood she'd given me, reminding me that she was mine, through and through. And that her death would shatter me in ways I'd never have imagined. She started toward the smell of smoke, her back to me. I followed, as I would follow her always.

"No, Frostbite, it won't be okay. Not if I lose you."

CHAPTER 18

Diana

How did I make Raven see that if saving the realms required my death, it was a small price to pay?

Not that I wanted to die, but seeing Myrr speak to Raven in Elhimna's voice had weirdly not been a surprise. I'd survived Edmund's attack as a child, and while I fought to live, I'd always known that death lay in wait for me.

At least this way, my death would mean something.

We weren't there yet though. I weaved my way through the piles of rock—an old landslide—and headed straight for the smoke. Here and there, I lost sight of it, but the smell drew me on.

The others were silent.

Well, not quite.

"I don't know why you're all so blue," Myrr grumbled. "We're alive. And I smell dinner cooking."

"It's not even lunch!" Maverick spluttered. "Where do you put it all, woman?"

"Sometimes my bra, sometimes just in my pockets."

My lips quirked. Myrr would never change. Nothing fazed the old Oracle, and that was a constant in this world that gave me a small comfort.

Voices floated in the air, coming from ahead of us. A man. A woman. Children. The bark of a dog.

Kevin gave a low woof and took off running. "Kevin, no!" I tried to grab him as he bolted past me, taking Myrr for another flat-out gallop.

"Weeee!" Myrr lifted one hand to the sky, her body bouncing. I took off after them, chasing them through the piles of rocks, skidding to a stop as the path opened into a vista I hadn't expected. Raven was at my heels, Nicholas and Maverick not far behind him. Theo...well, Theo would catch up eventually.

A two-story stone house was built into the base of the mountain, smoke curling from out of the chimney. The yard was not sand, but green, and lush, as if we'd stepped into another oasis. Only this one was not created by a wily god. I hoped.

A garden to the one side of the house was overflowing with produce and fruit, chickens with two heads pecked at whatever grubs they could find, and a low moo snapped my head to the side.

A small herd of cattle—mind you they had flames in their eyes which was more than a little disturbing—were penned up in a field that spilled out and away from the house.

Kevin though, he was what really commanded attention. Because he'd found another hell-hound to play with. One whose eyes were as crooked as his.

Myrr bobbled on his back, finally managing to slide off one side. I scrambled forward and caught her before she fell, dragging her away from where the two hell-hounds romped around each other.

"Looks like he found his brother," Myrr grumbled.

I held tight to her as the door to the house opened. A woman with long, sleek, black hair and forest-green eyes stepped out, a long spear in her hand. "Who are you?"

Letting go of Myrr I slowly held my hands up.

It was Maverick though who stepped forward to take point. "Jade. It's...been a long time."

Her eyes and the weapon swung toward him as he held his hands wide. "Maverick? How...how is it possible?"

He shrugged. "You know me, I'm a survivor."

Her eyes narrowed and her dark brows furrowed. "Like a cockroach." She pulled back as if to throw the weapon and Maverick waved his hands.

"Stop. Jade...I tried to save her. You know that!"

Jade's green eyes hardened. "No. You came and got me and left her alone! I'd have found her eventually, but that will never happen now, will it? You left her because you're a fucking coward and couldn't stick around through the hard stuff!"

"Couldn't agree more," Raven muttered under his breath.

I wanted to elbow him, but it was Nicholas who took the next step.

"I can show you the truth, Jade."

She shook her head and opened her mouth to reply when a voice from inside hollered. "Mama! I'm hungry!"

"A child after my own heart," Myrr said with a sniff.

I sighed. "All of you, back up to the rocks. Right now. I need to speak to Jade woman to woman."

Raven glanced at me, and I gave him a quick nod. He could be on Jade in a flash, but I didn't want to scare her.

We needed her as an ally, not an enemy.

They did as I asked. Jade did not lower the spear, and I didn't approach her. "I'm sorry to burst in on you like this. But we need your help."

A tiny pair of hands circled around Jade's legs. "Mama?"

"Inside, Horace, I told you to stay inside." She didn't waver from her stance. "My mate will be back soon. You really should go, he doesn't like visitors."

"We can't," I said with a helpless shrug. "All the realms are at risk, Jade. And you hold a key to saving us all. I think you know what I'm talking about, don't you?"

How the hell was I going to convince her to come with us? She had a child. Even as I thought it, a wail from inside told me she had a second, younger child waiting for her. How could I ask her to leave them? We couldn't protect them all.

Slowly she lowered the weapon. "What is your name?"

"Diana."

Her hands began to shake. "Queen of the werewolves?"

I dipped my head toward her. "The very same."

The weapon clattered to the ground, and she caught herself on the edge of the door. "I dreamed of you. They told me you would come, and I would have to leave. Leave or..."

She started to sink to the ground, bumping her knees on the doorframe with a soft thud.

They?

"Nefir, or Elhimna?"

"Elhimna," she whispered. "I cannot leave...my babies are here. My mate. I cannot leave them." She covered her face with her hands and began to sob, her thin shoulders shaking. The wail of the younger child continued, spiking in pitch and fervor.

Approaching her carefully, as if she were a wild animal, I crouched next to her. "Maybe you should get your little one, and we can talk about this. Maybe there is another way?"

Still shaking, she pulled herself up. I offered her a hand, but she waved me off. "Wait in the yard. I will bring refreshments."

"Thank you."

Her eyes glittered with tears. "Do not thank me yet."

She closed the door and a moment later the wailing eased off. I turned to see the others watching. "Now we wait."

Only a few minutes passed before she opened the door again, a platter balanced on one hip, a small child on the other.

The little one was very obviously half human–half demon with the pair of tiny horns sprouting from the top of her head. Her milky white hair curled like a cherub's, despite her parentage. The older child slunk out after his mother, the same milky curls, the same horns, only he bore a scowl on his face.

"What are you doing here?" he growled.

"Speaking with your mother."

"This is our home," he all but hissed the words. "Go away."

Lovely.

Kevin and his newfound friend–or brother, if Myrr was to be believed–bounded between us, tumbling against the boy and taking him with them. Jade's eyes tracked them.

"They are from the same litter I think."

I waited for some smart-ass comment from Myrr, but she remarkably remained quiet.

Jade took us to an outdoor table, chairs placed all around the edge, right under a blossoming tree of some sort. The petals were pale blue and purple, very pretty.

"How is this all possible?" Raven asked, his voice gentle. "It is...heaven in a place known only to be hell."

Jade's lips tipped up in a soft, suddenly shy smile as she poured drinks for everyone. "My mate did this. He understands the earth, and how to pull water to places that are dry."

Nicholas let out a low whistle. "Waterborn demons are rare. I'm surprised the king allows him to be here and does not keep him closer."

Her face hardened, fear flashing clearly in her eyes. "The King doesn't know. No one does. You are the first to...to ever see our sanctuary."

I shook my head and held up my hands, palms facing her. "Your secrets are safe with us, Jade. I wish we didn't have to disturb what you have here, and we will tell no one when we leave."

She relaxed and passed out the cups. I took a long breath at the edge of the cup and smelled nothing dangerous. Still, I waited until Jade took a drink.

I noted that only Raven waited, as I did.

I set my cup down after just a sip. "The power you carry...it is a key to saving the entire world. Human and the Territories. You can bring your family, your mate, we will get you to the Werewolf Territory. You'll be safe there."

Even if I had no idea how we were going to do it.

Her shaking started up again. "Even if I wanted to help, I am bound to this place. I was a slave, and my mark was burned not only into my body, but into my soul. As long as Malach reigns, I cannot leave the Demon Territory."

There was no reason for her to lie. The truth was far too brutal to bother.

Theo sipped his cup of water, swirling it around. "What if there was another way?"

We all turned to him.

"What do you mean?" I asked, not sure why he was taking part in the conversation at all.

He shrugged. "You think that Akmon just kept me around all these years because I was good with the lighthouse? Anyone could do that." He rolled his hand, and a tiny bit of fire bloomed on his palm, then danced across his fingertips. "But I could produce a fire that as long as I was near, it wouldn't go out. Among other things. I do have a little magic..."

Our party of four just stared at him.

"How?"

He cocked his head, contemplating. "I captained a ship. The Marigold, after my mother. Shortly before the Veil fell, my men and I were lost at sea somewhere between the Territories and the Human Realm. It was a strange time. We'd find little islands with just enough resources to refuel us for a while but not forever, and we'd move on, in search of people. One of those islands that existed somewhere between fantasy and reality had these mushrooms. We ate them and–there were six of us left at the time–we all had different reactions. It was fun for a while. Craddock could make us a little rainstorm.

Old Phinneas could fly...for short spurts, anyway. But then we came upon Bathsheba's island, and—well, she had them for dinner, and I wound up alone."

"I'm so sorry for the men you lost, Theo," I murmured softly.

"Seriously?" Maverick spluttered. "You have magic, and you didn't tell us?"

"Didn't seem pertinent at the time. Now it does." He shot a glance at Myrr.

She leaned over and he leaned in as if he thought he was going to get a kiss. Instead, she whacked him right in the face with a gnarled fist. "Foolish toad! We almost died in the desert, and you did nothing!"

"What was I gonna do? I've been injured or near dead from thirst since day one. If I want to use magic, I need to be hale and hearty, or I'm as useless as I look. Until I drank that magic water of Nefir's, I couldn't have helped if I wanted to."

I pushed my way between them, my back to Myrr, my front to Theo. "Tell me, exactly, what you're capable of."

He scratched at his white chin stubble and squinted. "Well, it's hard to say for sure. I haven't had much cause to use any of that in a long while. Once I realized I wasn't strong enough to escape the island, it didn't matter much. That said, I had a pretty good handle on working with elements. I think I can call the shard to the surface of her skin. Granted, we might have to create a small cut to remove it, but—"

"Do it," Jade said. "Now. Take it out of me now!"

Her outburst caught me off guard. "What?"

She leaned forward on the table. "If you can take it out of me, do it. This...thing inside me killed my sister. It is the reason why the demons stole me away and brought me here. It has done me no favors in this life. It feels like a foreign entity inside me. I sense it always, writhing, pulsing. Like a restless beast. If I give over to it, I know I will lose myself forever. I don't want it. I never wanted it." Her eyes closed and she swallowed hard. "Take it and be gone before my mate gets back from his hunting trip." She turned to face Theo. "Are you sure you can do it without it killing me on the way out?"

He pursed his lips. "I'm not certain, but I swear I will stop if I feel taking it will do you irreparable harm."

"Alright, then." She nodded. "That is worth the risk to be free of it."

Raven broke the spell, sweeping the table clear. "Nicholas, the sheets on the line, grab them."

Nicholas ran to do as he was told.

Maverick stood up. "Wait. Jade...I don't—"

"With your track record, you don't get a say," she snapped.

I felt a stab of pity for Mav as her arrow hit home, but there was no time for mending hurt feelings. If her mate was dangerous, we needed this done before he was back.

Nicholas flipped the sheet over the table and Jade

walked over to me and handed me her child, then climbed up and laid down.

"Just like my dream. I saw this part too."

Theo went to her side, a distinct red mark on his cheek from Myrr. He rubbed at it absently. "Good, then you know how it all turns out?"

"I do." A tear tracked down her cheeks. "My family will be saved, and I will be free."

The baby snuggled her head against my neck and stuck a thumb into her mouth. I went to stand next to her mother. Jade reached out and I took her hand. It seemed so strange to find myself comforting a woman I'd just met.

"We need something to put it in once I retrieve it," Theo said. "A box or something similar?"

"The jug" —Maverick pointed at the silver jug Jade had served us with— "has a lid."

While I didn't think it was ideal, there was no time for arguments. It seemed clear that we didn't want to be here when her mate came home to find a troupe of strangers on his doorstep, his wife bleeding and prone on a table.

Last thing we needed was another fight.

I squeezed her hand. "It will be okay."

Theo held his hands over her body, skimming along maybe an inch above her skin. He paused and frowned. "Flip over."

Jade did as he asked without question.

"Ah, there it is." Theo's hands ghosted over her back

and stopped just below her shoulder on her left side. "Behind your heart. Tricky."

Jade hiccupped. "I can sense him drawing closer. You have only minutes. Do it quickly."

Minutes. Fuck me. I held the child and Jade's hand as Theo began to work his magic. "When I tell you"—he pointed at Raven— "you make a small incision. The item—"

"Shard," Maverick and Nicholas said in tandem.

"Fine, the shard will be able to slide out. Myrr, if you'll have the jug ready."

The others stepped up to their places and Theo began to hum under his breath, a steady drone that ebbed and flowed, tugging at something deep in me. Jade trembled from head to foot, and she gripped the edges of the table with her free hand.

"There" —Theo pointed, and the back of Jade's shirt rose as if something was trying to get out— "Raven, cut—"

Only there was no cut needed. The shard shot out of Jade's back. She stifled a cry and went limp.

The shard hovered in the air, as Theo tried to cup it. "Come here you slippery thing."

I couldn't look away from the shard as it slowly rotated in the air, avoiding Theo's grasp as if it did not like him. The color was like nothing I'd seen; pearlescent and darkness, a rainbow of colors and then...nothing. It changed with each beat of my heart, mesmerizing me.

The child squirmed, and I let her slide down my body to the ground, entranced by the spinning shard.

Someone was yelling. Theo. Theo was yelling. Trying to command the shard.

It wasn't even that big, the size of a short pencil, sharp at both ends, like a crystal.

The world slowed down as Myrr climbed up onto the table, straddled Jade's prone body and tried to scoop the shard into the jug.

But that wouldn't work. I knew it as surely as I knew what came next. It didn't want to be inside an inanimate thing.

Will you accept me? I need a host if I am to survive.

I breathed out. For the safety of those I loved, for all the realms, I held out my hand. This was the death that awaited me. The shard did not want to be in me—not truly. It wanted Jade. So, like her sister I could carry it... for a time. But eventually it would kill me.

I knew it in every fiber of my being. This was the cost. This was how we got it back home.

Yes.

The shard spun toward me, then like an arrow, shot straight at my chest. The blow knocked me backward and I hit the ground hard, struggling to breathe.

Sound and light came back to me in a burst of noise and bodies rushing toward me. Raven scooped me up and we were running. Or he was running, and we were weaving our way back through the rocks.

"The others...." I gasped and touched my chest. The

wound was small, like a pinhole really. It hadn't torn into me like it had leaving Jade.

"They're coming right behind us. Her mate was close. We had to leave."

"Why? Is he evil?"

"I don't know, but he wouldn't have to be. If I saw you lying there like Jade, I'd strike first and ask questions later."

"He could have stolen all the water in our bodies with a thought if he chose to," Nicholas said as he caught up to us.

We were out of the rocks. When I turned around, Theo and Myrr were riding Kevin.

Kevin didn't seem to care. If anything, he seemed energized by his visit with his fellow cross-eyed litter mate.

Maverick was running behind them.

"Is she alright? Is Jade going to be okay?"

"She's fine. Relieved, actually. Like we'd freed her from an anvil around her neck."

Thank gods.

Raven didn't put me down, and I didn't ask him to. My body felt...strange. Like it wasn't quite my own anymore.

We made our way around the base of the mountain, to find ourselves up against another desert. Or maybe the same desert, just the other side of it.

"We could get to the coast," Nicholas said. "I don't think it's far from here. Sneak to our boat...assuming nothing else goes wrong."

Maverick wiped sweat from his face. "What's the chances of that, man?"

Raven held me a little tighter, his whole-body tensing. "Oh fuck."

I didn't want to know, I didn't. But I looked and saw what had him freaking out.

Oh fuck, indeed.

CHAPTER 19

Raven

"Haboob," Theo gasped as Kevin began to wind in circles around my knees.

"A what boob?" Myrr demanded.

"Sandstorm." And it was a doozy. Like a tornado of whipping winds and sand. A terrible storm, so massive, it was impossible to see where it started and where it ended. If it continued on the path it cut, we'd be flayed to the bone.

"She knows," Diana said, squirming until I let her down. "She knows we found Jade. Damn it. I'd hoped to have some time to—"

She wobbled on her feet, and I made a move to steady her, but she held me off. Her eyes were trained on the incoming storm that seemed to be moving faster with every passing second.

"If this hits us, it's curtains," Myrr said, scooting closer to Theo.

"Doesn't take an Oracle to see that," Nicholas replied, meeting my gaze with a questioning one of his own.

I knew without words what he was asking. Should we snatch up Diana and Myrr and make a dash for it? But as tempted as I was, I knew she'd never forgive us if we left Maverick and Theo behind. I was pretty sure Kevin could keep up if he wasn't burdened with riders. No matter how we split it, there was no way we'd all make it out of this.

The winds whipped, and the sand screamed as the haboob closed in.

"What do we do?" Nicholas called out to be heard over the sound of the growing storm.

"Not we," Diana replied with a grim smile. "Just me. It's time to see exactly how powerful this piece of Veil truly is." She shot me a look over her shoulder, mouthed the words, "I'm so sorry," and then broke into a sprint.

Toward the storm.

"You want me? Come get me, bitch!"

What the hell was she doing?

My feet were anchored to the ground in sheer terror for a single instant before I leapt toward her, arms outstretched, as if she were going to literally embrace the storm. Before I could reach her, she let out a primal scream that rang through my head so loud, it nearly felled me. The sound climbed around us, building in strength instead of waning, unnatural in its reverberation.

At the peak of her scream, a light exploded from her

chest, momentarily blinding me before the storm swallowed it. And her.

"Noooo!"

I was in motion again, hurling myself into the whipping sands after her. Razor sharp grains tore at my cheeks and neck, forcing my eyes closed as I reached blindly, grappled wildly to find her. A wrist. A shoulder. A handful of hair...nothing.

And then, it was silent, deafening in the quiet that shouldn't have been.

The sand fell harmlessly to the ground, joining the rest. The wind but a memory as if it had never been. I blinked, sand stuck to every piece of bare skin, my eyelids crunching as I tried to see...anything.

"Diana!"

I searched the desert floor, howling her name. "Answer me, damn you!"

I could have reached for her with my bond if I'd thought of it, but I was too panicked at first.

"She's there!" Nicholas ran forward, gesturing wildly to a lump covered in sand a few yards ahead of me. The angle of her body, I'd have never seen her.

I stumbled toward her, muttering incoherent pleas under my breath. When I reached her, I bent and scooped her limp body into my arms.

"Diana? Can you hear me?" As the sand trickled away, her eyes remained closed, but she looked unharmed. No signs or scent of blood, her nostrils flaring lightly with each breath. "Why isn't she answering me?"

Myrr toddled closer, with a whimpering Kevin at her heels. She pressed two fingers to Diana's forehead. "It took Sienna's body years to process the shard and access her powers. She still doesn't know the extent of what she can do. Diana forced the issue on day one. Maybe her body couldn't handle that kind of power."

"Diana is strong. She can handle anything," I shot back with a growl, ignoring the pity in Nicholas's eyes as he looked on. "Now stop talking and start walking, old woman. Diana will wake up."

Myrr grimaced. "And if she doesn't?"

The thought of Diana not waking up was...I wouldn't think about it. It wasn't a possibility as far as I was concerned. "Then we need to get her to the ship and back home as soon as possible so Sienna can fix this."

Sienna was a healer, it was a part of her gift. If anyone could bring Diana back from whatever this was, it was her.

But as we marched along in eerie silence, I couldn't shake the little voice inside my head...

What if it couldn't be fixed?

The next few hours passed in a haze of grief and regret, and it was dark by the time we reached the shore. The few demons we saw looked away from us, as if we didn't exist. Fine by me.

We made it back onto the ship, and I was almost numb.

Almost.

I kicked open the door to the captain's quarters with Myrr on my heels.

I looked around. The place had been cleaned, everything set to rights. I laid Diana on the bed.

"What is this?" Nicholas said from the hall. "From what I can smell, the ship has been cleaned, repaired and re-stocked. Why?"

A thump from the deck above had me running, fangs bared.

General Algrin stood on deck, his wings tucked behind him along with his hand. "I thought you might come back this way. Figured you'd need your boat ready."

"Why are you helping us? Not that I'm complaining."

He drew a deep breath, his chest and wings expanding a little. "Things are shifting. I can feel it in the air...know that...know that I am on your side. As much as I can be when it comes to my king. I am bound to him in ways I cannot change. The sands of our territory have spoken to me in the darkness that it won't be long..." He shook his head. "Go swiftly, I have told those on the docks to forget your passage."

Without another word he sprang upward, into the sky and flew away.

I turned to Nicholas. "Get us out of here."

I ran back down to the captain's quarters.

Myrr had started the water into the tub. "Put her in, and then go drink some blood and clean yourself up. It's been a long day in the sun, and you'll need your strength to stay on watch overnight in case we run into you know who on the trip back," the Oracle muttered, waving at me to set Diana in the bathtub. "I'll wash her down and make her comfortable."

She turned off the water and stood back expectantly.

But I didn't want to leave. I wanted to sit on the floor with Diana in my arms until she woke up. The whole walk I'd expected her to snap out of this, to tell me to put her down, she had legs and would use them

The longer she was out cold, the more the fear grew that she wasn't coming back. That this was the cost.

"Fuck," I snarled, tightening my grip on her as I stared down into her soft, expressionless face. "It feels like a bad dream. How did this happen?"

"It happened because it was meant to happen, boy," she snapped back. "The sooner you can get with the program, the better. It will save you a lot of heartache."

"And what is the rest of the program, Myrr? Is this the end of Diana's story?"

Of our story?

Better if I knew now so I could make a plan to join her...wherever she might be.

"I wish I could tell you, but you know that isn't how it works. Go, Raven. Let me take care of her, and you let all that emotion out so that when you come back, you can be strong for her."

Her tone had shifted, and she sounded so gentle, I almost wondered if she herself had been possessed in some way.

The two of us stripped away Diana's clothes and I set her gently into the warm bathwater, pausing to press a kiss to her forehead.

"I'll be back soon, Frostbite. Come back to me."

With that, I rushed headlong out of the room before I couldn't force myself to leave at all. Myrr was right, though. Despite the fact that Diana had defeated Lilis in the moment driving the haboob back, we had no idea how long Diana would be out of commission. One thing was for sure, we were on borrowed time. Nefir had said as much. We could hold her at bay, but we couldn't stop her forever.

Algrin had given us a shot at surviving though.

My footsteps had carried me to the galley and I was surprised to find Theo standing by the stove. If I hadn't sensed the man or the stew, I definitely needed to recharge if I wanted to stay alert on watch all night. He glanced at me. "Stews bubbling in the pot, and Nick has got the ship on the proper course. He figures we should be in Werewolf Territory by tomorrow."

"Thanks," I said with a clipped nod. He looked like he was about to say more, but I held up a hand. "Look, I know you mean well, and I'm sure you have some amazing wisdom to share, but I just need to be alone for a while."

"Understood," Theo replied. "While I've spent enough time alone to last an eternity, I will leave you to it. I'll be at the wheel if you change your mind."

I paused and realized with a start that the old man

would likely be captaining a ship for the first time since he'd crashed onto the island. So far, so good, as he'd managed to get us on our way without me even realizing he'd taken command.

"And Theo?" I called to his retreating back, forcing him to turn around. "Thanks. I appreciate everything you're doing." I popped off a salute, which he returned with a bittersweet smile.

"My pleasure."

In an effort to get a few minutes with Diana before night fell, I made quick work of helping myself to one of the jars of blood in our supply. I eyed it, smelled it and then carefully tasted it.

Human. Not demon. Demon blood could be unpredictable at best if I was foolish enough to drink it. I did not need to go on a killing rampage, thank you very much.

Satisfied, I tipped the jar back and guzzled the entire thing.

Surging with renewed energy, I scrubbed myself off in the shower, and made my way back to Diana's room, armed with two steaming bowls of stew, and two hunks of bread.

Just in case.

I found Diana laid out on her bed in a nightgown with Myrr snoozing in a chair beside her.

"What the—" Myrr sat up and let out a snuffle. "Oh. Only you." She perked up as she squinted in my direction and caught sight of the bowls.

"How did she get out of the tub? Did she..."

But my hopes were dashed as Myrr scuttled toward me, both hands outstretched. "No, she won't be needing the stew, Raven. Maverick came and helped me put her in bed. But I'll eat both, if you please."

I didn't bother to hide my disappointment as I handed her the bowls and made my way to Diana's bedside. As before, she looked at peace, which was a small comfort.

"Captain says we'll be home tomorrow, Frostbite, so unless you want Lochlin and the Duchess out there making heads roll, you better plan on waking up soon."

My teasing brought no response, and I bent low to press my nose to hers, chest aching.

"I love you, Diana. Please don't leave me."

A loud slurp echoed through the room, and I let out a puff of air as I turned to the Oracle who had a spoon in each hand as she chewed in delight.

"Hard to have a tender moment when you're around, isn't it?"

"Some might say I'm having my own tender moment right here with this stew," she said around the mouthful. "Food rarely lets me down, bloodsucker. I can't say the same for people."

I couldn't argue. Instead, I gave Diana's silky cheek one last kiss and headed out.

I made it to the main deck just as the sun fell off the earth. As bad luck would have it, we were just approaching the area where we'd found the mermaids, and I couldn't help but search the seas for signs of life. But as I scanned the waves, it looked like nothing at all out of the ordinary had happened. So vast and unpredictable, the ocean and the creatures in it had all but erased the carnage. But it would forever be branded in my mind. I let myself remember Xefia's impish smile. Her eyes full of excitement. Her childish giggle.

Gone for whatever revenge Lilis was taking out on the world.

The hate flared hot again in my heart, and I relished the feeling.

Anything beat the terror that came with the thought of Diana never waking up...

"I fucking hate that she loves you."

I turned from the railing to find a slightly drunk Maverick sidling up next to me. In no mood to spar with his dumb ass, I faced the sea again with a sigh. "Well, it's a good thing I don't give a flying shit what you think, then."

"Me hating you makes perfect sense. The thing I don't get is why you despise me so much." He leaned his back against the railing and craned his head to meet my gaze. "You won. It's you she wants."

My gums ached with pressure, and I tried to remind myself that Diana would be super irritated with me if I separated him from his larynx while she was asleep. "This is exactly why. This conversation right here. You are sitting here prattling on about winning and losing, while she is—"

I broke off, at a loss for how to continue. Because what was she doing, exactly? Fighting for her life? She all but told me she didn't have any regard for that which was most precious to me. That she'd throw her life away in a heartbeat if it meant saving the realms. Did she even want to wake up, or did she consider stopping the haboob her grand finale? Did she think we could take her back home with the shard intact, and everyone would be okay with using her to fix things, so long as the realms survived in the end?

Because I would never be okay.

I couldn't wait to tell her that when she woke up. And tell her how pissed I was at her for thinking I might be.

"Look, Maverick. Even if she was just a friend, I wouldn't like you on principle. You used her and then broke her heart."

"That was a long time ago, Raven. I'm not the same person I was back then—"

"The way you continue to use her sympathies to try to sway her affections tells me otherwise."

"I'll do whatever it takes if I think there is any chance at all that she will see me the way she used to. And what about you, Mr. Above it All?" For the first time since we'd met, his eyes snapped with something like fury. "You know her people would revolt the second she openly chooses you as her mate, yet you persist. There are factions of wolves that have never accepted her. Not to mention the assassination attempt right before you left for this journey that killed her father. And yeah, she told me about all that. Being with you would be painting a target on her back for all eternity. But that's okay, is it? That fits in with your 'principles'?" he snarled.

My fingers itched to curl around his neck and choke the life out of him, except there was no point. He'd laid the truth bare already.

"I would protect her. I have always protected her," I managed, my voice nothing but a hoarse whisper.

"Like you did today?" His laugh was low and humorless. "You might have an ego like one, Raven, but you are not a god. You can't promise her protection against what's coming her way. No one can. And being with you only adds to the dangers she will face. Maybe if you truly look at this situation without rose-colored glasses on, you'd see that the greatest act of love would be for you to help figure out how to heal her, and then walk away."

My insides churned, and I squeezed my eyes closed. "I suggest you take your own advice and walk away yourself. Before I forget that Diana cares for you and do what I've been dying to do since I first laid eyes on you."

He was motionless for a long moment, but then he nodded. "Fine. I'll go. But remember what I said, Raven. Assuming we all survive this nightmare and when all is said and done, the safest place she can be is away from you. Allowing her to think it can be any other way is far more cruel than anything I've ever done."

With that, he stalked off, remarkably steady on his feet for someone who was supposedly deep in his cups.

Tricksters tricked, after all.

But I couldn't get his words out of my head, even hours later as I sat at Diana's bedside, head bowed in something like prayer.

Was the bastard right? Was I as bad as he was...Or worse?

And if I was, did I even have the strength to walk away?

CHAPTER 20

Raven

The second we stepped foot on the dock at dawn, finally back in the Werewolf territory I knew something weird was going on. Not just the snowflakes drifting lazily from an overcast, early morning sky, or the fact that I could see my breath. The weather had been volatile for a while now and was escalating daily. But what had me on high alert was the fleet of ships in the harbor. Half a dozen packed high with crates and turned out with a full array of weapons from catapults to cannons.

"Raven?"

I turned toward the call, laced with a Scottish brogue, and hefted Diana higher in my arms.

"Fucking hells!" Lochlin roared, his tree-trunk legs churning as he broke into a run my way, pounding down the dock. "What's happened, man? Is she—"

"No," I cut in, gripping her more tightly as he slowed

to a stop, arms extended. She might be his Queen and longtime friend and packmate, but she was mine to carry. "She's...fine. Let's get her to the keep and once she's resting comfortably, I'll fill you in. We need to get Sienna here immediately."

He tore his gaze from Diana's motionless form. "She's here already. Dominic as well. All of us, besides Will and Bee, who were putting together a second fleet to launch from Vampire Territory."

"A second fleet?" I shook my head, nonplussed. "For what? Has a war begun?"

His bushy, auburn brows rose high on his forehead. "Raven, we were preparing to come after you. We thought either the Vanators might've captured the lot of you, or those feckless demon bastards had pulled a fast one. Where the bloody fuck have you been?"

I frowned. "What are you talking about? We've been looking for the gem... as planned." I wasn't going to go into detail about how Maverick hadn't had the right gem, that it had been in Jade. Time for that later. "And we found it. Pretty quickly, in my estimation."

"Quickly? You've been gone and completely out of touch for nearly two months."

"What the hell are you on about, man? We've been gone a couple of weeks at most." Not that I'd been keeping track, precisely.

"Even less than that, twelve days by my count," Nicholas chimed in as he and Myrr pulled up next to me, with Theo trailing behind.

Lochlin shook his head, expression grim. "Either you've got the scurvy and are all addled from it, or that goddess bitch is playing games, because you've been gone nigh on eight weeks. We spoke to the demon Gabriel, and he said you left Isla Naranja over seven weeks ago. Hamish and the others returned and confirmed that message."

My mind raced as I tried to piece together what had happened. Had Ludimon Island somehow managed to steal time from us? Or maybe—

"Nefir," I snarled, an image of the puckish god floating through my mind. *Time is a construct,* he'd said. How long had we been at his oasis? We had assumed his magic water had healed us. Had it kept us asleep long enough for us to heal ourselves? Or had he warped time to make it seem like a day when it had been far longer? How strong was his magic that even Diana hadn't been triggered to shift by the full moon? Or had we all just slept through it?

I couldn't be sure, but as I looked over my shoulder at the ships prepared for battle, one thing was clear. We'd narrowly avoided starting an all-out war.

Lochlin put a hand on my shoulder. "We can discuss exactly what happened after. Let's get to the keep and let the others know you're alright. The Duchess has been fairly climbing the walls with worry."

By the time we got to the keep's great hall, the news had already reached the others. We stepped into the room to find Dom, Sienna, and the Duchess waiting.

"I can't lie. You've aged me a hundred years this time, old friend," Dominic said as he stepped toward us, his eyes going to Diana in my arms. "What happened to her?"

"I am hoping Sienna will know." I let myself inhale Diana's sweet scent one last time before allowing Dominic to take her. Not because she was his more than mine, but because his wife was the best chance we had of figuring out how to fix what had been broken inside her.

"Let's get her to her quarters," Sienna said, concern etched on her pretty face. "It will bring her comfort to be in her own bed."

She led the way, and Dom and I followed, but Sienna turned and shook her head. "You stay here and fill the others in on exactly what happened. Dom will join you as soon as he gets her into bed. I need to focus on Diana and Diana alone. I can't have you two hulking over me. When I'm open and healing, I can sense the emotions of others so fully, it can be incapacitating. Myrr," she called, craning her neck to find the old Oracle. "You can come and give me the rundown."

It was actually a good call on her part. Myrr didn't have many emotions, so she was a pretty safe bet.

"Can do." She pointed a gnarled finger at Nicholas and said, "Just make sure they send some breakfast in. I'm nearly starved."

She toddled after them as they all disappeared up the stairs.

"If anyone can fix her, it's Sienna." It was the

Duchess who spoke, but when I turned to face her, I flinched. Gone was the strong, vibrant woman I remembered, always the same since my childhood. I'd seen hints of her decline after Lycan's death. The loss of her beloved had been a shocking blow. But the past couple of months had not been kind. Her face was gaunt, her skin and hair dull, as if someone had drained her life force. I couldn't help but wonder when she'd last taken blood...

"Yes," I agreed as I crossed the room to take her hand. "Sienna's powers are unmatched. Diana will be alright."

She squeezed my fingers, eyes pleading. "She must be. Lycan gave his life to save her. I refuse to let it be for naught. Thank you for bringing her back to us, Raven."

I cleared my throat, unable to speak, settling on a nod.

"Let's all sit so our weary travelers can introduce us to their new friends and bring us up to speed," Lochlin said with curious glance toward Theo, Maverick, and Kevin, who still stood by the entrance. Uncertainty written across their faces.

Dominic re-entered the room and joined us as we all took a seat.

For the next half hour, we took turns telling the tale of our travels. From the Vanators with their new and enhanced magic, powered by the goddess Lilis, to meeting up with Gabriel at the Wild Queen. From the battle with St. George's undead army, to rescuing Maverick from Sal the water dragon. By the time we got to the mermaids and giant spider people, they were all just staring, open mouthed.

"If I didn't know that Nicholas didn't have a dishonest—or humorous—bone in his body, I would think you were putting us on," Dominic said, shaking his head in disbelief. "And this all happened in the Human Realm, you say?"

"Some of it," I said, getting impatient now. Where the hell was Sienna with an update on Diana's condition? "And some in what I can only describe as the space between. The longer the Veil is down, the weirder things have become. If we add..." I paused, still hesitant to say her name aloud, "the evil goddess's twisted games to the equation, things get even more unpredictable. And I only expect it to get crazier until we find the rest of the keys."

"Raven?"

Sienna's soft voice had me jerking my head toward the doorway. "Yes?"

"Can I speak with you...alone?"

I lurched to my feet and rushed to join her. I would know it if she was gone. Surely, I would feel the loss of her light on this earth—

She tugged me further from the room, and still lowered her voice. "It's clear that something has...changed between the two of you on your journey. Myrr confirmed it for me, so I hope I'm not overstepping in assuming that you are the person to consult on the matters of Diana's health?"

"You're not overstepping."

She let out a sigh and rested a hand on her lower back. It was only then that I remembered that she was pregnant. Selfish bastard that I was—I'd only thought of Diana.

"Raven...I've tried everything I know to reach her, but it's like she's in shock. I don't sense any internal trauma. I can feel her life force, and that of the shard. I just can't connect to her in the way I'm used to being able to do." She gnawed on her lower lip as we made our way down the hall. "I still have work to do when it comes to mastering my powers. If I was better at it, maybe—"

"It's not your fault, Sienna." As much as I wanted to rail at the world and everyone in it for this injustice, adding to Sienna's suffering wasn't going to help Diana. "I know you're trying your best."

When we stepped into the room, Myrr was gone, and it was just my Frostbite stretched on top of the sheets. She looked so small...so fragile...nothing like the woman I knew her to be.

"I'm going to go talk to the medical team here," Sienna said. I had been so focused on my own feelings; I also hadn't noticed until now how exhausted she looked. She'd likely not been taking care of herself these past weeks as their concern mounted for our party. She was still in the early, most crucial part of her pregnancy and here she was devoting all her remaining energy into Diana. A better man might have told her to rest. To revisit this in the morning once she regained her strength.

I was not a better man.

"They're a brilliant group," she continued, rubbing at her tired eyes. "I want to run a few thoughts by them. I'll be back shortly."

She left the room, and I moved to Diana's side. For the next hour or more, I knelt next to the bed, head resting on her chest as I listened to the steady thump of her heart.

Please come back to me, Frostbite.

"She looks so...normal."

I scrubbed a hand over my face and turned to find Dominic standing in the doorway, gaze locked on his sister.

"Like she's sleeping."

"She is," I growled, trying not to take his head off for the insinuation otherwise. "Sienna said she couldn't sense any internal injuries. Maybe just needs to rest...adjust to the shard inside her."

To his credit, Dom didn't argue. "She can do that, and we will all be here waiting when she wakes up. Why don't you come on out for a while. Feed. We can talk. You can't just kneel at her bedside and—"

"As if you wouldn't do the same if it was Sienna?"

"Ah, so that's how it is now? I wondered," he said with a wry smile. "I will read you the riot act for taking liberties with my sister once this crisis has passed. But you're right about Sienna. I wouldn't leave her side if I was in your shoes. There is nothing I wouldn't sacrifice to save her. Which is why I need you to give this some space.

Sienna can sense your worry...all our worries. Along with her healing abilities comes a heightened sense of empathy. The more she absorbs of that, the more pressure she puts on herself. I love my sister dearly, even though we didn't grow up together. But we must find a balance here. I can't risk Sienna and our unborn babe..."

To save Diana.

Fucking hell, I knew he was talking sense. But that didn't stop my fists from clenching at my sides as I resisted the urge to pummel his face in.

Before I could say anything more, Sienna swept into the room, jaw set, eyes steely with renewed determination as a male and female dressed in lab coats pulled up behind her. "We've come up with an idea. We think it has a fair chance of success. But Diana isn't going to like it one bit..."

I'd done a thousand and one things Diana hadn't liked all to keep her safe and alive. She couldn't be consulted for permission, so I'd just have to hope I had the opportunity to beg her forgiveness.

"Let's hear it."

"We've been toying with the idea that perhaps it is Diana's blood—half-vampire, half-wolf—that is causing this issue. The shard was such a shock, and this third element is very likely too much for her body to handle."

I eyed Sienna and then Dominic, who shrugged.

"And what are you suggesting, exactly?"

Sienna looked at Dom and then back to me. "We think that the healing property of her mate's blood could help bring her back. To push her wolf down enough so that the balance is no longer split evenly within her."

"How sure are you?" I asked.

Sienna closed her eyes and then gave a slow nod. "As sure as we can be. The medical team thinks that being turned into a werewolf didn't fully erase every part of her that was vampire. If we must choose her to be one, more than the other, then we can push her wolf back. Allow her vampiric side to rise again. This may be the only chance she has."

Diana might hate me forever, she'd think I'd done it so we could be together...but if Sienna was right, at least she would be alive to hate me forever.

The answer was clear.

"Let's do it."

CHAPTER 21

Diana

The black willows swayed all around me, the soft rustling of the dark leaves, the long tendrils reaching for me, tugging me further and further into their midst.

I lifted a hand and ran it down the length of one of the slender branches. "Am I really here?"

There was no answer from the trees, not that I expected one.

I slowly put my hand to my chest, remembering the shard.

The decision to take it in, the sharp pain that had exploded in my chest.

The sandstorm I'd stopped and then...here. Nothing between the haboob and this place that I could not possibly be in unless I was dead.

Was I dead? Too many questions, and no one to help me answer them.

I pressed my fingers to where the shard had pierced me. Only now I felt it in all my bones, as if it had spread out.

I am a part of you now, my power is yours. The earth will bend to your will, Diana.

I shuddered as the voice of the shard seemed to come from the trees around me. "You...you are a piece of the Veil connected to the earth?"

We are.

"Am I dying?"

Yes.

I went to my knees there in the grove of willows, where we wept for our dead. A construct of my mind, perhaps, but it was a place of grieving, and I let the tears fall.

Here, where there was no one to see my fear and trepidation, I cried for all that could have been, and all that would never be. For never being able to say goodbye to those I loved, to never see Raven again...

"How...long?" I whispered the question, not really sure I would even get an answer.

"That depends, daughter."

I shot to my feet at the sound of his voice, flinging myself in his direction and letting him catch me before I even fully saw him. "Father."

Lycan's arms were strong and firm around me, holding me up as if I were a child again. For long minutes he held me, then finally he spoke again.

"Diana, let me see you."

He held me out at an arm's length and peered into my eyes. "Yes, I see the difference now. The power within you is more than you have ever known. More than that of a vampire's speed and strength. More than the grit and fire of a werewolf." He smiled. "Walk with me."

He tucked my hand into the crook of his arm and drew me away from the black willows, past the graves of those we'd lost. And then, in a blink, we were in a different part of the territories.

A beach I saw in my nightmares. The beach where Edmund had tried to drown me. In the distance I could see the castle where I'd been born, half-vampire, half-human.

"Why did you bring me here?"

"This is your past, Diana. And it plays a role in all this, just as your present as the Werewolf Queen plays a role."

"And my future?"

He stared out at the waves as they crashed across the rocks. "The shard is your future."

We stood there, and I almost didn't want to ask him the question, because I felt like it would shorten my time with him. Time that I wouldn't give up for anything.

I turned him to face me. "Do you understand what is happening, Lycan? Do you know what we must do? Are there others who carry pieces of the Veil too, is it that simple?"

He slowly shook his head. "I think that you must speak to the shard, it is...living...sentient, even if it does not exist the way we would understand something to exist."

I tightened my hold on him. "You will stay with me?" I didn't care if I sounded like a child afraid of the dark. I wanted my father at my side for as long as I could have him.

His smile was gentle as he patted one of my cheeks. "Yes, I will stay with you."

Once more, I let him lead the way, and we were walking across the rocks. I glanced to the beach where I'd nearly died.

A figure stood on the beach, a little boy with dark hair. He looked over his shoulder at me.

"Who is that?"

"You don't know?"

I stared. The boy was too far away to make out anything but his dark hair and diminutive frame. He was young. Skinny, the way so many little boys were.

"No."

"That is your mate, Diana. He loved you from the moment he saw you. He fought for you then, knowing he'd die if he were caught."

My heart lurched. Raven had told me that a boy had been killed, a boy that had saved me from Edmund, but it had cost him his life.

"Why show me this?"

"I am not. This is...this is the shard showing you things it believes you need to see."

I didn't understand how seeing a future that could

never be, was of any help. Maybe if I was going to die, at least I would know the identity of my true mate?

And then what of Raven? Pain roared through my chest as if I'd been pierced by the shard a second time. Once I was gone, he would move on; I knew he would. He was not a man who would live a life without the comfort of a woman, no matter how many pretty words he gave me. But then the idea of him with another was...gut wrenching.

But that was a wolf for you, once they decided they loved someone, that was it.

My feet stilled, as if I'd been frozen to the spot.

Loved. Is that what this was? Did I love him?

No, that...that couldn't be. Could it?

"Diana?"

"I'm coming," I whispered, and did all I could to push Raven from my mind.

Lycan took a step, and I moved with him, blinking as the world shifted around us again.

We were no longer in the Alpha Territories.

Huge standing stones rose around us in the dark of a black night, with nothing to light our way except the distant flickers of stars.

"Stonehenge," I whispered. Even to those of us in the Alpha Territories, ones who'd never stepped out of our realm, we knew of this place. Of the innate power within it. No one had understood the role it played though, that it literally kept the Veil between the human realms and us intact.

Lycan gave me a gentle push, toward the center of the structures.

I took a step, then another and another as the stones around me began to shift and move. The missing stones of the circle reappeared, until the broken structure was once more fully intact.

And I stood in the middle of it. Slowly turning, I faced the entrance to the holy ground. There were no footsteps, and yet I felt a presence drawing near.

The energy was strong, warm, and it drew me toward it. I took one step, and the ground softened, pulling me to my knees.

A glowing light spun slowly into existence, a deep green threaded with gold and copper. It flickered and held steady at my eye level.

You came.

"I...did. Are you the shard?"

As best I can show myself to you, yes. You are the shard now. We are the shard.

This was my chance to ask the questions, to get the knowledge we needed to stop Lilis.

"Can we save the world, all the realms?"

Possibly. There is much that stands between us and victory over the goddess. Death. Life. Joy. Pain.

"Can you tell me how to stop her? If I live, I will face it all to save those I love."

Warmth flooded from the floating orb, gathering around me like a massive warm blanket.

I knew I chose wisely. I waited a long time for you to arrive, Diana of three worlds. Human. Vampire. Wolf.

My heart was beating faster, the longer we spoke. I clutched my arms around my middle. "Please, tell me."

You already know. You must find the other pieces of me. They went to those I chose to help protect the realms from Lilis.

"Like Sienna."

Yes, like the one who holds the first piece of me. You carry the second.

I swallowed hard. "And if I were to say there were three pieces, is that all?"

More than three.

"Four pieces?"

A pause, the gold within the orb flashed and I could tell—I don't know how, but I knew—that the shard was considering the question deeply.

More than four.

I swallowed hard and took a leap as my mind told me that I already knew the number. "Less than six?"

Once more the orb flashed and danced. Again, I felt the understanding in me. The orb that embodied the spirit of the shard could not give me a straight answer.

Less than six.

Five. There were five shards all together. So we had three more keys to find. Girls that had all been at the same point as Sienna? All there at Stonehenge?

And were the others where they were originally

placed, or had there been other situations like Opal and Jade, where the shard had to move in order to survive?

"You're killing me, aren't you?" The question popped out of me before I could catch it.

That's not my intention. I am trying to bond with you.

Not really an answer, but it wasn't malicious. I sighed, my chin dropping to my chest. "And will you find another to take you if I cannot bear it?"

There is no other who can carry me, I am too strong. You are the one, Diana. I contained myself all these years to protect Jade. You must find a way to live. You must connect with me and find a way to wield my power, or all the realms will fall.

"No pressure at all," I whispered. "Maybe you could tell me where to start?"

How could I save myself when I wasn't even conscious?

The orb spun and the colors began to fade. No, not fade. They were shooting toward me one at a time, sinking into my skin. Again, I felt the strength of the shard. The biggest piece, this was the biggest piece of the Veil. I knew it as surely as I knew myself. And that was why it struggled so much, why Opal had died. Too much power hummed through it, I could sense it, even now, threatening to overtake me completely. There was no way for me to wield something like this...no way anyone could...

Slowly the interior of Stonehenge went dark.

Lycan stepped into the doorway. "Did you gain the answers you need?"

"Not all. I don't...I am not ready to die yet, father. Even if it means being with you, it's not my time. I have too much left undone. But if I don't find a way to connect with the shard..."

He gave a low hum under his breath. "Walk with me, Diana. Perhaps we will find the answer together."

I stepped and reached to take his hand, only he wasn't there. I tumbled forward, over the edge of a cliff. Screaming, I clawed at the rocky edges and managed to stop my free fall. "Father!"

"Diana!" he called from far away, somewhere below me. I tried to twist and see but the distance to the bottom was hidden beneath a layer of fog that I couldn't see through.

Clutching the rocks, I began to pull myself up, fighting to get to the top. But every time I reached up, I lost ground.

Slid further down.

A new voice spoke softly. "There will be a choice to come, Diana. That is the answer to all your questions. A choice only you can make."

I stared up into Nefir's face, his blond hair swept up into a strange beehive hairdo that did not suit him. "What are you doing here?"

"I was sent to tell you that a choice must be made." He shrugged. "That's all I know."

I blinked and he was gone. What kind of non-answer was that?

But I couldn't worry about it now as I clung to that rock face, my father calling below, his voice frantic.

"Hold on!"

I sobbed into my upper arm. "Father!"

"Diana!" Raven bellowed my name, and it cut through the panic and fear.

I gasped. "Raven! I'm here. Down the cliff."

"Diana! I need you to reach for me. Come on, Frostbite, reach for me!"

If I let go of the cliff, I'd fall. I didn't know if I could die here, I didn't know where here was, and I wasn't willing to risk the world because this *might* be a dream.

Every muscle protesting, I tried once more to climb to the top. But the rocks just kept sliding away, shoving me right back to the place I'd started. Sobbing in frustration, I leaned my head against the cliff face. "Raven, please...I can't...I'm afraid...."

"Frostbite, I need you to trust me. I need you to... take that leap. I'll catch you, I promise."

Tears streaked my cheeks, my back muscles were starting to spasm, and I knew I didn't have long before the choice would be taken from me. I would fall, because I couldn't move.

But to leap for the top, when I couldn't even see him? It was insanity.

"Raven..." Did I trust him enough to reach blindly,

to push once more for the top and leap for a hand that I couldn't see?

In all our time together, he'd not lied to me. He'd not failed me no matter the task that had been laid at our feet. A burning certainty rolled through me. I could trust him, of all the people in my life, Raven was the one I could trust above all.

"Ok, I'm going to jump. And you'd better fucking catch me!" I scrambled hard for the top, clawing and fighting for purchase, even as I felt myself begin to slide. I dug in with my toes and pushed off, leaping for the top of the cliff, both hands outstretched. Letting go completely.

For a moment, I thought...I thought I was going to fall.

I screamed his name, one last desperate plea. "Raven!"

Unseen hands wrapped around my wrists and yanked me up and away from danger. Away from Lycan.

My eyes flew open, and I sat up, gasping. Blankets pooled around my waist, the bed sunk under me in a familiar way, the smell of my Keep wrapping around me in a flash. Was this real or just another dream?

It wasn't until I heard Kevin's low whine, felt the moisture of his nose as he nuzzled my face that I knew the truth. I was home. And I was alive.

For now.

Shaking, sweat still coursing down the sides of my

face and neck, I turned to see a physician staring at me open mouthed. "Your Majesty!"

"Where is everyone?"

He shook his head. "You cannot go to them, you have been unconscious for days, my queen..."

I stood and pointed at him. "Tell me now. Where is Raven?"

He dipped his head toward me. "He is with all the others."

"I know you're stalling." I grabbed a pair of pants from the closet and began to yank them on. "What's going on?"

"They are down at the shoreline, my queen."

That didn't seem so bad, only my gut told me he wouldn't be holding out if it was a joyful occasion. "Spit it out."

"I cannot...I promised I wouldn't and that vampire... he...I won't cross him."

Fucking Raven.

My lips quirked. "Fine. I can look out the window myself."

I should have been weak, should have been exhausted from being out cold for days and yet I felt like I'd had a shot of energy, as if I were ready to take on the world.

I flung the window open and stared at the shoreline. Saw my people, saw a contingent of the vampire army, my brother Dominic at its head, Raven beside him.

And in our harbor, in the skies above the water...

I could barely take it in. The king of the demons, and his entire army were here, and I doubted it was for a political visit. If there was any question that Malach was being controlled by Lilis, his bellow erased them.

"You will give me your queen, or I will destroy you all!"

CHAPTER 22
Raven

The horse under me shifted, stomping a front foot and huffing a breath that blew out in a cloud of vapor before scattering in the brisk night air. I didn't take my eyes from the amassed army on the shoreline of the Werewolf Territory. This was Diana's home, and I would defend it for her.

I just couldn't believe who we were facing.

Malach, king of the demons, stood at the prow of a warship. The front figurehead just below his feet was that of a gorgon, her hair made of snakes streaming outward, her head thrown back in a silent scream.

The King pointed his finger, sweeping his arm to encompass all that had gathered to oppose him. "You will give me your queen, or I will destroy you all!"

Dominic's hand on my arm was the only thing that held me back. I snarled at him. "Let me go so I can cut his head off and feed it to the sharks! Maybe that psycho witch can speak through one of them instead."

"Hold it together, man. We cannot defeat them. There are too many."

His assessment was not far off. There were hundreds of demons, and within their ranks I saw Malach's general, Algrin.

He caught my eye and shook his head. He knew as well as I did that Malach was being controlled by Lilis, but there was nothing he could do about it. He was bound to his leader, the same way the vampires had been tied to Edmund.

Malach took a few steps forward. "And while you're at it, give me the girl who speaks to dragons. I want her too."

Whatever calm had settled on Dominic was gone in a snarling flash. "You dare threaten my mate?"

Malach laughed. "They both belong to me. Their lives are *mine!*"

Wrong words.

Lochlin stepped in front of Dominic. "Our queen is indisposed, or she would speak to you herself. Regardless, she'd tell you the same thing. Get stuffed, Malach."

Not exactly the height of diplomacy, but it got the point across.

Malach laughed, his skin moving independent of his frame, as if something crawled beneath it.

"I will rule all. And those bitches are MINE!" The

words were howled, a feminine shriek on the last word that I felt all the way to my bones.

Lilis was getting pissy.

"General Algrin," Dominic called to his peer. "This is insanity. Surely you can talk sense into your king. He's clearly not of his own mind–"

"Do not speak as if I am not here!" Malach strained forward, as if he were barely able to contain himself, his face white in the dark of the night. One wing hung at an angle, and he looked even worse than we'd seen him in his throne room. As if he were slowly falling to pieces.

General Algrin again shook his head. "You will all die if you do not surrender. While you carry strength and speed, you do not have magic. Not as we do."

Fucker was just rubbing it in now.

But that was not what started the fight. Nope, weasley, fucking chickenshit Maverick managed to do that all on his own.

"You aren't taking her! I won't let you!" His voice drew everyone's eyes as he rode hard across the beach, his horse churning up water and sand at a flat gallop. As he drew level with Malach, he swung a crossbow, hidden from the king, pulled back and loosed in a single smooth motion.

The bolt sailed true, driving straight through Malach's throat.

He garbled and flailed, ripped the arrow out and bellowed. "KILL THEM!"

The demons paused for a half breath, then surged forward.

All Maverick had done was throw the rest of us into the oncoming path of our enemies. What a fucking moron.

I leapt to the sand and sent my horse away with a slap to the rump. I was no cavalry man. Pulling my two swords free, I met the first demon head on.

The water at the edge of the ocean turned red in a matter of minutes as the demons fell in front of me. Over and over, they came in waves.

"I'm here. We've got this."

Dom's assurance as he stepped beside me gave me another jolt of energy as we cut through our enemies. These were the infantry, sent in to slow us down, to fatigue us before the trained fighters descended from the skies. Blood splattered across my face, but I restrained myself from biting into a neck or two.

For now. When that time came I needed to be ready to end it all.

I dared a glance to where Algrin and his men waited well above the water. Most of them stood on the high rigging of the ships, out of range of the arrows that flew.

Slowly but surely, I fought my way to the ship where Algrin stood. He watched me approach, but didn't do anything to stop me.

A demon launched at me as I got waist deep in the water, seizing me around the middle and biting my hip.

With a backward swing I cut his body in half, but he didn't let go.

"Fucker!" I drove my second sword through his neck, and he finally released his hold on me.

I shoved both bloodied swords into their sheaths and grabbed a rough edge of the boat. Then, I began to climb. There were no ladders. It was hand over hand, all the way to the top. The fact that they'd run the ships aground said it all.

Malach and his friend Lilis had no intention of leaving.

I flipped myself over the rail and onto the deck. There were a few lesser demons who scattered when they caught sight of me, and I let them.

My eyes were trained on the General high above me.

Did he fucking well expect me to climb up there to talk to him?

"Algrin, stop this madness! You know who controls your king!"

"Do you?"

I spun to see the king himself behind me. He'd jumped across from the other ship.

Fuck me. Not that I was afraid of him but...he held a goddess inside of him. Controlling him.

I did what I did best. I tried to piss her off. With a mocking bow, I swept my arms wide. "I would say it's a pleasure, Lilis, but my mother taught me not to lie."

Malach's face twisted and he gasped. "Your mother? Why would you speak of her to me?"

The question caught me off guard. It was not the response I'd expected, but seeing the reaction...I dug into it. "What does it matter if I speak of my mother? She was a woman of honor. Unlike you. You are no goddess, you're just a piece of shit who has no morals."

He snarled, his body lurching toward me like a broken wind-up doll. There was no way he could fight, no way he could stop me if I just cut his head off. I pulled a sword free and Malach flicked a hand at me, casually, as if swatting a fly.

A blast of energy sent me hurling through the air, and smashed hard into the main mast, snapping it in half. I hit the deck and rolled out of the way as the sails and splintered wood fell around me. I couldn't breathe, wasn't sure if it was broken ribs or just the wind knocked out of me.

Stumbling to the side, I flipped the sail off me and stared across the deck, pulling my swords free. "You cannot beat us, Lilis."

"You know nothing!" The screamed words, the rage in them...she was close to a breaking point.

I tried another angle. "Nefir told us about you. And the stars...they watch, Lilis. They see *everything*."

Malach stared at me, but I knew it was Lilis watching me. "How dare you..."

I kept her eyes on me as another figure climbed over the deck, a crossbow in his hands. I'd give Maverick credit; he was a quiet fucker when he wasn't faking injury and limping about like a wounded elephant.

"You think we don't know your plan?" I laughed, made myself throw my head back. "You walked right into our trap."

Maverick loosed the crossbow bolt, the trigger clicking ever so slightly. It was all the warning Lilis needed.

Malach stepped sideways which left the bolt free to sail straight across, and right into me.

I managed to dodge just far enough to the left that it missed my heart, and sunk into my sternum instead, burrowing into the bone. I grabbed at the bolt and yanked it free before I could feel the pain of the entry.

"You think *that's* a trap?" Malach laughed as he reached to the side and drew Maverick up by his throat. "This…this is a trap. I have the two men she cares for and you both came to me. She will be here to rescue both of you. Or maybe just one? Wouldn't that be a delicious choice to force upon her? Allow one of you to live, but she must choose!"

My chest throbbed as it hit me. Lilis had no idea that Diana was still unconscious, had no idea that she was dying. That I would follow on her heels. But until then, I would defend her people and land as if they were my own.

"Nothing to lose, Mav," I said.

Maverick's eyes closed and even held by Malach's hand he gave me the nod I needed.

I sprinted toward them, hit Malach square in the chest and took all three of us over the side of the boat.

Malach bellowed as we fell, I grappled for his face. Found his eyes, dug my fingers into one of them as we broke through the shallow water.

I kept on grabbing at him, trying to find his vulnerable points. Remove whatever pieces of him I could to weaken him.

To weaken Lilis.

Something grabbed my wrist and yanked me deeper in the water. I fought the hold as I broke the surface in water that was chest deep.

I blinked several times, not sure if I was dead already, or I was just seeing things. "Xefia?"

Her long green hair was piled on top of her head, woven around a crown of shells and gold. Her eyes flashed with a mix of pain and fury that aged her far beyond her years.

"Queen Xefia now that death took the rest of my line. I am all that's left to rule."

Diana would have been so happy if she knew the young mermaid was still alive...

Now to make sure she stayed that way.

"You need to go. Now! It's far too dangerous." I tried to push her away, turning toward where Malach had been. Only he wasn't there. And neither was Maverick. "Xefia, go. It isn't safe..."

A big head rose out of the water behind her, and I reached for my blade only.

"Sal?" I murmured, gaping at the water dragon.

"She saved me. I've gathered my remaining people,

Raven. We are here to help. To join you in your battle against the evil that killed so many." Eyes narrowed, sharp little teeth gleaming, she looked exactly like the predator she truly was.

I nodded and pointed to the warships. "Drag the boats out," I said, "get them as far from the shore as you can."

"We can do better than that." Xefia flipped backward and was gone with barely a splash.

I slogged forward, heading for shore. The demons were like ants on a hill, more and more seemed to appear no matter how many were downed.

As I reached the sand, the sound of wings was the only warning I had. I spun, pulling my sword and parrying a blow from the skies, our swords ringing as they bounced off one another.

Algrin remained two feet above me. "I tried to stop him."

"Not hard enough," I growled as we went back and forth. He had the literal high ground advantage. But he wasn't as fast floating in the air as I was on the ground.

I shot around him and cut a sharp blow down the middle of his back. "If you don't want to lose your wings—"

"I am sworn to him. I have no choice." He dropped to the ground, wincing as he folded his wings back.

"Stand down then."

"I can't." Algrin shook his head. He launched himself at me and I found myself wishing I had let him remain in the air. Because on the ground...he was easily as fast as me, and I wasn't sure if he was holding back or not.

Back and forth across the beach we went, time sliding by, neither of us giving quarter.

But her voice...her voice cut through everything.

"Lilis! You will leave my land and free the demon king from your possession now!"

Diana.

She was alive. She was alive and strong enough to talk shit to a goddess. The block of ice sitting on my heart lifted, and it took everything I had not to roar her name.

"You will set him free, or I will make you!" Her words carried across the battle. More than a few demons stopped fighting.

I heard the question over and over as it rippled through the remaining soldiers. Was the king possessed? Was this war even his will?

Algrin lowered his sword. "Can she do it? Can she... can she free him?"

I took a step back, out of reach if he decided to try and cut me down. "If anyone can, its her."

The demon general sheathed his sword. "Stand down! If the Wolf Queen can do as she says and free our king, then we will stand down!"

Malach stood a hundred feet down the beach, his hand still impossibly gripping Maverick, who was on his knees.

"You like this one, don't you?" Lilis hissed the words

through Malach's misshapen mouth. "Then I will take him with me."

The crowd of fighters parted as Diana stalked toward them. She wore her dark leathers, but her top was a flowing white shirt that opened and showed off a healthy amount of skin only...I did not think that was why she'd worn it. In the center of her chest was a mark. Like a tattoo that hadn't been there before. Even at this distance, I could see it clearly, as if it glowed and drew not only my eye, but the eye of everyone near her.

Including Lilis.

A willow tree with its long tendrils sat between her breasts, the black leaves that of the trees that held the pathway to the dead of the werewolf clans.

Diana came to a stop in front of Malach. "Let him go, Lilis."

"Only if I can have you."

Diana impossibly found me in all the werewolves and vampires around her. I saw in her eyes what she was going to do, and I started toward her, already knowing I was going to be too late.

"No!"

"I agree."

CHAPTER 23

Diana

I had to block it all out. Dominic's shout of warning. Raven's howl of fury and disbelief. The connection between us that crackled with his fear for me. I could only focus on the entity in front of me, and the information I had been given.

A choice must be made.

The Wolf Queen must die.

This was it. This was the crossroads, here and now. I just needed to be brave enough to meet the moment, and that would drive Lilis away...for a time.

Now, to get her solemn vow.

"And if I come to you, you'll leave the rest of them alone and sail back to the Demon Realm, swear it on the stars?"

I stared deeply into Malach's eyes—No, *Lilis'* eyes. The figure no longer fully registered as the once-proud

Demon King. His life force waning, his body a twisted mess.

The monstrosity gestured impatiently for me to come closer, "Yes, yes. I already agreed."

"*Swear* it."

"I see someone has been meddling in my affairs." The demon's face contorted in anger, but it did not delay him for long. "All right, then, I swear it on the stars."

I let out a breath, and a cold peace settled over me as I strode toward him, hands raised. The choice had been made, the prophecy fulfilled. What exactly that all meant, I couldn't be sure. But if I was unable to drive Lilis out when I laid hands on Malach, at least I would be with Lycan soon, and my friends would live to see another day. It had to be enough.

I winced as Raven's enraged scream cut through the air, but I couldn't bring myself to look at him.

I could not waiver.

Malach tossed Mav aside and surged forward, closing the remaining distance between us before Mav could even hit the ground. He cackled, face curling in a hideous mockery of a grin as his eerily cold fingers found my throat.

"One down, four to go."

"Diana!"

Anger flashed in Mav's face as he hefted his sword and took one, single step forward, before five soldiers stepped in front of him. Anger gave way to pain as he stared at me a moment longer, and then let the blade drop to the ground, the fight fading from him as quickly as it had come. He was just doing as he always had; looking out for number one–but damn, it stung.

A white blur crossed into my field of vision, surging toward the demon, and a wave of horror rolled through me.

"Kevin, no!" But it was too late. Malach's foot whipped out, slamming directly into Kevin's jaw. The hell-hound flew back like he'd been hit by a car, smacking into a tree with a pained yelp. And then nothing.

"Not my dog, you fucking bitch!" My hand shot up on pure instinct, and my heart thundered as I tore the cold fingers from my neck. I might die today, but not before I took my pound of flesh. I scrambled back, narrowly avoiding the demon's grasping hands. I hit the ground hands-first, slamming my leg backward, aiming a full-throttle horse-kick directly to his sternum. Bone snapped under my foot, and I whirled, preparing for whatever was coming next.

Malach staggered, keeling over, as the ringing of blade against blade echoed all around me. Demons resumed their profane, horrifying chants as the battle reignited, sending waves of magical flame at our scattered troops. I winced as my attention shifted to Raven. He'd cut a path to reach me, and now stood only a few yards away. Countless corpses littered the ground in his wake, but a dozen winged demons–the strongest of their kind– had surrounded him, weaving in and out as they stabbed at him with spears.

Malach rose, flashing me that wicked grin, and I refocused myself on the task at hand. He was on me in the blink of an eye, blade slicing through the very tip of my nose as I stumbled backward in the nick of time. Bone crunched from the force of his strike, and his sword-arm dropped, hanging unnaturally at the elbow. His body was weak and broken from Lilis's presence, but he paid it no mind, unleashing a whirlwind of vicious attacks as his arm snapped back into place. He danced as much as fought, each limb seeming to move with a mind of its own. I staggered backward, fighting frantically to keep him off me.

Just one opening, and I could try to shift and use my wolf to force her out.

His leg whipped out as I dipped under a sword thrust, smashing his shin directly into mine. I flailed, howling wildly from the pain, but he simply continued the onslaught, like some kind of demon-puppet. Kevin's pained whimper replayed in my mind, and I growled, rolling sideways just in time to evade another attack.

But I was done fighting on my heels. It was time to attack.

I tore my knife from my belt, lunging toward his neck. His sword clattered to the ground as twin gouts of black flame erupted from his hands, blasting me backward as the heat consumed me. I let out a feral scream, scrambling to my feet as he leapt right onto me, smashing his fist into the side of my skull. My vision blurred, and I rolled away, arms raised.

"You're finished, she-wolf."

It was Lilis' voice, now, not his. She'd twisted it, as surely as she'd twisted his trademark blue fire magic.

The demon's fingers gripped my neck once again, now blazing with heat. I thrashed in a wild attempt to free myself, but, with her full attention on me, she was simply too strong. My neck screamed in pain as his burning hand raged even hotter, the smell of burned flesh filling the air.

But the fire didn't come. Malach's face shifted, returning to something resembling the demon he had once been for an instant. His eyes pleading, as he croaked out a plea. "End this, Diana. You *must* kill me. Whatever it takes." His arm shook and vibrated as he fought madly for control, but the grip on my neck remained firm. The goddess was too strong.

I reached for my wolf, calling to her with everything I had in the brief window the proud demon had managed to create for me. If I could just—

Panic rolled over me as the realization struck. My wolf was out of reach, not too different from that day in the desert. Except, this time, it was like she was actively retreating from me...shrinking away from me.

I roared as something else washed over me, flooding my body with power like nothing I'd ever felt. Filling my heart with pure, unadulterated, *rage*. For Kevin, for Malach, for my father. For everything this bitch had done. Vengeance would be mine.

A crimson haze blurred my vision, and I latched onto his wrist.

Malach's face contorted in agony, and he was gone as quickly as he'd arrived. "Silly woman," Lilis spat, heat and magical power flaring more with every word.

I screeched as my muscles tensed and the shard inside me throbbed, my newfound magic forcing its way to the surface to match Lilis'. I pushed, calling on every drop of this new strength. And the goddess did the same. Droplets of rain hit my face as electricity surged through Malach's husk, twisting his mouth in a silent scream.

Thunder cracked overhead, and I roared as my body lit up with pain. But pain didn't matter. Not anymore. "You don't stand a chance!" Lilis screeched.

A familiar figure flashed into view behind Malach and a mad laugh split my lips as I shoved back at her. "You're right, I don't. Not alone, anyway."

I threw caution, and any thought of defending myself, to the wind, directing my rage and power *through* Malach, right to the source. My ears rang as I smashed into her, pushing and tearing at the goddess with everything I had. And, for the briefest of moments, she faltered.

That was all Sienna needed.

"Both of us together!" she shouted, seizing the opportunity. And, in that moment, the twin lights of our magic, equal but opposite, seemed to fuse into a single, blinding star. And together?

We were unbeatable.

The rage amped up even further as I continued my chaotic assault on Lilis, somehow tempered by the aura of peace and control emanating from Sienna. No words were needed between us. She reached out to Malach, seeming to latch directly onto his soul.

The demon dropped me to the ground, and I gritted my teeth as I was enveloped in wave after wave of electricity. I stepped forward nonetheless, continuing my assault through the agony; my role in this was set.

"This won't change a thing!" The goddess' voice came from above, now, rather than from Malach's mouth. Thunder boomed, drowning out her agonized screams. "You stupid cows. This ends the same way no matter what you do. I'll kill every last one of you—"

I stumbled back as the storm clouds overhead fizzled into nothing in the blink of an eye, consumed in a flash of light. Malach's body dropped to the ground like a broken bag of dried leaves and sticks. What looked like a black bruise formed around his neck and spiraled outward, forming spikes. Lilis' mark, same as the Vanators under her control had shown.

But this time, when Malach spoke, his voice was his own.

"Thank...you."

I dropped to my knees as the all-consuming fury faded, replaced by the screaming of every nerve-ending in my body alight. My vision swirled as I glanced at Sienna. The magic had receded, but the strange one-ness was still there. And stranger yet?

I was still alive.

I reached for her arm, searching frantically for Raven as I struggled back to my feet.

His wild eyes met mine as he wrenched his sword from the neck of the final demon that separated us. Blood poured from countless wounds; his face nearly unrecognizable through it all.

"You will pay for putting me through that, Frost-bite," he managed, before wheeling around and dropping into an unsteady dueling stance. Demons roared and began to stomp and snarl as cries of their King's demise spread.

Dom appeared at Sienna's side. Once he made sure she was unhurt, he quickly joined Raven to form a wall in front of us.

"Nicholas managed to get to the mutt. Kevin is injured, but alive," Raven said over his shoulder.

I breathed a sigh of relief, but the feeling left as quickly as it had come as I caught sight of the ritualistic war-dance the demons had begun.

"Whoot. Whoot. Whoot! Whoot!" The chants grew louder as they began to pound on their chests in time and formed a circle around us.

Every one of them looked prepared to die.

"Defensive formation," Dom's voice cut the battle-field like a knife as he moved away from Raven to face the other half of our enemies. "I'll hold these off. You handle them. We can outlast them."

But the attacks never came as a second voice cut

through, with just as much gravity. I looked up to see a lone demon, massive wings spread, hovering above us.

Algrin.

"Retreat!"

Roars of protest split their ranks, and fire flared from his palms, silencing them.

"You saw it with your own eyes; our king was not himself."

A bold voice rose above the rest. "We *saw* those two kill him, Algrin. Someone must pay."

Algrin flickered out of view, reappearing directly next to the younger demon in an instant. The fire in his palms burned even hotter as he pressed one against the other one's throat. He made sure to speak loudly enough for the rest to hear as he continued.

"I don't give a damn whether you agree. Our king is dead, and the dark goddess is to blame. I will not continue a war Malach did not believe in." He threw his arm to the side, blasting a gout of flame in the direction of the ocean.

I followed the fire, heart skipping a beat as the wreckage came into view. Sal rose up, next to their final ship, and Xefia called out from beside her. "We left you one ship to take your leave. Now get out before we take care of that one for you, too."

The energy was sucked out of the remaining demons in an instant. No more shouts of protest, no more fire or rage. The one who'd contradicted Algrin dropped wordlessly to one knee, and the general withdrew his hand.

Algrin uncinched his belt, letting his sheathed sword drop to the earth below, and began marching directly toward me. A group of younger wolves began snapping and growling at him, and I held up a hand.

"Let him approach."

Raven didn't budge, but the demon stopped a few feet short, dropping to one knee. "I am in no position to ask this of you, but I will do so anyway: allow me to take Malach's body back to our homeland so we can give him a proper burial. Do this, and I'll be forever in your debt."

I faltered, taken aback. Demons were, by and large, a selfish bunch, looking out for themselves above all. So what was this?

"Y-yes. You may take him with you."

He exhaled, dipping his head in thanks, then called for a few other members of the King's Guard. And, when they arrived, every one of them was wearing the same, solemn expression. They folded his arms and hoisted him into the air. As their wings unfolded, Algrin turned to look at me a final time.

"Thank you, for putting that to an end."

"He died a warrior's death, fighting back against her control. I would've died if he hadn't."

He grunted in understanding, then took flight with the other members of the King's Guard. "The Heir apparent is *not* going to be happy to hear of this, but we should send word right away. We will need him to take the king's place as soon as possible."

Raven's hand dropped to my shoulder as Algrin, and his men retreated.

"You did it," he murmured, his gaze drilling into mine. "You did it and you're still alive. You've foiled the prophecy."

I nodded weakly, leaning into him. In a way, he was right; my new abilities had allowed Sienna and I to send a *goddess* packing...

And yet, even as I soaked in the warmth of his comforting embrace, I couldn't shake the awful feeling in the pit of my stomach. Because something was still very, very wrong. I reached for my wolf once again, and she cowered, sending a shaft of agony through me.

As grateful as I was for what the shard had done *for* me this day, I couldn't help but wonder...

And what had it done *to* me?

CHAPTER 24

Raven

I licked the last bit of blood from my fangs, shoving the empty goblet to the center of the table. It was my third of the night, and although it had mended my beat-up body nicely, it was equally as unsatisfying as the previous two. The uneasiness deep in my gut wasn't something food could fix.

Nicholas drained a glass of his own to my right, his sips audible in the otherwise-silent room. Theo's gaze snapped away from the goblet of blood as I glanced over, his attention shifting back to Myrr, who was slurping the marrow from a beef bone.

It had only been a few hours since I'd almost lost Diana. The scene replayed in my mind for the umpteenth time. Being forced to look on in horror as demon after demon threw themselves between us, making it impossible to get to her fast enough. Feeling her resolve to die when Malach took her by the neck.

Seeing that bastard, Maverick, accepting her sacrifice like the coward he was.

My hand twitched as I looked over at him, and it took every shred of self-control I had not to leap across the table and strangle him. I exhaled, turning toward Diana's empty seat.

She'd avoided me, and everyone else, since the battle. The haunted look in her eye after the demons had made their exit left no doubt that something was very wrong. She'd brushed the concern aside when I'd pressed but instead had gone to her quarters to bathe at the first opportunity, locking the door behind her.

It was hours later when a messenger had summoned me and the others to the great room on her behalf. And she still wasn't here, despite the rest of us, barring Sienna, having come nearly thirty minutes ago. So what was it that was bothering her? Something to do with the shard? Or perhaps seeing our enemy's full power firsthand had taken its toll on her.

I clenched a fist, looking at Dom as I leaned forward in my chair.

"How is Sienna?" I asked, breaking the silence that had hung over the room since our arrival. She'd healed up dozens of werewolves after the battle. By the end of it, she'd been so tired that she needed Dom to carry her back into the keep.

"She was sleeping when I left our room, but her color is already improved. I doubt she'll be out of commission for too long. She's gotten a lot more comfortable with her powers."

The door creaked open before I could respond, and I turned to see Diana striding into the room, a limping Kevin close on her heels. Her eyes flitted to mine for a fraction of a second as she settled into her chair, but they didn't linger.

Her voice was monotone as she spoke. "We've driven Lilis back for now, but it was only a minor skirmish in the war to come. She will be back, of that we can be sure, and we need to be ready to face her. I need to find a way to contact Nefir again. He knows more than he's letting on, and we need him to commit to helping. We also need to set up a meeting between the monarchs of every faction in the realm."

"What about the demons now that Malach is dead?" Nick interjected.

"Gabriel is their Heir apparent, fortunately, and will serve as King going forward. I've already sent word to him about a potential meeting and have asked him to investigate Lilis' corruption of Malach. Things will get a lot more difficult if we need to suspect even our allies, so I hope to learn more about how she is able to gain control of people. How she got into Malach in the first place."

"It's been a long time since we've had a meeting like this," Evangeline said, concern lacing her words. "The angels will suspect foul play, since the demons are involved, and the fae are flighty and secretive at the best of times."

Diana tossed up a hand. "That's part of why I brought you all here; we need to select a neutral location and figure out how to reassure them that this isn't some trick."

Myrr's hand shot up, the chicken thigh she'd been holding clattering onto her plate. "We can use the ruins near my old hut."

The ruins laid in the central part of the Empire of Magic, just north of Wolf Territory.

"That could work. We wouldn't have too far to travel, then, no one would," Diana said with a nod.

"It's as good a place as any," said the Duchess. "If they'll even agree to a meeting at all."

"The situation is more dire than any we've faced before," Lochlin said. "We have to show them that this is bigger than our grievances with each other."

Diana pushed a small pile of papers in his direction. "I was hoping to have you spearhead that, actually."

He dipped his head in assent. "Of course, Your Majesty. I'll begin reaching out as soon as we hammer out the details."

"We'll want to keep attendants to a minimum," I chimed in. "We can't expect a whole army of angels and demons to keep it civil if they're in close proximity for very long."

"We'll keep it to a maximum of ten attendees per realm," Diana replied, hardly looking at me, then turned to Myrr. "If you'll agree to it, I'd like to use your position as Oracle to make sure everyone feels safe to come without weapons."

Myrr looked up from her food, shrugging. "Sure, just let me know when we're doing it."

"I wonder if they even trust in The Oracle's neutrality anymore," Evangeline said. "They've certainly gotten word that you've been traveling with her."

"It'll still count for something, at least with the fae," Loch replied. "They have always held her in even higher esteem than the other magical races. It's the angels that will be difficult to convince."

The Duchess' hands went to her temples. "Then we must make sure they know it was Diana the Wolf Queen who killed Malach. Their distaste for him was even greater than toward the demons as a whole. I'll get to work on spreading rumors about what happened. We can embellish the story and try to entice them."

"Excellent," Diana said. "I'd also like to have Myrr share the prophecy about the other keys. They need to know that we either work together or it means death to us all."

I sucked in a breath, trying to keep my fangs from extending as Maverick began to speak.

"We seem to be taking the attendance of the demons for granted. Personally, I wouldn't be so sure. There were many that left here none too happy. Malach kept them in line with his strength as a leader, does Gabriel have what it takes to do the same?"

I rose, no longer able to hold back the fury that'd been growing every hour since his betrayal.

"I don't even know why you're talking right now. And about *strength*, no less? We all saw what you did out there, you fucking coward." Pure rage washed over me in waves, and I fixed my eyes on him.

Just give me one more reason. Anything.

He turned, averting his gaze. "The prophecy said she had to make a choice. I was trying to help by not interfering with fate—"

I was halfway across the table before I'd even consciously decided to move. His chair smacked against the ground as I slammed into him, my hand wrapping around his neck.

"Trying to help?" I pushed his head against the ground, pulling my arm back to bash his cowardly fucking face in. Just one punch and this could all be over. We'd already found the gem, so what did we even need him for?

My fangs popped through my gums, at the ready to drain him into a husk. Until Diana's hand dropped to my shoulder, tugging me gently back.

"Chickenshit," I muttered, brushing off my shirt like just being close to him had sullied it.

Diana shot me her trademark, icy stare, and I allowed myself to be pulled away.

"I understand how you're feeling right now, but this is not the time for it," she murmured. "It's just like the meeting with the clans; we need to put aside our differences and work to defeat Lilis together."

Loch, Nick, and Dom had all stood to break up the fight, and I pushed past them as I moved back to my seat.

"It won't happen again. Especially if he keeps his fucking mouth shut."

Maverick shot me a venomous glare as he and the others retook their seats.

"Now that that's settled, let's get to our second order of business..." Diana shot a look around the table, her questioning gaze touching on each of us in turn. "Why am I still alive? I remember stopping the haboob, but then I was in some strange limbo between life and death after that. So how did I get back here?"

My anger at Maverick took a backseat and I met Dom's grim gaze. It was time to come clean and face the music. Resolving myself, I turned back toward Diana.

"You were—"

A loud creak cut me off before I could finish, and Sienna stepped through the doorway. As Dom had predicted, she didn't look that fatigued. Very interesting. Would Diana's powers evolve to this extent, too?

Dom rose to greet her with a kiss and lead her over to the empty seat, but Diana was first to speak.

"How are you?"

"Okay, I think." She cocked her head. "It's hard to explain, but something about us using our magic together was different. More powerful. I feel energized, in some way, even though I used up a ton of energy. It's my first time feeling like this."

"I felt it too...when we connected. But I don't feel it anymore."

"What do you mean by 'connected'?" Evangeline cut in.

Sienna looked to the ceiling for a second, pondering, then back. "It was like we were acting as two parts of one thing. Different, but the same. I could tell what she was doing, and even thinking with no words being exchanged. Her emotions felt like mine."

"It was the same for me," Diana agreed.

"I think it has something to do with the Spirit. I can feel it inside me, like a second presence that sometimes calls out to me or offers me aid. I think yours was entangled with mine, somehow. It was sort of what it feels like when I communicate with an animal."

"Can't say I've experienced that, though I do have a stronger sense of Kevin's emotions than before. It feels like he's" —she shrugged and let out a strange little laugh — "I don't know...mourning for me, somehow, even though I survived."

A wave of nausea ran through me as a silence settled over the room. I hadn't allowed myself to focus on what I might have deprived her of. How did we tell her that we'd pushed her wolf down?

Diana continued, "I can't be sure, but I don't think I'll be able to heal anyone or talk to animals like Sienna can. It's more like the shard is just allowing me to be more in tune with other living creatures."

"Elhimna said that each key will have a unique ability," Sienna said. "It will become clearer as time passes. At first, it's so overwhelming and weird that it's hard to know anything."

Diana nodded. "I'll have to get the hang of it quickly. I fear we haven't got much time before Lilis is back."

"I will say that I did get some sense that your power was very different while we were connected. Mine was driving me to comfort Malach...to heal his heart and mind and prepare him for a death that was beyond my powers to stop. And yours..." Sienna's throat worked as she held Diana's gaze, "There was an edge to it that I've not felt with my own. A deep desire to punish Lilis for all she's done. If I was the calm, you were the storm."

Diana folded her hands in front of her, the picture of calm now. "It's true. The anger was driving my power. It went beyond anything I've ever felt in terms of strength. Like I could do anything. It was scary, but it made me feel like I could survive, even against Lilis."

"We should take tonight to recover, but I bet we can learn a lot if we spend some time practicing together."

"I was thinking the same. We should see if we can recreate that connection. If Lilis attacks again, it'll be our only chance at beating her." She shuddered. "If we have any chance at all. Did you feel how strong she was?"

"We were lucky. She was hindered by being in someone else's body, I think," Sienna agreed. "Especially since Malach was trying to resist her. I can't imagine what she would be capable of if she controlled someone with great strength who welcomed her presence."

"Or worse, if she could face us herself. It's something we should've pressed Nefir on. What's keeping her from facing us head on?"

It was a question that had been haunting me too. Why hadn't the bitch attacked us with all her might?

"The most proactive thing we can do right now is find the remaining keys." Diana turned to Lochlin. "The other monarchs might be able to help on that front. Let me know if there's anything I can do to help you win them over. Getting their support is crucial."

"I'll get to work the second this meeting ends."

"Once they've all gathered, I can show everyone what happened at Stonehenge if Maverick will allow it. Maybe they'll recognize one of their own from inside the memory?" Nicholas offered, glancing at Maverick.

Chickenshit nodded. "Anything to be of help."

I scowled but held my tongue.

"At least we've got a path forward. Now, let's get back to the question of the day." Diana patted the table with a tight smile that was more like a baring of teeth as she circled back to the question I'd hoped she'd forgotten.

"How the hell am I still alive?"

CHAPTER 25

Diana

If I hadn't been certain that something was sorely amiss before, the way the air left the room in that moment sealed the deal. I tried to mask my emotions as I waited, guts churning. Kevin whined, pressing closer to my knees, and I reached down to stroke his warm fur.

Just breathe. Whatever it is, you can face it.

"Diana..." Sienna began, her eyes filled with worry. "I tried to heal you on my own. But there was nothing I could do—"

"It's alright, Sienna," Raven cut in with a shake of his head. "This isn't on you. I need to be the one to tell her...although I'd hoped I could do so when we were alone?"

The question was plain in his voice, but even though some part of me knew whatever was coming was best heard in private, I couldn't wait another second.

"Tell me," I managed to keep my voice calm, even while clenching my fists under the table.

He flinched as if I had yelled at him, and shot a glance around the table, holding Lochlin's gaze for a long moment.

"Not everyone here knows exactly what happened, and I'm sure I don't have to say it, but what is shared here and now stays in this room. If this got out to the general public..."

Lochlin frowned and then nodded. "Of course. I would never betray my Queen's trust."

"He is my trusted confidant, packmate and friend. Damn it, Raven. Out with it!" So much for my attempt at calm.

His face fell as he dropped his head. "You weren't waking up. Sienna couldn't connect to access your spirit to heal you. We were out of options. It was let you die, or..."

"Or?"

Raven raised his head and met my gaze, the grief in his green eyes palpable.

"Or have you feed from me."

I drew back, absorbing his words like a physical blow.

"Feed?" I managed in barely a whisper. "I-I took blood from you?"

"You didn't take it...I gave it. But, yes."

A wave of dizziness overtook me, and I let my eyes drift shut. What did it mean that I'd drank vampire blood? Was that why my wolf was no longer accessible? Fuck me...

"You think *that* was the choice the prophecy spoke of? How could you even know for sure?" The unfairness of it all nearly stole my breath. "And even if it was, it should've been *my* choice." I jabbed my thumb against my sternum. "*My* decision. Hells, why do you think I was so keen to become a true wolf and leave my vampire life behind? This. This is why. Because this is what *your* kind does! They take advantage of others for their own gain!" I spluttered, wheeling around so I didn't have to look at his stricken face.

The fury inside me would not be denied. I needed a place to aim it, and Raven was my target.

"*Your* kind fucks with people's minds and lives. You take what you want, consequences be damned. You think you're the top of the food chain. The best of the best. But you're really just a bunch of selfish, parasitic narcissists. And because you *think* we're fated to be together, you used this as your in to make me one, too!"

The words loosed from my lips like poison-tipped arrows, leaving behind a bitter taste in my mouth. I was being unfair, not to mention cruel. But I couldn't bring myself to take any of it back. I just stood there with my back to him, shaking from head to toe as I tried not to fly into a full-blown panic.

Was it taking me over, even now? Raven's blood cells, consuming my own. Would I slowly transform into a facsimile of him? My murderous brother Edmund? Of what used to be me?

And what of my wolf? Once so majestic and powerful. So cocky and brave. Even now, I tried to reach her, and she cowered from me.

When Raven finally spoke, his voice was barely a whisper.

"You're angry. I can accept that. But you need to ask yourself what you would've done if you were in my shoes. I don't do it, you almost certainly die. I do, and there is a chance that you live. I won't apologize for choosing you, Diana. I will always choose you."

His retreating footsteps sounded louder than gunshots in the too-quiet room.

"Come find me whenever you're ready. I'll be there. No matter how much time it takes."

The door opened and closed an instant later and I forced myself to do what I did best. To lead my people. "Loch...start contacting the monarchs. We'll reconvene first thing tomorrow." I kept my eyes on the floor as I stalked toward the door. Dominic's voice called after me.

"Diana..."

But I had to keep moving if I had any hope of making it to my quarters before the dam inside me broke.

By the time I slammed my bedroom door shut a few minutes later, the fear and panic had turned to rage. I let loose a howl as I swept the contents of a side-table onto the stone floor. A large vase shattered, and the satisfying *crash* only made me crave more destruction. I tore through the room like a cyclone, destroying everything in my path. Curtains and bedding shredded to bits; every piece of decorative glass obliterated.

It wasn't until I whirled around in search of something more to break that I caught sight of myself in the full-length mirror on the wall. I looked like a madwoman. My once upswept hair in a wild tangle around my shoulder. Chest heaving. Eyes that had turned ice blue in the wake of my father's death, were now emerald green again, glittering like gemstones against my too pale skin...bright with unchecked fury.

And the very tips of two, pearly fangs poking from beneath my upper lip.

"Nooo!" I balled up a fist and drove it into the mirror. The glass exploded in a crystalline rain even as the stone behind the mirror crumbled.

The smell of blood reached my nose almost instantly, and those new fangs ached. My wolf let out a low, warbling growl and a pain like I'd never felt gripped my insides.

"Please, no...I can't lose my wolf," I whimpered, dropping to my knees as I began to cough. The razor-sharp glass lashed at my skin, but I barely felt it as blood filled my mouth.

Fear gripped my chest as I sucked in a rattling breath that again set off a fit of coughs that spattered my palm with blood before finally ceasing.

What the hell was happening? Was it the shard, or

was it my own body turning on me...one half consuming the other?

A low knock at the door had me mopping my mouth and hands with the tattered bedsheets on the floor beside me.

Raven.

I refused to let him see me like this. I was both furious and terrified. If I spoke to him again, there was no doubt I would say something awful to hurt him even more than I already had.

I might be a monster, but I didn't have to act like one.

"Please go. I want to be alone," I called.

"It's Sienna. I have Myrr with me." Long pause. "Can we come in? We won't stay long. It's important."

I wasn't mad at Sienna for her part in this all. As a healer, she did what she thought she had to in order to save my life. I'd expect nothing less—or more—of her. She might be my sister-in-law, but she didn't know me. Not like Raven did.

Correction. Not like I'd *thought* he did.

But just because I wasn't angry at Sienna didn't mean I was in the mood for a heart to heart with her...or the Oracle, who never seemed to truly grasp the seriousness of any situation.

"Come on, Diana. Open up," Myrr grumbled. "My gouty toe is killing me standing out here in this drafty hallway."

I sat there for another moment, feeling sorry for

myself, but then I remembered; I might be more vampire than wolf now, but for the time being, I was still queen. There was no time for self-pity. Not with Lilis still at large and the realms at risk. I had to pull my shit together.

"Come."

The door squealed open, and I pushed myself to my feet.

"Holy tornado...Did you and that bitch goddess have another throw down in here or what?" Myrr said with a low whistle as she stepped into the room.

I gingerly made my way over to the fountain and pool that took up the center of the room and rinsed my bloodied hands.

"We can sit over here. Just watch the glass on the floor," I said, pointing to the seating area in the corner.

Once the three of us were comfortable and I'd removed a chunk of the mirror from one of my knees, Sienna spoke.

"It wasn't Raven's fault. Or, not all his fault," she amended quickly. "Your doctors agreed, and I knew I didn't have the ability to save you. I truly believe you would be dead right now if not for Raven's blood."

Her expression was so solemn and sad, I didn't have the heart to tell her the truth. I was pretty sure I was dying anyway.

I was saved from having to reply when my lungs went tight again, and my body was wracked with coughs. By the time I was done, blood coated both hands and dripped down my forearms.

"I know you're angry, but Raven did not choose for you," Myrr murmured, the expression on her wizened face so unfamiliar that it took a second to recognize it.

Pity. Kindness.

"*This* is the choice, child. And it is yours and yours alone."

I stared at her, some part deep inside me knowing exactly what she meant, but my mind refusing to accept it.

"The *Wolf* Queen must die. The question is, will you choose to go with her?"

The animal inside me let out a long, mournful howl, and my stomach roiled.

"I choose anything but this," I croaked, a sob breaking free before I could stop it. "You don't understand. You couldn't possibly—"

"Oh, but I do." Myrr managed a half-smile. "Do you think I was always a shriveled old hermit?" She shook her head. "Once, I was young and pretty. Maybe not as pretty as the two of you, but damned close. And I had a love of my own. We were to marry and have children. Twins. A boy and a girl. One dark, one fair, both born plump, squalling and perfect. I know because I saw them with my gift. I saw snippets of our whole lives, and it was..."

Myrr swallowed hard and Sienna took her gnarled hand. I could almost see her lending the Oracle the strength to continue.

"It was a beautiful life. But my gift also showed me

what would happen if I chose that life. And while I'd have been happy in a little cottage tucked in the forest with my family, much of the rest of the realm would've suffered in ways that I cannot describe. War after war that saw tens of thousands of our people dead. Hundreds of years of discord and strife. The worst part of every race exposed."

Myrr pulled away from Sienna and took my bloodied hand in hers.

"The moral of this sad tale? Sometimes, Diana, both doors lead to pain. And we still must open one. I'm so sorry this is your burden to bear."

I couldn't speak. I just sat there, letting the truth of her words wash over me as Sienna wept. Myrr was right about all of it. Except one part.

There was no choice to be made.

Not really. The Wolf Queen must die. But I, Diana, must live if we had any hope of saving the realms because I was the only one strong enough to wield the shard inside me.

Or, I would be, as soon as...

"One more run." I stood and swiped my bloodied hands on my thighs. "Me and the old girl will go on one more run. And then, I'll let her go."

I moved toward the door, suddenly desperate to escape. No one else needed to see this. The desperation as my wolf began to prowl, still afraid of this new thing inside me, but also heeding my call. Maybe she already knew this would be our last time together.

I headed out my bedroom door and sprinted down the hall, heart pounding. Hell, maybe once we started running, we just wouldn't stop. We'd just go and go, the brisk wind in our fur, freedom unparalleled...

Distantly, I heard Dominic call my name as I passed the Great Room, but I didn't slow my pace. When I reached the entrance to the keep, I yanked the door open. Before I could launch myself down the steps, I stopped short with a gasp.

There, standing before me, was a slumped, and clearly exhausted Nefir, knuckles raised to knock.

"Nefir? What...what are you doing here?"

"I came to warn you."

I waved him inside, confused. "Warn us? It's too late. She already attacked with Malach's army. Luckily, we were able to hold her off."

His grim expression told me lady luck was no longer in our corner, and I braced myself.

"When you told me what she'd been doing...about the mermaids and the babes...I went to find her. To see if I could talk sense into her. You were right, though. She's too far gone."

"But you were able to get her to share her next move with you?"

"Not exactly..."

"Damn it, Nefir, it's been one of the worst days of my life and my patience is gone! Just tell me."

"Fine! Okay!" he said, holding up both hands in surrender. "My parents had her imprisoned after she destroyed the Veil and I just...I accidentally set her free. Are you happy now?"

"Am I happy?" I managed a few moments later, once I'd caught my breath. "My wolf is dying, I just had to help kill the king of my ally, and you're telling me that you've loosed your psycho sister into the world where she can act all on her own, without a meat puppet slowing her down. Am I happy?" I let out a harsh laugh. "I'm fucking ecstatic. This is perfect. Couldn't be better."

"I'm sorry, alright? It wasn't like I meant to do it. She is very wily, that one. And—"

Suddenly, his head lolled to one side, and his eyes went wide.

"Two sides of a coin, each pair must be,
    Key one and two, then four and three
    The fifth to bind them all as one
    Only then can the will of the Veil be done

Hard of Head, Vengeance dealing
    Soft of Heart, with hands of healing
    Fiery passion, Righteous Fury,
    Savior's touch of Tender mercy

Next will come keys four and three,
    As different as any two can be,

One deals only in pain and death
The other, more like spring's first breath
A taker of souls, the bringer of night
Her opposite like dawn's first light

And then key five, soul of the Veil
To make them one, who can prevail
In their success, our salvation lies
Or a new world begins...as this one dies."

Nefir slumped even more, but before I could grab him, Raven was there, hauling the god to his feet.

"Where is all the blood coming from?" Raven demanded, barely giving Nefir a glance as he took in my crimson stained clothes.

"Me. It's fine," I said, waving off his concern for me. We had bigger fish to fry. "Did you just get here, or did you hear the prophecy?"

"I heard it, and what he disclosed before that. Lilis is free?"

"Apparently." I nodded, a renewed sense of purpose filling me as the shard inside me pulsed.

Fiery passion, righteous fury.

I'd take it over misery and heartache any day.

"But in spite of the unfortunate news, this new prophecy foretells our potential victory. Raven...we can still win this war if we assemble all the keys and fight her together."

And I would finally meet her, face to face.

"She is weakened now, from more than a decade of imprisonment," Nefir whispered. "It will take her time to build up strength."

Time was all we needed.

I would mourn for my wolf and life as I knew it later. For now, I would focus on what mattered most.

Finding the rest of the keys so we could restore the Veil...

And then make that bitch pay for what she'd done to me and mine.

Also By Shannon Mayer

The Forty Proof Series

MIDLIFE BOUNTY HUNTER

MIDLIFE FAIRY HUNTER

MIDLIFE DEMON HUNTER

MIDLIFE GHOST HUNTER

MIDLIFE ZOMBIE HUNTER

MIDLIFE WITCH HUNTER

MIDLIFE MAGIC HUNTER

MIDLIFE SOUL HUNTER

MIDLIFE VAMPIRE HUNTER

ROBERT

The Honey and Ice Series (with Kelly St. Clare)

A COURT OF HONEY AND ASH

A THRONE OF FEATHERS AND BONE

A CROWN OF PETALS AND ICE

World of Honey and Ice (with Kelly St. Clare)

THORN KISSED & SILVER CHAINS

IVY TOUCHED & BRONZE BLADE

BLACK ROSE & GOLD QUEEN

RECURVE

BREAKWATER

FIRESTORM

WINDBURN

ROOTBOUND

ASH

DESTROYER

Questing Witch Series

AIMLESS WITCH

CARAVAN WITCH

MAZE WITCH

ELEMENTAL WITCH

The Nix Series

FURY OF A PHOENIX

BLOOD OF A PHOENIX

RISE OF A PHOENIX

A SAVAGE SPELL

A KILLING CURSE

The Desert Cursed Series

WITCH'S REIGN

DRAGON'S GROUND

JINN'S DOMINION

ORACLE'S HAUNT

WYVERN'S LAIR

EMPEROR'S THRONE

DEN OF THIEVES

KINGDOM OF STORMS

REALM OF DEMONS

The Golden Wolf

GOLDEN

GLITTER

GOSSAMER

The Alpha Territories

TAKEN BY FATE

HUNTED BY FATE

CLAIMED BY FATE

CAGED BY FATE

Hi

FOR A COMPLETE BOOK LIST VISIT

www.shannonmayer.com

Connect With Me

Email me at Shannon@shannonmayer.com or find me on social media.

Join my newsletter for updates on upcoming books, behind the scenes info, and exclusive content.

facebook.com/ShannonMayerAuthor

instagram.com/hijinksink

bookbub.com/profile/shannon-mayer

tiktok.com/@hijinksink